Celebrity Crush

CHRISTY SWIFT

FOREVER
New York Boston

Forever
Hachette Book Group
1290 Avenue of the Americas, New York, NY 10104
read-forever.com
@readforeverpub

First Edition: February 2025

Forever is an imprint of Grand Central Publishing. The Forever name and logo are registered trademarks of Hachette Book Group, Inc.

The publisher is not responsible for websites (or their content) that are not owned by the publisher.

Forever books may be purchased in bulk for business, educational, or promotional use. For information, please contact your local bookseller or the Hachette Book Group Special Markets Department at special.markets@hbgusa.com.

Print book interior design by Marie Mundaca

Library of Congress Cataloging-in-Publication Data

Names: Swift, Christy, author.
Title: Celebrity crush / Christy Swift.
Description: First edition. | New York : Forever, 2025.
Identifiers: LCCN 2024034400 | ISBN 9781538767764 (trade paperback) | ISBN 9781538767771 (ebook)
Subjects: LCGFT: Romance fiction. | Novels.
Classification: LCC PS3619.W537 C45 2025 | DDC 813/.6—dc23
/eng/20240729
LC record available at https://lccn.loc.gov/2024034400

ISBNs: 9781538767764 (trade paperback), 9781538767771 (ebook)

Printed in the United States of America

CCR

10 9 8 7 6 5 4 3 2 1

of the four hottest male celebs from everybody's favorite sci-fi dance TV show is the inspiration for my celebrity crush romance novel and that I'm about to go onstage to talk about it *right now*. It should create some last-minute buzz for the show.

The best memes are all right there waiting for me in my favorites. I take a moment to feed my addiction. My BFF, Josie, says the devil is going to drag me to hell by way of *Lost Star* memes. I disagree. Everyone knows the road to hell is paved with Henry Cavill memes.

Terica says something I don't catch. Was it my name? Oh God, did I miss my cue?

"Go, go, go!" Angry Nat gives me a shove, and suddenly my feet are moving, and I'm onstage smiling and waving like I'm Princess Kate. The applause is a giddy ocean in my head, and I blink in the bright lights. All the rules Nat barked at me earlier rush back to me: *Don't trip on the taped-down wires; approach Terica from her left; don't look at the backstage crew...don't look at them!*

When I shake Terica's hand, I feel like I'm getting sucked into her brown, perfectly made-up eyes surrounded by her brown, perfectly made-up skin. A copy of my book rests on the knees of her bone-colored pantsuit. Sliding into the cushioned chair across from her, I gaze out at the blurry sea of faces. Everyone is still clapping, so I wave some more, this time with both hands. I'm smiling so hard that I can't feel my face.

"Welcome, welcome, Emmy Ellison! How does it feel to have your novel on the *New York Times* bestseller list? You're a *New York Times* bestselling author! Let's give her another hand, everyone!"

As the audience claps and cheers some more, my chest balloons, and I don't even know what to do with myself. When the applause dies down, I let out a deep breath. "It feels amazing,

Terica. Thank you for having me on the show. Can I—" I hesitate but then just go for it. "Can I say hi to my daughter?" Terica's tight, dyed-blond curls bob a quick *yes*, so I wave at the close-up camera. "Hi, Peyton! I love you! I miss you!" I know my tweeny-bopper will love that I gave her a shout-out.

Terica holds up my book. "For those of you who don't know her yet, Emmy is a novelist and social media influencer. Over the last month, her posts around her rom-com *Hashtag Celebrity Crush* have gone viral, propelling it to number ten on the *New York Times* bestseller list, and it's also been optioned for film. You may have seen her popular vlogs *Dolphin Tells Your Fortune* and..." She looks at her notes. "*Random Yoga Poses*. Those sound fun."

My nerves have started to settle. I've been interviewed about my romance novel a bunch of times already for the publishing industry, but general audiences never paid attention until I had that extra glass of wine on vlog-taping night and admitted that the book was based on my *actual* celebrity crush. Authors like to imagine which actors might play their characters all the time, so it shouldn't even be that big a deal, but in the world of social media, you never know what's going to take off. When it does, you've got to jump on that rocket and ride it all the way to the moon.

My rocket was a viral internet poll. Boy, did that thing go nuts! Over six million responses. Oh, and I'm pretty sure Terica's expecting me to reveal today who my celebrity crush really is. I don't know if I should fess up or not. I could milk this thing for another couple of weeks if I wanted to. Although revealing him might bump sales even higher.

Meanwhile, Terica's still telling the audience about me, because being a social media influencer with a book deal isn't the same as being a bona fide celebrity. By Hollywood standards, I'm still a card-carrying nobody. No matter how well I do with my social media business, no matter how many sales my book gets, I'll probably still see myself as Rhett Castle saw me thirteen years ago when I tried to peddle him my first screenplay at that swanky LA party: some young woman, no, *girl*, in last year's slinky dress. Not blond enough but not brunette enough, either. Carrying a knockoff Chanel purse. Too loud. Too excited. Unpolished. Good enough to lure into bed, but not good enough for anything else.

Hollywood's not for everyone. What was your name again?

All those feelings came rushing in on me this morning when I lifted my chin and saw those famous, colored LAX pylons staring down at me from a better-than-you blue sky. Even the air had a threatening nip to it—Cali showing me who's boss.

I may not belong in Hollywood, but at least for today, I'm here, and nobody can take that away.

"Emmy's on TikTok, Instagram, Facebook, and several more platforms. Wow, and you write books and screenplays, too. That's a lot to keep up with."

I clear my throat. "Yes, Terica. My philosophy is to take off and nuke the entire site from orbit..."

Terica stares at me. It's my favorite Sigourney Weaver quote from *Aliens*, but she doesn't recognize it. What a heartbreak. I have to finish it myself. "It's the only way to be sure."

Someone in the audience whoops, and I toss them a thumbs-up. At least there's one sci-fi fan in the house.

"Where did you get your idea for the novel, Emmy?"

The honest answer is from real-life memes, Duran Duran songs, and maybe an itty-bitty bit of my crush's personal life that I probably shouldn't have put in there. But what I say is, "I love the Hollywood scene. I studied screenwriting at UCLA for two years before I got—before I realized what I really wanted was to write books, so I meshed that with the work I'm doing now in social media, and *voilà!*"

"That's great." Terica winks. "But that's not what everybody's talking about when it comes to your book, is it, Emmy?"

I shake my head, grinning.

"The male character, the love interest, is based on your actual celebrity crush, am I right?"

"'Based on' is a strong way of putting it." I rub my knees. "I would go with 'inspired by.'"

"Ah yes, the lawyers have gotten involved. Fair enough." Terica looks to the audience, and they're ready with the laughs. "The poll you created has narrowed it down to one of the four male members of *Lost Star Dance Troupe Saves the Universe.* Let's take a look at those guys."

The screen behind me flickers to reveal the vlog post introducing my poll. The unattractive thumbnail has me sporting pursed lips in midsentence and a sloppy bun with wavy highlights escaping. Behind me are the familiar living room walls of the travel trailer where Peyton and I live on the west coast of Florida. Can anyone tell it's a trailer? The video crackles to life.

EMMY: Okay, friends and fans, it's time! I'm Emmy Ellison and the *Hashtag Celebrity Crush* poll is up and ready for your votes! Which hunka hunka dancin' love is my book inspired by? Let's take a look at what we're working with.

First, there's Sean O'Sullivan with that one lock of yellow in his raven hair strategically bouncing as the world explodes behind him. O captain my captain! Gotta love that unshakable self-assurance. You also gotta love how half his shirt is ripped off. Anatomy students, do you want to name those muscles for us? Hold the phone, here comes the Irish smolder! Look at that mouth. So pouty and sensual. I'll just give you a moment on your own with that mouth.

Next, it's our gentle giant, Jason "Mount" Ramirez. Pretty nimble on his feet for a big guy. I swear he's Mario Lopez and the Rock's love child. Those brown eyes are like pools of infinity...I can't look away. I. Just. Can't. Here he is curled up in his sexy space underwear, presumably lost in a shuttle floating away for eternity. Who didn't cry during that episode? On a side note, I hope the men's underwear industry is taking notes because *that's* a future I want to live in.

Next in line is the other Jason, Jason Connor, our charmer with his endless facial expressions. Let's run through a few of those. The fierce face. The worried face. The confused face. The sweet-slash-shy face. There's the million-dollar smile. Oh, the curls! Don't you just want to cut them all off and make a little nosegay to lay on your pillow at night? It can't just be me. And the famous "Hey, buddy" photo, where he's holding his newborn son. Excuse me, I think I just received a lethal dose of *awwww*.

And last, but not least, Andrew Valentine, our long, lean cowboy. His *Lost Star* character is a bit shady, but Andrew himself is an awesome guy! Really musical. Here he is playing guitar...cue the swoon! Still spends time on the family ranch. Look at that wink! Mmm. Not available, of course. Andrew and his wife just celebrated their tenth anniversary. Congratulations, you two! I'm still allowed to have a harmless fangirl crush on him, though, so don't count him out.

All right, so here's what you do... read the book, see if you can figure out who my celebrity crush is from the clues, and place your votes. Thanks for tuning in! Don't forget to like and subscribe. Emmy Ellison signing off!

The video ends, and I startle to see Terica leaning in toward me. Her voice drops a register. "Now, Emmy, I don't think you know how big this has gotten."

The numbers on my Fitbit tick up. "Wh-what do you mean?"

"These four are in actual competition for this title you're offering. They're trash-talking each other. It's like *Fight Club*. I think there might even be a Ferrari in it for someone."

I know she's joking, but I'm giddy and thrilled all the same. "They wouldn't know unless they'd read the book."

"Ah, yes, the clues. I spotted a few when I read it."

I swallow hard. A terrifying thought occurs to me. If Terica has read my book and figured out who my crush is, there's a chance he could actually be here. Maybe she brought him here to meet me!

I cough into my fist. Hell to the no, I'm not prepared for that. This is about a poll. This is about a book. This is not about meeting the man I've swooned over through screens for years. He can't be here today. That can't happen.

Although, this *is* Hollywood. And he does live here.

I spy a glass of ice water on the table next to me and gulp half of it down.

"Time for a commercial break!" Terica announces.

Once the cameras are off us, I brace for her to drop the bomb on me or to at least give me a clue that my freaking celebrity crush is here, but she just turns to the side and checks her phone instead.

I spit ice back into my glass and take a couple of cleansing yoga breaths. I'm overthinking this. I've been away so long I've forgotten that, here in Hollywood, it's all about the hook. Terica's teasing is just fun and games for the audience's benefit. She doesn't know who my crush is. He's not hiding in the back, waiting in that little area behind the screen where I was a few minutes ago. Still, I crane my neck for a look. I can't help it.

"You ready?" Terica tucks her phone away as the camera-person cues her.

I grin and nod. I'm starting to feel a bit like the girl I used to be back in college. Bright, shiny Emmy with a bright, shiny Hollywood future ahead of her. The Emmy I was before I realized that my little mistake with Rhett was growing bigger every month. Before I turned tail and ran.

The cameras roll, and Terica catches up those just tuning in before focusing back on me. "Emmy, celebrity crushes are all about fantasy. So, if you were to get the opportunity to meet your actual crush, what would you do?"

Suddenly cocky, I drop my voice. "What would I *do* or what would I *want* to do?" The audience laughs, and my heart flutters in a good way.

"It's a family show, Emmy," Terica says in comedic deadpan. "You know that, right? Let's keep it clean."

The audience is really going now. She's a great wingwoman.

"Well, Terica…" I tap my finger on my lips. "I don't expect him to carry me off into the sunset on a horse or anything, but I *would* like…a hug."

"Awww." Terica draws it out in a way that cues the audience to *awww* with her.

"And it would have to be a long hug, long enough to make everyone else in the room a little uncomfortable."

"Hmm." She raises her eyebrows.

"Not because I'm trying to be creepy, or not *necessarily* because I'm trying to be creepy..."

Laughter. I'm on a roll.

"But because, when it happens, I'm going to be totally freaking out for the first several seconds, and if the hug ends too quickly, I won't have had a chance to enjoy it. It needs to be extra long, so I can let all that nervous energy work its way out, and I can relax and—" I pause, searching for the right word. "Appreciate it."

"That's nice." Terica turns to the audience. "All she wants is a hug."

"Not just any hug. A quality hug." Well, maybe that's not all I'd want, but that's all America is getting out of me today. Honestly, I don't know why I'm telling the whole world the secrets of my heart. But then again, why not? Maybe my crush will see this show and... No, that's crazy.

"I don't think that's too much to ask of a perfect stranger," Terica says. "What do you guys think?" The audience hoots and hollers.

Then something changes. Terica is quiet for longer than usual. I feel it. The audience feels it. A kind of tenseness envelops us, like we're all waiting for someone to jump out and yell, *Boo!*

"Okay, Emmy," Terica finally says. "You know I read your book, right? I loved it, by the way. And you're right, there are a lot of clues in there, but I still couldn't figure out who your celebrity crush was. So..."

She pauses, and I stop breathing. "So, what?" I gasp.

"So, I invited them *all*!"

A tsunami of screaming rises from the audience, and I jolt in my chair.

No, this can't be! I search Terica's face for a sign that I'm being punked. *Wait for it, Emmy. Any second, it'll come.* But she's not even looking at me. In fact, she's whipping the audience up into even more frenzied applause, and oh hell in a handbasket, she isn't joking! This is real! This is happening! I'm about to meet my celebrity crush and three other superhot megastars.

Icy prickles ripple across my skin in the wake of a terrible thought. What if he's a jerk? What if he blows me off, and I'm here looking all smitten and dumb, and I humiliate my twelve-year-old on TV, and all my new fans decide I'm too cringey to subscribe to? The lights on my dashboard click on, one by one. The ship's computer warns me there's a perimeter alert, a singularity forming, a bogey on my tail.

"Should I bring them out?" Terica shouts to the audience above the din. "Sean O'Sullivan is probably chewing off his very sexy foot back there! Let's put him out of his misery, what do you say? Come on out, guys!"

"Wait—" I start to protest, but my voice is drowned out by a wall of noise. If I thought the audience was excited a moment ago, it was a paltry shadow of what they are doing now as the *Lost Star* men emerge from stage right. I may go deaf from the decibel level in the studio, but thank God and Tom Hanks I'm not blind, because it would be a damn shame not to see this.

Four specimens of manly perfection make their way across the stage, preceded only by a breezy mixture of their respective colognes. Andrew Valentine comes out first in skinny jeans, snakeskin boots, and a sport coat over a retro Las Vegas T-shirt. His trademark white cowboy hat is perched on his head, and his lopsided smile doesn't falter as he spins away from the audience, shakes Terica's hand, and then sets his sights on me. As he closes the distance between us, I consider standing up, but my legs don't get the message, and it's too late to move as he takes my hand and shakes it before falling into a chair that has (magically?) appeared beside me. A crew member mikes him up.

I pull my gaze away to find Mount Ramirez already towering over me in a pin-striped button-down shirt that is trying not to tear itself to pieces over his huge pecs. I mean, all these guys are muscled, but this dude is Chris Hemsworth muscled. My hand is swallowed by the warmth of his as I nod into his clean-shaven, dimpled face with those soulful dark eyes. *God almighty.*

I don't even catch a breath before the *Lost Star* captain himself, Sean O'Sullivan, is in front of me in a three-piece gray suit with *that mouth* and his one wavy lock of blond hair practically glowing. I swear, if someone told me the world would end in a fiery blaze of pain and destruction unless I tore my eyes away from him, I'm still not sure I could do it. He raises my captured fingers to his lips, and I'm pretty sure my eyes go wide, because one corner of his mouth tweaks up in a knowing grin and a wink before he, too, shifts to the side and finds a seat.

But they saved the best for last.

Jason Connor saunters my way, his easy smile aimed at me like a weapon of mass destruction. He's in jeans and a silk Hawaiian shirt that is so wrong for the decade and so right in every other way. He captures my hand in his, and when my gaze locks onto his azure eyes, it's like I'm in a free fall through a cloudless sky because suddenly there's no oxygen in the air, just citrus-musk cologne and adrenaline. A brown curl falls across his forehead as he leans in and says, "It's nice to meet you, Emmy," his voice cracking on my name. It's the sexy, vulnerable little crack that comes out when he's doing an emotional scene. That little voice crack kills me.

He's already moved aside before I can reply, and I check to make sure that (a) I'm still breathing, and (b) I haven't melted into a puddle on the floor that Angry Nat will have to mop up later.

Did I just meet Jason Connor? Did he just touch me? Did that happen?

Maybe it's happening to a version of me in an alternate universe, like in *Lost Star* season one, episode eleven. Maybe a rift in the space-time continuum has caused our energy signatures to align. God bless you, quantum physics.

The coolness of Terica's hand on my forearm yanks me back to this dimension. Her crocodile grin is wide. "That was kind of mean of me, wasn't it?"

I'm about to agree, but then something occurs to me: how much fun this is. This is so freaking fun! Whoever gets to do this? Me, that's who. And I'm going to enjoy every nanosecond of it.

Leaning forward with obvious relish to get a better look at the four superstars to my right, I reply, "On the contrary, Terica, you're officially my new best friend. A woman named Josie in Florida is going to be very upset." I glance around for the close-up camera. "Josie, hon, I'm sorry! I'm really sorry!"

Terica laughs along with everyone else. My chest swells to see the guys chuckling, too, especially Jason Connor. He's made me laugh so many times that it's kind of nice to return the favor.

"I've been meaning to have some of the *Lost Star* cast on to talk about the charity work they've been doing. I didn't think you'd mind hanging out while we do that. You don't mind, do you, Emmy?"

"I think I could carve the time out of my schedule, Terica."

More laughs, and then Terica turns her attention to them. I'm grateful because it gives the blinking heart on my Fitbit a chance to catch its breath. Plus it's fun to watch these guys just be themselves as they talk about raising funds for children's hospitals and all the escapades they've had while taping their show with the *Lost Star* female cast members, Amanda and Kayla. I try not to stare too hard at Jason Connor, but he's right there, looking better than any person has a right to, talking with his hands, joking with his costars, laughing with those gorgeous blue eyes. These guys love working together, and you can tell. I can't help but wonder if I had stayed in LA—if I had *been able* to stay—could I eventually have been part of something like this, too?

Then my stomach twists up when I realize that, in a few minutes, I'm probably going to be telling Jason Connor face-to-face that he's the inspiration for my book. How is he going to react? Is it going to be weird? I'll probably blush. God, I hope I don't blush. Maybe I shouldn't do it today after all.

He catches me looking at him, fidgets, and looks away. Does he already know? Great. I haven't said anything yet and already it's weird.

I don't know why I'm so nervous. He's just a person. They're all just people. The fact that they do a job that puts them on my living room screen at the press of a button doesn't change that. And I'm pretty sure none of them really cares whether they're my celebrity crush. I mean, why would they?

But I care. Because I've loved Jason Connor forever.

The conversation winds down as the screen behind us announces all the different ways people can donate to the fundraiser. Then everything shifts.

"Okay, now we're going to find out who *Hashtag Celebrity*

Crush is based on." Terica holds up my book and homes in on me. "Emmy, it's time to come clean. Which one of these hotties holds your heartstrings?"

I tilt my head in what I hope is an endearing way that hides how desperately I'm scrambling for a way out of this. "Terica, they're all so awesome. I don't want to hurt anyone's feelings."

Terica makes a snorty laugh that shows I've actually surprised her. "Oh, I wouldn't worry about that. These guys have the discomfort tolerance of a bed of nails. They're bulletproof. Just have fun with it, 'kay? Now, who is it?"

I clear my throat. Terica is staring at me, and so are the four celebrities, the audience, and all the camerapeople and crew. Everyone in this entire, enormous studio is waiting for me to say something. I feel like a person strapped into a bungee, toes on the edge of the platform, overcome by the desperate need to *not* do what they are about to do.

I could lie. I could say it's the other Jason. Or I could play games and not admit one way or the other. I could even flat-out refuse—for marketing purposes. Nobody has a blaster to my head, right?

But Jason Connor's ocean-blue eyes are trained right on me, and this is a chance I'm never going to get again. Plus, I'm tired of running away from my dreams. I've been doing that for thirteen years, and I don't want to do it anymore.

"Emmy?" Terica presses. It's more like a gavel strike than a word. I can't stall any longer.

I open my mouth and say a name.

Chapter 2

I still don't know if there's a llama farm in my future.

Jason (five days earlier)

I STRESS VAGUELY over the last text Margarita sent me as I push open the hotel doors, my red Nikes padding across the worn carpet on the way to the staging area for the *Lost Star* fundraising event.

> **Margarita:** Matthew has been invited to a birthday party next weekend. You'll need an appropriate gift for a four-year-old girl.

It's the first time a birthday party has fallen on one of my weekends, but I guess I need to get used to this sort of thing. Will the whole family be expecting some big expensive gift because Mattie's parents are actors? Do I need to look up a local pony farm? Or maybe llamas? I heard somewhere that llamas are the new ponies.

"Hurry up, *Hard-On*," Sean says out of the side of his mouth, staring up at the ceiling as a makeup artist paints black eyeliner around his eyes.

"*Hadron*," I correct him for what feels like the thousandth time as I search the conference room turned hair and makeup studio. "Hey, what do four-year-old girls want for their birthdays?"

"Diamonds," Sean replies, "in the shape of Elsa."

I ignore him and make a beeline for the curtained-off dressing rooms. I run into Mount Ramirez on the way.

"Sup, Snack?" He slaps me on the back as I pass him.

I cough involuntarily. It always surprises me how huge the dude is, and I'm not a small guy. "Life's good!" I call over my shoulder.

Slipping out of my jeans and T-shirt, I shuffle into my Hadron costume. It's not the one we use for the show; it's the media version, which is less sweaty and itchy, but just as shiny and purply brown. Eggplant is the official name for my color, I think. The long zipper makes a satisfying noise as I yank it from groin to neck and then add the pleather jacket. At least I don't need two people to dress me in this costume. A man takes pride in being able to dress himself from time to time.

"What do four-year-old girls want for their birthdays these days?" I ask Kathy, my makeup artist, while she's covering up my imperfections. All the ones you can see, anyway.

She shrugs. "Dolls?"

Not particularly helpful, but I thank her anyway.

When the final touches are done, we assemble in the hotel courtyard for go time. All six members of the *Lost Star Dance*

Troupe are in costume and ready to sizzle the proverbial fajita, this particular fajita being an autograph party for sick kids. Sean as Captain Footwork is all slit-eyed in black, Jason "Mount" Ramirez as Diggit is larger-than-life in chartreuse and gray. Then there's red-clad Andrew acting bored as Quasar, Amanda all green and fierce as Maelstrom, and little Kayla rocking the spunky purple thing as Ruby. Oh, and I'm here, too—Jason Connor as Hadron, the funny one. In eggplant.

The gates to the hotel courtyard open, and the kids and their parents surge toward us in a flood of primary colors and autograph books.

"Hey, buddy." I accept a book from a skinny kid wearing a T-shirt with my face on it.

"Just like the meme," his mom says, grinning ear to ear.

I give her the million-dollar smile, but inside I cringe. The photo from the "Hey, buddy" meme was taken during what was seriously my lowest point, but this lady doesn't know that. How could she? Anyway, it's not her fault. I assembled that shit sandwich all by myself.

I pose for their selfies and get ready for the next visitor. This time I'm attacked with a hug—from the mom, not the kid. "Whoa there!" I pat her back awkwardly and peel her off me when she won't let go.

"You're my favorite, Hadron," says the daughter, who looks about ten years old. She's wearing a scarf on her head and yellow, star-shaped glasses.

I ignore the mom's mountain of exposed cleavage and give the little girl all my attention. "What's your name?"

"Sarah."

"You look beautiful today, Sarah."

"Will you do the dance with me?"

I cock an eyebrow. There's a lot of dancing in the four seasons of *Lost Star Dance Troupe Saves the Universe*, go figure. "Which one?"

"This one." She shuffles her feet and thrusts out her arm.

I do it. The little girl squeals and claps. The mom leans her bleached-blond head right up to mine and whispers what she'd like to do to me to show her gratitude, punctuated by a squeeze on my butt cheek. Really, lady?

I can't totally blame her. A few years ago, I would've been game for it—the touch, the sex, the invitation to feel something, anything. But I don't do that stuff anymore. Not since Mattie was born. Besides, I have to figure out what's going on between Margarita and me. I don't know what you'd call what we're doing. I've heard things like *co-parenting* and *friends with benefits*. It all sounds so pragmatic. But I don't want to think about that right now. These kids are here, and they're sick, and they deserve this little thing I can offer them—being present for them, showing them a fun time. Being Hadron, not Jason Connor.

"Hey," I ask the little girl, "do you like llamas?"

But it's too late. They get swallowed by the crowd.

I catch Sean's eye over the heads of the mob, and he makes a quick motion like he's hanging himself. Sean's been in the business too long. Just to bust his chops, I burst into the theme song for *Lost Star* and start to dougie. Once I do this, the others are obligated to join in. I think it's even in our contract. Sean's eyes turn to daggers, and Mount Ramirez looks like a parent who's given up. Kayla's into it, though. She wiggles over in her space-age silver cornrows and bumps hips with me. The kids are laughing and joining in. I grab a little girl by the hand and twirl her. When it comes to the forearm bump, I pick a kid in a wheel-chair. The song ends, and I get ready to launch into another one, but Amanda's brown eyes flash under her Popsicle-red hair as she says, "Jason," in that way that really means *no*.

A second later, Sean is beside me with my head pinned under his arm. "I think Hadron needs a little talkin'-to!" His operatic Captain Footwork voice rings across the courtyard.

I punch him a few times in the kidney (lightly, 'cause, hey, there are kids here) until he lets me out of the headlock. "The hair!" I complain, but I can feel the shit-eating smile on my face.

"Just sign the autographs," Sean says in the same tone of voice he might use to say, *I'm going to slit your throat in your sleep.*

It's all good. There's love there.

As I'm adjusting my collar, I notice a family of three off to the side, huddled in the shade of one of the courtyard columns. The littlest one, pale with dark circles under her eyes and ragged strands of dark hair, is eyeing me, clutching a stuffed Orbit plushie. I lope over to them.

Crouching down to her level, I put on the serious face. "Do you have a proper alien handler's license, miss? Those things are dangerous, you know."

She hides her smile in the toy's fur.

"Thanks for coming over," her dad says. "She can't handle too much heat and sun."

I sign her branded eight-by-ten *Lost Star* photo and hand it back to her. "This counts as your license. If anyone gives you any trouble, you tell them Hadron authorized it."

She throws her skinny arms around me, and I'm careful not to squeeze too hard. "Hey, what do you want for your next birthday?" I ask her a second before her father's face falls. Suddenly, I realize what an ass I am. This kid might not see her next birthday. "Never mind," I whisper, patting her bony back. "Who do you want to see next? I'll send them over."

An hour later, we're all wiping the makeup off our faces in front of a long mirror, and I still don't know if there's a llama farm in my future.

"So, which one of you is it?" Andrew asks as he plunks his cowboy hat back on his head.

"I beg your pardon?" Sean smooths out his goatee and stuffs the blond streak under his jet-dark locks.

"That celebrity crush poll. For that romance book. It's all over social media. Which one of the *Lost Star* troupe is the book based on?"

"What the hell is he talking about?" Sean's palms are up as if the planet itself has offended him.

I pull out my phone. I'm not terribly active on social media. I find it overwhelming, not to mention a lot of people are jerks, but I swipe around until I find it. There's a poll posted, and I've been tagged on it several times. Who is @authorEmmy's #Secret CelebrityCrush? is accompanied by four photos: Andrew, Sean, Ramirez, and me. If I tap one of our names, it will take my vote.

"Here it is!" I announce.

"Oh, I've heard about this!" Amanda snatches the phone from my hand. "It's fun. The book is a rom-com. You guys should read it. Find out if she based it on you."

"I don't read romance novels." Sean throws his makeup-soiled cloth into the trash with more force than necessary and flexes.

"Don't worry, it's not you." I grab my phone back from Amanda, tapping my name to place my vote. The percentages pop up. Mount Ramirez has 47 percent, which makes sense because he's a demigod, and I'm in second place with 30 percent. Sean's lagging at 15 percent. Andrew has 8.

"Hey, Sean, I'm ahead of you," I crow. "I have double your score!"

"What the—" He snatches the phone from me and glares at it.

"The character must not be a total asshole." I laugh.

Kayla digs out her own phone. "I'm voting for Everest."

"Don't call me that," Ramirez grumbles.

Amanda has found it on her own device and taps the screen. "There! I voted for Connor."

"You haven't even read the book!" Sean protests. "It could be me. Why wouldn't it be me?"

"Hey, can I have my phone back?" I chase it. "I need to screenshot the moment I beat Sean O'Sullivan at something."

"Gloating is an ugly look on you, Snack. You're supposed to be the nice one." Sean slips his rings back on his fingers, making him look even more kingly. "Dinner anyone?"

"Nah, Margarita is dropping Mattie off tonight," I say. "I gotta go."

"How are things going between you two?" Amanda asks quietly while I check out of the conversation and stuff my things into my bag. "Still fighting?"

I rub the back of my neck and stand up. "It's a never-ending battle."

"You're a good guy, Jason," she says. "And you're a good dad. You'll figure it out."

Her light pat on my shoulder is more comforting than it should be. Amanda and I started out together in LA doing commercials and bit roles. She's always been a good friend to me. I give her a tight-lipped smile. "See you at the studio."

On my way out, Miles, one of the *Lost Star* directors, stops me. "Got a minute, Connor?"

"Not really, Miles…"

"Let me rephrase that. I need to talk to you."

I blow air out of my cheeks. This doesn't sound good. "What's up?"

Miles holds out his phone. He has the *Celebrity Straight Talk* gossip show paused on it. My heart sinks as he presses PLAY.

AMIL: Let's start the show off today with one of my favorite things ever...Jason Connor's butt! Hello, everyone, I'm Amil Nair, and this is my cohost, Isla Wallace.

ISLA: Hi-la, it's Isla! A question, Amil. Is that a hand I spot on that very shapely rear end?

AMIL: It is, Isla! This is a photo of Jason Connor trolling for moms at an autograph party for sick children less than an hour ago!

ISLA: Wow, that's...inappropriate.

AMIL: He could have chosen a better venue, I agree.

ISLA: I guess he's at it again, isn't he?

AMIL: His butt is, at least.

ISLA: Has it got a name? I feel like Jason Connor's butt should have its own name. It's practically sentient.

AMIL: We can call it Ronald. Anyway, Ronald is liable

to get Jason Connor in big trouble, and he can't afford that.

ISLA: I know, right? Jason's on, like, strike seven with *Lost Star*'s network. And I heard through the grapevine that they've already got Zachary Tay lined up to take his place if he screws up again.

AMIL: Oh no! The same Zachary Tay who beat Jason out for the voice of Prince Reese in *Tower Diaries*?

ISLA: The same!

AMIL: Ouch, that would hurt.

ISLA: I'm sure it would. Those two appear to have a friendly rivalry going.

AMIL: I'd like to see it get less friendly. Maybe with Speedos in a mud pit. [*laughs*]

ISLA: [*laughs*]

AMIL: Speaking of Zachary, did you see that amazing video he posted earlier this week?

ISLA: The one where he was holding that koala and announcing that he's launching his own personal campaign to save endangered species around the world? I sure did.

AMIL: Are koalas endangered?

ISLA: I don't think so.

AMIL: Well, who cares, right? That video was adorable. And at least Zachary Tay knows how to get the world's attention with something other than his Ronald!

ISLA: So true.

AMIL: You know, Isla, I'm going to come right out and say it. I kind of hope the old Jason is back. That sexy thang was game for anything. You just had to be in the right place at the right time to get your invitation.

ISLA: Remember when he got drunk and fell off the Santa Monica Pier?

AMIL: Yes! Someone photoshopped an orca into that picture.

ISLA: I saw that, too! Remember the tagline? He's just as yummy as they say!

AMIL: I bet he is, too.

ISLA: [*laughs*]

AMIL: [*laughs*]

Miles pauses the video midcackle. I wipe my face with my hand. "'Yummy' is an exaggeration. I think 'palatable' is a more honest assessment."

Miles does that thing where he presses his lips together so his mustache takes over his whole mouth. "It's not funny, Jason."

I know it's not. I'm actually pissed because, out of all that time spent trying to make sick kids feel good, it's a photo of a woman's hand on my ass that makes the news. It's been three years since I went off the rails, but I can't seem to live it down. Yup, that's me, Jason Connor. Everybody's favorite train wreck.

"Look, Miles, I could understand if I did something wrong. But that's *her* hand on *my* butt. I'm the victim here! I've been keeping my head down. I've been working hard. I can't control what other people do."

Miles sighs, and suddenly, I'm overcome with memories of my dad. My dad was the kind of dad who threw a baseball with you in the front yard and whose "talking-tos" left you feeling sheepish but still loved. Looking back, I wonder if there was some kind of magic to it. Like, how was it that the feeling of his hand on my shoulder was enough to give me the courage to swing a bat again after striking out six times in a row? How was it that when he said, *Son...* and followed it with anything, anything at all, I believed it—really believed it, down in my DNA?

I don't play baseball anymore, and my dad doesn't say, *Son...* to me anymore because he passed away right before Mattie was born. Now, when I screw up, there's nobody to make me believe in myself again.

"You've got to be the cleanest guy on the block, Jason," Miles says, and I'm already nodding. "I mean no screwups. Nothing that even *looks* like a screwup. If you don't, you could lose your contract for next season, and as your director and your friend, I don't want to see that happen."

"Does the network really want to replace me with Zachary Tay?"

Miles's mustache twitches. "They don't want to do anything. But they like Zach because he's not always being photographed with women's hands all over him, and he doesn't sucker punch random husbands and get thrown in jail while home on vacation. I practically had to donate my left nut to keep that quiet."

I wince into my fingers. "That was a long time ago."

"Funny, to my scrotum, it feels like yesterday."

I shake off the image of Miles with only one cherry on his stem. "Fine. Look, Miles, I won't let you down. I won't touch another woman unless it's in front of a camera for work purposes, I promise."

"And the drinking?"

"I've got it under control."

He nods. "Let's get some more good PR shots and clips, preferably ones where your ass isn't playing the starring role."

"That's gonna be hard. My ass auditions for everything."

He laughs, and it's one of those weak, almost-doesn't-make-it-out-from-under-his-mustache laughs, but I grab on to that sucker, swing on up, and ride it into the sunset. "Don't worry, Miles. I'll be your poster boy for good behavior. Teacher's pet. Sam Beckett. Boy Scout. All of it. I'm your Huckleberry."

He frowns and nods. "I know you are, Jason. And don't worry. I'm on the lookout for the kinds of projects that'll help you turn things around. If I find one, I'll send it to Cameron."

I want to hug him, but instead I shake his hand and head for the exit. Truth is, I just made a promise I don't know how to keep because, when I do something right, nobody notices, but if I trip up even the tiniest bit, the wolves are always there, dressed as grandmothers, ready to eat me alive.

Outside, aviator shades rescue me from the dazzling sun reflecting off the sidewalks and buildings. A couple of women with shopping bags stop me for selfies, and I oblige, hurrying away with a polite wave. I always park far away because walking feels good. My shiny black Alfa Romeo is there waiting for me on the curb in front of Starbucks. I love this car. It's warm and comfortable and fast and nonjudgmental. Just falling into the driver's seat makes me feel 30 percent less shitty.

I don't want to blame my dad's death for why I beat the crap out of that guy or why I did all the other awful things I've done, like missing Mattie's birth. Especially that.

I pull out my phone and scroll through my social media feed until I find that celebrity crush poll again. Looks like I'm bravely hanging on to second place. At least some people out there don't think I'm a total jerk. Maybe I should buy the book. I don't have to actually read it, but I feel like I owe the author that much for giving me something to lord over Sean. I plan to draw every ounce of blood out of that unicorn.

I tap the link embedded in the post, and it takes me to a web store. Wow, I think I grew an ovary just looking at that cover art. I read the blurb:

When dolphin trainer Nora is hired to oversee the filming of animal actors in a major motion picture, she doesn't know that her celebrity crush is playing the starring role. Then the leading lady suffers a shark attack, and Nora finds herself polishing up her acting (and flirting) skills . . .

"Geez." I laugh but tap the link for one-click ordering anyway. Now the book is mine. It'll arrive by mail tomorrow, but I can start reading it now on my phone if I want. Why not? I launch the e-book app.

Although it's not my typical reading material, I find myself hooked a few paragraphs in. By the fourth page, I'm introduced to Mr. Celebrity Crush himself, a character by the name of Gage. It's a romance novel, so of course he's all muscled and chiseled and rugged.

Am I rugged? I like to hike, so I'm thinking that counts.

Then I get to the part about the memes. The girl character, Nora, is watching memes of the guy character, Gage, and whaddayaknow? They're mine.

Okay, maybe that's jumping to conclusions, because a bunch of us have memes where we're saying *okay* and *what?* and *nope* and things like that. But she describes a couple of others in there that aren't standard one-worders. Subtle things clue me in. There's one especially that I can tell is based on a scene from a movie I did early on in my career, where I deliver the line *Whoever cares most gets to win*. It's not one of my better-known performances, but I'm really proud of the work I did in that film. The meme isn't exactly the same, but the way she describes it, there's little doubt in my mind. I'm 90 percent sure it's me.

I smile. I don't know this person, but it sure feels good to be chosen for something other than Most Likely to Seduce Your Mom at a Wedding.

Out of curiosity, I click her personal link. It takes me to an author web page with links to her social media accounts. "Emmy Ellison," I say out loud, studying the picture of her squinting out to sea. She's pretty in a beachy sort of way. Her wavy, light brown hair is highlighted by the sun, and her hazel eyes have a golden clearness to them. Her bare shoulders are sun-kissed and glittering, as are the tops of her breasts rising sensually from her low-cut bikini top. The way she stares at the sea makes me think of mermaids and sailboats, buried treasure and longing.

My phone rings, snapping me back to reality. It's a number I don't recognize. "Hello?"

"Hey, Jason." The voice is perky and fun. It sounds terribly familiar.

"Yes?"

"It's Terica. You know, *Terica*. Don't you have me in your contacts? Never mind. I have a favor to ask. Have you heard of the book *Hashtag Celebrity Crush?*"

Well, well, well, I was right! Immediately, I want to mentally celebrate, but my conversation with Miles floats back into my consciousness. While the media is adept at spinning things to my detriment, seriously, what could it hurt? I haven't done anything wrong. *She* chose *me*. And this whole celebrity crush thing is just good, harmless fun. Maybe it could even help my image.

What would Dad say? I close my eyes and imagine it. Before he got sick. Before hospitals and tubes and fighting adjustable beds through narrow doorways in my childhood home. *Son*, he would say, *you've got a good heart, and anyone that matters will see it*. I hold my breath, letting the words sink in. Do their magic.

Yeah, I don't buy it, either.

But with a little effort, maybe I can play this to my advantage, show the world that Jason Connor is really a good guy who just made a mistake. Or a few mistakes. Or one enormous mistake that kind of overshadows every other aspect of his life. The point is, this could be my path back to sweetheart status. Besides,

I'd be lying if I said I wasn't curious to meet this Emmy Ellison in person.

"Jason?"

A tiny chuckle escapes me like a scrappy underdog with a heart of gold who never gave up on his dreams. "Absolutely," I say before she can even ask. "Count me in, Terica. Whatever it is, I'm there."

Chapter 3

Maybe that's part of the medical emergency
I'm experiencing.

Emmy

AS SOON AS his name leaves my lips, my face explodes into a flush
of heat, and I have to look away. Oh to the crap. I did it.

"It's Jason Connor!" Terica throws her hands up in the air in
excitement. "Congratulations, Jason!"

The screen behind us transforms into a vanity shot of Jason in
his Hadron costume. He stands up and trades a variety of handshakes with his colleagues. Then he's coming toward me, and the
background blurs as I home in on all the little details I missed
before—how tall and thick chested he is in real life, the sexy
dusting of stubble on his cheeks and chin, the little curls peeking
out behind his ears.

My internal organs do a Klingon fire drill, jumping out of

the airlocks, zipping around, and reboarding in all the wrong places, all the while shouting and cursing in a very throaty language. When he reaches for my hand, it's in slow motion, or maybe that's part of the medical emergency I'm experiencing. I don't know if I stand up or if he pulls me out of the chair, because all my senses have shut down and my brain is like a scratched record, repeating, *Oh my God, oh my God, oh my God.* He folds me into a hug, and I'm pretty sure I gasp and just stand there in freak-out mode with Jason Connor's arms around me, all my dashboard lights exploding with sparks and tiny fires, and the AI screaming like a cybernetic teenage girl at a Taylor Swift concert.

It takes a few seconds to settle into it, just as I predicted. My body relaxes, and I press my hands into his back, forcing myself not to trace the muscles there with my fingers. My nose fills with his scent of citrus and musk, and I probably sigh before realizing that the standard elapsed time of a normal human hug is ending right about now, and, tragically, I'll miss 90 percent of this one, just as I'd feared.

But he doesn't let go. Instead, he continues to hold me tight, my cheek against his chest while the audience loses their freaking minds and Terica is saying, "Wow, wow, wow," and the entire front of me is steadily growing warmer with our trapped body heat.

Jason Connor is giving me the long hug I asked for! He's not being a jerk. He's being... amazing.

God, this makes me feel even worse about putting his personal life in my book. It was just one tiny scene, but it's way too much like the small-town Ohio police record that somehow never drew the eye of Celebrity Sauron. I tried not to use it. I really did. But when my love interest needed a painful and reputation-ruining moment for the plot's sake, it was perfect. After I read the police report, I couldn't think of anything else.

But why am I letting this moment get ruined? He probably doesn't even care about that stupid incident. It's years in the past, and he's a super-successful movie star. And he's hugging me! Right now! If there was ever an argument for living in the moment, this is it.

The dashboard alarms silence themselves as I surrender to his embrace. I let myself feel all the feels, let all the straining parts of me go slack. That's what fantasies are for, right? I melt against him. He senses it and adjusts, pulling me in even tighter. It's freaking paradise. I don't even care if I look like a dope on TV.

Then he chuckles.

It's so slight it doesn't even make a sound. Instead, I feel it in his body, a jerking movement of laughter, as if he's just heard the punch line to an inappropriate joke. Is he making fun of me?

He pulls away, arms still around me, and I find myself looking straight into those eyes, deep and blue as a summer sky. A playful smile dances on his face. I know that smile. I've seen it a hundred times on screens and in memes. He murmurs, "You okay?" and when I hear the little crack in his voice, I understand what's happening. He's not making fun of me. He's saying, *Terica is right. I'm bulletproof. But what about you? Can we have some fun? Can we put on a show? Can we give the audience what they want?*

My heart is all kinds of all over the place. I think it's the only organ that hasn't given up on me completely. But I need to keep it in check. This isn't real—it's Hollywood. I can't forget that. I'm onstage on *The Terica Show* wrapped in Jason Connor's embrace, but it doesn't mean anything. It's all about the *ooh*s and the *aah*s from the audience. It's about millions of women living vicariously through me. My best strategy is clear. Play along. Go with the swoony celebrity crush thing. And never forget, we both have an agenda—I'm selling a book, and he's selling an image.

But Jason Connor is looking into my eyes, deeply, and I'm not sure I can handle any of this.

Emmy, this is your chance. This is the wormhole to the Hollywood universe, and Jason Connor is holding it open. Close your eyes. Hold your breath. Jump in.

I'm pretty sure my smile is as sloppy as a 2:00 a.m. taco run. My voice is raspy and not my own. "I'm bulletproof, too," I whisper. "Do your worst."

The smile widens. He sweeps me off my feet and into his arms.

Chapter 4

Did you say somebody owes me a Ferrari?

Jason

THIS IS GONNA be fun.

I whirl Emmy around in circles in my arms, and the audience goes wild. Honestly, she's even prettier in person than in her author photo. I turn up the charm to the max. "Where's the horse, Terica? I thought I ordered up a horse. And a sunset."

Terica looks apologetic. "Sorry, Jason, there's no horse, although, considering the time, there might actually be a sunset outside."

I set Emmy down, and she makes a show of her knees buckling so I have to steady her. It's perfect. "Whoa there."

She holds on to my arm with one hand and brushes the hair out of her face theatrically with the other. Apparently, she's got some acting chops. Awesome! I flex that arm to make sure she has something steady to hold on to. She's a little short, so I have to lean to the side, but that's okay.

"I'm all right. Not swooning at all," she says.

I knew this was going to be fun.

Terica's voice is all faux concern. "Jason, can you get her over to the chair, please? I think the poor woman needs to sit down."

"I'm not sure I can walk." Emmy's grin is careless and wanton. It's a total turn-on.

"I'll handle this." I give a confident nod and then sweep her into my arms again. The audience explodes into more whistles and applause. I walk her over to the chair slowly, with a cowboy swagger, noting Sean's aggressive eye roll on the way. I toss him my best *suck it* face.

"Before you put me down..." She pauses.

I stop, and we all go silent, hanging on her words. "Yes?"

"Would you do the memes for me?"

"Wh-what?"

"Yes! Just like that."

I'm still confused. Terica clarifies. "She wants you to act out your internet memes, Jason. She wants to see you do them in person."

Emmy's eyes shine as she nods. "Please? Do the one where you say, *Okay*."

Oh. I get it. I dip my head and raise my eyes. "Okay," I say.

She grins. "Do the one where you wink."

I wink.

"Do the smolder."

I purse my lips and darken my gaze. The camera is right there, capturing both our faces.

"Do the one where you say, *Whoever cares most gets to win*."

So she likes that one, huh? I dig deep, find the feeling. "Whoever cares most gets to win."

A sleepy, satisfied smile pours across her face. I find myself matching it. "Thank you."

"My pleasure." Gently, I place her in the chair.

"So, Emmy," Terica says as I relax into my seat. She has to say it twice and then add a *yoo-hoo* to pull Emmy's attention away from me. The whole thing is really working for the audience.

"Sorry, Terica. I'm finding myself slightly distracted."

"I think we can all forgive you for that," Terica says. The laughter surges. "But, you know, there are about three billion folks out there who are dying to know what it feels like to be hugged by Jason Connor."

"Oh, it was okay." She fans herself with her hand. The audience loves it. She steals a glance at me, as if maybe her comment has hurt my feelings. Meanwhile, I'm having such a great time that I forget to pretend to look offended. The bright stage lights illuminate her eyes so that they sparkle like beads of amber in her heart-shaped face. I spot a little mole on her lower left eyelid that I didn't notice in her author pic. Her bare arms are smooth and golden, and her hands are completely naked—no rings, no nail polish, nothing.

"Just kidding," Emmy continues. "So, a hug from Jason Connor...how would I describe it?" She taps a finger on her lips in an über-cute way. "Have you ever been on one of those rides, like Mission: Space at Disney, where they put you in a capsule and spin you really fast, and all you see is a little screen so you don't know what's happening to you? But you feel all funny and disoriented and like there's no air in the capsule?"

"Yes?" Terica leans forward.

"It's like that. And then you time travel to another dimension." She crosses her legs and leans back, obviously pleased with herself.

"Wow!" Terica looks at me, impressed.

I shrug and do the nonchalant thing. I feel like a million bucks. Correction: I feel like at least five million bucks. I didn't know I was that good at the hugs.

The guys have been pretty polite up until now, but this is too much for Sean.

"Okay, okay. Now wait a minute!" His ringed forefinger goes up, and he looks like an annoyed prince in a suit. "Somebody's got to say it, and it might as well be me. This woman is obviously confused." He turns his attention to Emmy, his voice going up an octave. "Miss...*Ellison*, is it? Have you seen a medical professional lately? Why'd you pick this guy?"

She shrugs and smiles. "Sorry, guys. You're all awesome. Truly, you are. I guess I just like the funny, charming ones."

Sean puts on his conservatively offended face. "I'm funny!"

"I'm funny, too," Mount Ramirez adds.

"I'm charming," Andrew says blandly.

The gloat in my voice is extra thick. "Did you hear the part where she said hugging me is like time traveling to another dimension?"

Sean looks like he just tasted some bad sushi. "That's not fair. She doesn't have anything to compare it to."

I give him my *oh well* face.

"I demand a competition!"

"Let it go, Sean." I grimace to the audience. "You're embarrassing yourself."

Emmy leans forward in her seat. "I'm up for the hugging competition!"

"We're out of time for everyone but Emmy and Jason," Terica cuts in. The cameras keep rolling as the crew removes the mics from the rest of the gang and carries away their chairs. "Thanks for coming, guys."

"Next time you're in LA." Sean points his finger at Emmy as he exits the stage. "We'll do it. Remind me. See ya, Snack!"

Ramirez and Andrew pat my shoulder genially before waving to a cheering audience as they make their way offstage. I have to stand up so the crew can rearrange the seating. When everything finally settles down and it's just the three of us, I turn to Terica. "Did you say somebody owes me a Ferrari?"

"I'll look into it." Terica puts on a serious face. "So, let's talk about the book. Jason, now that you know you're the inspiration, are you going to read it?"

All the playacting is officially done, and we're in business mode. "Actually, I've already started reading it," I reply. I turn to the audience. "I got sucked in right away. I can't wait to read the rest."

"You don't have to finish it," Emmy says, shifting in her seat. She looks flattered and terrified at the same time. "I mean, I know you're really busy..."

I grin. "Oh, I'm going to finish it. You can count on that."

"Did you suspect you were the celebrity crush?" Terica asks. "No spoilers!"

"Yeah, the memes gave it away. Some of those memes—it was pretty obvious they were mine."

"And what did you think?" Terica asks.

Emmy's cheeks are flushed, and she can't look at me. It's adorable, but I don't want to embarrass her too badly. "I thought it was cool." She tosses me a grateful look. "It was *really* cool," I emphasize, and I mean it. It was.

Terica gets a cue from her staff. "Okay, folks, that's it for today. It's dance party time! Let's have some music, and in honor of Emmy's book, let's make it Duran Duran!"

"Girls on Film" bursts out from the speakers, and all three of us get up and start dancing as dictated by *The Terica Show* format. Emmy's dancing is not technically impressive, but it's carefree and sexy. I throw out some of my best *Lost Star Dance Troupe* moves. When she glances at me over her shoulder, I grab her hand and give her a spin. I mouth, "Dip?" at her, and when she nods, I drop her low, hyperaware of her compact, muscular body in my arms. At the bottom, she lets her head hang back, and I follow the long, sensuous line of her throat to her smooth chest and the curve of her breasts under her coral-colored top. I pull her up again and hold her against me, forcing her onto her toes. When the momentum dies, she's in my arms, our faces inches away from one another. Her lips are parted, and her eyes are half-lidded and sultry. She doesn't look like she's playacting anymore.

Oh crap, I almost forgot that I'm her celebrity crush! This isn't just fun and games for her. There are real feelings here. Real-ish anyway. I shouldn't play with them.

And my feelings? Technically, I'm not allowed to have any of those right now, so we don't even need to go there.

The taping stops. The music cuts out. It's all over.

I drop back, putting space between us. Something that feels a bit like guilt is transpiring in my chest. Emmy falls back onto her heels, looking shaken. Terica gabs with her crew and isn't going to rescue us. The audience is ushered out row by row.

I clear my throat. "You were great." I say it like I'm made of wood.

"Thanks for being a good sport." Her face is doing funny

things, like it's fighting with her brain. Then we both look around, even though there's nothing to look at.

"Okay, guys, that was really fantastic. Thank you so, so much. Angela's going to take you back now." Terica's got an obvious rush in her voice. It's showbiz, after all.

Angela leaves us in the hallway by the hair and makeup room, where we stand like abandoned souls. This is the part where I usually turn left and hightail it out of the studio. For some reason, I don't move.

"Can I get a selfie?" Emmy asks.

"Of course!"

She pulls out her phone, and I put my arm around her carefully, lean in, and smile. She snaps and shows me the picture. We look good.

"A silly one?" she asks.

"You bet." I do my best Hadron face. She twists her mouth to the side. She shows me that one, too. Then we just stand there again.

"Can I tag you?" she asks.

"You better." I point a finger gun at her. God, that's so lame. She does it back. Now we're both standing in a hallway, pointing finger guns at each other. It must be noon at the Awkward Corral.

My phone buzzes. It's a reminder to pick up Mattie from Margarita and a sort of auditory rubber band on my wrist, snapping me back to real life. "I have to go pick up my son," I tell her. "This was really fun."

"Yeah, it was." Her smile is a bit naughty, though I don't think it's meant to be. It feels dangerous and thrilling. Forbidden. Tempting. One of those moments I'm supposed to steal a bike and pedal away from at a very fast pace.

"Okay. Bye!" I give a wave.

"Wait!" she says, and I steel myself. Here it comes. The *Hey, do you want to go get a drink?* The gentle sidle into my personal space. The suggestive touch. The invitation for something, and, later, something more. I don't want her to do it because I'm going to have to say no, and I don't want to have to do that.

"Yes?" I ask in a careful voice.

"I'm kind of stuck here, time traveling in this other dimension. Do you think I could get a lift back?"

Huh?

Her arms open hesitantly, and then I get it. The hug thing.

"Absolutely," I say, stepping forward. "Bring it on in." I try not to notice how her curves fit against me, the smell of coconut in her hair, the pressure of her hands on my back. Without the lights and cameras and energy, all the small, subtle things make themselves known.

"Thanks," she says when our bodies separate. I can see her struggling to restrain a big grin.

"Anytime." Everything in me wants to offer her an actual lift, too. Or suggest that drink myself. Then that *something*, and maybe that *something more*.

I think the bike I was supposed to steal and pedal away on just turned into a motorcycle painted with flames of self-sabotage. But we don't have to get on it. It would be better to just keep it all profesh. Better for me. Better for her. Better for Miles's balls.

"Okay, goodbye!" I turn and walk away, a heavy, stifling feeling pressing against my back. The hallway seems to go on forever. *Don't turn around, Jason.*

The exit door opens into a sky the color of a missed sunset.

Chapter 5

That's a lie from the pit of hell.

Emmy

JOSIE BRINGS THE champagne, and Peyton and I have all the hors d'oeuvres lined up on trays like prisoners, ready to be devoured. We're celebrating yet another week of insane book sales. Ever since my appearance on *The Terica Show* a few weeks ago, *#CelebrityCrush* has been flying off the shelves.

"Moooom!" Peyton shouts from where she retapes a falling streamer to our trailer's polymer walls. "Has Jason Connor followed you back yet?" My daughter's braces glow pink under the thick, black curls she got from her dad. She's kept the place in celebration mode ever since the show, with dollar store party supplies and balloons. Other than that, it's dressed in its perennial beach-boho style with surfboard-shaped throw pillows, a sea-glass-studded floor lamp, and 3M hooks securing a string of Japanese lantern lights above the kitchen cabinets. I let her pick the "party candle" for tonight, one of a collection of Bath & Body Works winners we bought during the last candle sale. I believe this one is called Christmas Sweater. It's only April, but around here, we court anarchy.

"Not yet," I say with forced cheerfulness.

I can't stop thinking about being with Jason Connor on the show. God, that hug really was bliss. I expected a hug, of course. But I expected it to be polite. There was nothing polite about it.

In fact, my insides still go liquid thinking about how he squeezed me just that little bit tighter at the end, like he couldn't get close enough. Dancing with him was nice, too, the way he dipped me and pulled me against him so tightly I had to lift up on my toes. Really nice.

Gah, I'm an idiot! It was for the show. He made that clear. In fact, he couldn't get out of there fast enough after our second hug backstage—the second hug I asked for like a total fangirl. What was I thinking?

Anyway, it's all over. I have book sales—fantastic book sales. But that's it. Jason Connor hasn't followed me back or interacted with me in any way on social media even though I tagged him as promised. Did I really expect him to?

A sea breeze meanders through the back screen door, tarries a bit, and then wanders out the front. Josie is appraising a bacon-wrapped scallop on a toothpick with skepticism.

I plop down next to her. "It's cooked," I assure her.

She looks guilty before taking a nibble and grimacing. She's a natural blond, but with her artsy, dyed-purple haircut and brown eyes, she's got a beatnik Brie Larson thing going on. "I had a bad experience once. You know that."

I snatch it from her and shove it in my mouth. "Shellfish has apologized to you so many times. When are you going to forgive it?"

"*¡Nunca! ¡Jamás! Never!*" Josie's always trying to teach Peyton and me Spanish. She claims hers isn't perfect, but the Latinx women at the salon where she works say her accent is great even though she's from Central Florida. She learned to speak Spanish in Mexico, where she lived as a kid, although she's never told me the details.

"*¡Repitan*, por favor!*"

"*¡Nunca!*" I shout.

"*¡Jamás!*" Peyton bellows.

Shouting in Spanish is more fun than shouting in English—all three of us agree on that.

"*¡Excelente!*" Josie praises us. "And now we celebrate!" She grabs a champagne bottle and shakes it. She pops the cork before I can protest and puts her thumb over the mouth, spraying Peyton and me with foam. We cry out and try to grab it from her, but she's too fast. She tilts her head back so far that the choppy ends of her hair graze her shoulders as she drinks directly from the bottle.

I grab a kitchen towel. "God, can you please be more fun, Josie? You're such a downer."

"I brought three more bottles."

I'm not sure if that's supposed to be a comfort or a threat.

"Mom, Aisha wants to know what Jason Connor smells like." Peyton holds her phone in one hand and licks champagne off the fingers of the other.

"Stop that!" I throw the towel at her. "Go and wash your hands. And tell her he smelled like pickles."

Josie coughs down a laugh and pops another bottle, this time like a normal human being. You never know when the chaos is going to show up with her. It's kind of like her art. It's either lovely, otherworldly beach scenes, like the one in my living room, or black hatch marks of rage, like the one in my closet.

"Here you go, my celebrity best friend." Josie pushes the stem of a wineglass into my hand. My kitchen isn't big enough to store proper champagne flutes.

"Nobody but you considers me a celebrity." I clink rims with her and think about how Jason Connor really did smell. I'm pretty sure it was Calvin Klein.

"Your modesty disgusts me. What's it going to take for you to be proud of what you've accomplished?"

I think for a second and raise my glass. "Movie deal?"

"You sure about that?"

I don't answer. I'm too busy hearing Rhett's voice. *What was your name again?*

"You'll get to Hollywood, if that's what you really want," she says. "You'll take it by storm."

"I doubt that." I blink away a pair of stupid, ungrateful tears.

"No!" Josie shouts, as she always does when I get whiny or sad or weepy. She stabs another scallop at me. "You have oodles of talent, Emmy. Just because some big shot director didn't see it *one time* doesn't mean it isn't there."

"That's a lie from the pit of hell," I grumble.

She sniffs the scallop. "The pit of hell is my primary news source."

"You shouldn't get my hopes up." I reach over to rescue her from this appetizer as well. "You should support me."

Josie's laugh is more of a snort. "Support you in your self-defeating attitude? Okay, I'll give it a try." Her brown eyes open wide, and her eyelashes flutter. Her voice gets soft and sweet.

"Oh, Emmy, I love you so much. You'll never amount to anything, but I support you in that. Keep reaching for the middle shelf. Actually, you're short, so keep reaching for the lower shelf, and I'll be there clapping real hard when you get the participation trophy that's sitting on it."

"Helpful," I mutter. "Mucho helpful."

"*Muy* helpful," Josie corrects me.

Peyton comes back from washing her hands. "Come on, Mom, do the Renegade with me!"

I plaster on a smile. It's a welcome distraction. "TikTok version or do we do it to 'Planet Earth'?"

"You pick. We're celebrating you!"

God, I love this girl. When did she get so considerate? "Alexa, play 'Planet Earth'!"

The trailer fills with Duran Duran music, which I bought the permissions for and purposely peppered throughout my book. We all free dance to the first verse. Then Peyton and I launch into the Renegade TikTok dance on the chorus. First, it's the *whoa, clap, scoop, wave.* Then the *bang, bang, push.* Josie tries in vain to follow along, but she doesn't know how many hours Peyton and I have put into our old-school TikTok choreography. I'm not a great dancer, but for me, it's not about being great or even decent; it's about spending time with my daughter. It's about movement and losing yourself in the rhythm, forgetting about all the crushing disappointments of life and grabbing on to something that feels good, at least for the moment. *Snap, swoop, offer it, offer it. Hip, hip, wrap, open,* then the *jump and flourish.*

By the final chorus, Josie's mastered the easy part (*offer it, offer it*), and she adds some step ball changes and a bona fide Charlie Chaplin heel click, which is a feat in my tiny living room. Peyton loses her mind.

"Tía Josie—woooo!" It's so cute the way Peyton calls her "Tía" instead of "Aunt." Her arms flail in the way of little girls who haven't learned to hold it all in yet. She's twelve, so I know there's not much of that left, and I gobble up every moment.

"And that's enough dancing." Josie sinks back into her chair. She switches gears, putting on her fun face. "So, your Lost Boy called. Jason Connor wants to see you again."

I've been avoiding letting on to Josie just how badly I've been obsessing over Jason, but I play along with her game. "Tell him I'm busy."

"He says you can tell him all about how busy you are...over drinks."

I nibble a carrot. "Coffee."

"Breakfast."

"Josie!" My eyes flick to Peyton, but she's staring at her phone. I'm about to make her put it away—right after I finish imagining morning-after eggs with Jason Connor, my hair tousled, his gaze sleepy and seductive.

But Peyton misses nothing. "Don't do it, Mom. He's a total man-whore."

I purse my lips at her. "Nobody's doing anything. And that's not nice. Why would you say that?"

"He went to jail for a bar fight. Over a woman. Who was *married*."

Josie feigns horror, but I know she's the one who told Peyton, because I'm the one who told Josie. It's like Six Degrees of Kevin Bacon, the celebrity gossip version.

I glare at my traitorous friend as I grab my phone. "He's not like that anymore. He went through a bad time. Look, here he is saving children from cancer!" I pull up an article on the children's hospital fundraiser to show Peyton. Everyone is smiling and posing with the kids, and Jason Connor is totally into it. In one shot, his face is practically lit from within as he high-fives a kid in a wheelchair. In another, he's kneeling down to a little girl's level. It's sweet and candid. I let out a wistful sigh.

Josie eyes me. "You're not still pining over him, are you?"

"Yes, I'm still pining," I admit. "You saw that hug. I'll be pining over Jason Connor when I'm on my deathbed in a morphine coma!"

"Mmmm, I do remember it," Josie moans. "But the show's over, honey. It's time to get back to real life."

My phone rings. The illuminated name indicates that it's my agent, Jill. I exchange a look with Josie. Seven p.m. on a Friday is not a normal time for a work call from a New York agency. I tap the speaker icon. "Hello?"

"Hold on to your britches, girl, I've got some news."

Peyton and Josie have the wide-eyed look of bad anime. I hold the phone out on my palm, like it's going to beam us all up to a starship. It's so quiet I can hear the seashell wind chimes outside tapping out their comforting, gentle song.

"Two things," Jill says. "One, you're up to number eight on the *New York Times* bestseller list. Congrats!"

Josie and Peyton bounce silently while I open my mouth in a wordless scream.

"Two…the studio got the funding for the film. *Hashtag Celebrity Crush* is going to be a movie!"

The aluminum and vinyl chair rattles as I shoot out of it, and I probably look like I've just found a snake in the toilet, which, incidentally, has happened more than once in this mobile home park.

"You'll have to sign off on it, of course, which I imagine

you'll do since they're looking at Jason Connor to play the starring role."

"Of…of course," I stammer. "Sign it! Sign it all! Approved!"

"I thought you'd say that. I already sent the screenplay version you wrote over to the director. It's Miles Gauthier. He probably won't use it, though. He's got his own people, and he insists on complete creative control. You don't have a problem with that, do you?"

I plop back down on my chair, miss the seat entirely, and crash to the floor. "Of course not. Miles Gauthier is great!"

"They want to fast-track this to ride the social media wave you've created, so they want to do casting all next week, two to three months of filming over the summer, and get this…they want you to do a kickoff photo shoot with Jason to play up the whole celebrity crush thing."

I start to stand up but crumple to the floor again. "I'm sorry, what?"

"You heard me, you disgustingly lucky cow. You're gonna get to do interviews and photo shoots with Jason Sexy-as-Hell Connor. It was all that hugging adorableness on the show. Fans loved it."

I cough and reach for Peyton's outstretched hand to help me to my feet. "When is all of this happening?"

"The *Vanity Fair* photo shoot with you and Jason Connor will be late summer. Then, when the movie comes out at Christmastime, you'll get to be part of the premiere hype. And, girl, if we play this right, I think we can make all our dreams come true."

My Fitbit is flashing like crazy. I plop down in my chair, this time successfully. "What do you mean?"

For a moment, I only hear Jill's breath in the phone. Then

her voice gets deep and her New York accent extra thick. "Listen, Emmy, this is a Cinderella story. Small-time author/influencer makes it big, goes on tour with her celebrity crush, turns it into something more…if you know what I mean. With Jason Connor, it shouldn't be hard. Guy's a total cad…"

I quickly take her off speaker and cross the trailer to my bedroom. "Please tell me you're not suggesting I…" I sink onto my bed and lower my voice. "Prostitute myself."

Jill chuckles. "This is Jason Connor we're talking about. I've asked you to do more painful things already, like cut that one cringey sex scene. Remember that one? With the unicorns?"

"They were *horses*, and they were running across the beach! It's romantic! Anyway, back to Jason Connor…"

"Nothing has to actually happen. You just have to make it look like something *might have* happened. Just like on *The Terica Show* with that hug. You have to tell a story and make people believe it. It's called marketing. We'll do an East Coast book tour this summer while they're doing the bulk of the filming and tag a West Coast one onto your photo shoot with Mr. Hot Stuff so you have some time to work your magic. Then a reboot in December when the movie comes out. Any questions?"

My head is spinning. "I guess not."

"Great! Congratulations, Emmy."

"Oh, wait, yes! There's something I want to change in the screenpl—" But she's already hung up.

Josie peeks through the crack of the doorway with two more glasses of champagne in hand. "Whoa!"

"Whoa is right."

She perches beside me on the bed and hands me a glass so we can toast. "To your upcoming movie and promo tour with Jason Connor. Aaaaaah!"

I toss back my drink, but I don't cheer with her. My stomach is a twisty mess.

"What's the matter?" Josie asks. "I expected you to be bouncing off the walls."

A sigh escapes me. "I'm excited about the movie and the promo tour, of course I am. But Jill's advice feels . . . *ick*." I pause and wonder if I should say the ridiculous thing I'm thinking. Finally, I just do it. "It'd be different if it was for real."

Josie scoffs, making me immediately regret my honesty. "Come on, Emmy. You don't really think that's in the cards, do you? I mean, Jason Connor? And isn't he sleeping with that goddess Margarita Ayala?"

I pout. "*A*, I don't even know if they're together right now, and *B*, is it really that crazy a thought? I mean, you were the one just giving me a pep talk about following my dreams."

Plus, she wasn't on the receiving end of that hug. That extra squeeze.

"Aww, honey." Josie tilts her head. "I'm not talking you off a ledge of insanity because of you. I'm doing it because of him."

I throw my phone behind me onto the bed. "I feel like you're trying to support me, but maybe you accidentally kicked me in the teeth instead?"

She straightens up. "Again? Okay, let me try a different approach. He's a fool. You're completely right. The fact that he's a movie star doesn't factor in at all. You will have him, you determined little vixen. I have spoken!"

"That's better." I nod. "And thank you for quoting *The Mandalorian*. You know, they're pretty unfair to Jason in the press. All that partying he did was like three years ago."

"You're welcome." She takes another gulp of champagne. "Now don't stop me, I'm on a roll supporting you. You're going to get another crack at Orgasmic Hug Ken at this photo shoot, right, Barbie?"

A little bit of champagne bubbles out of my mouth from laughing, and I lick my lips to catch it.

"That's perfect! When you see him again, lick your lips just like that, but constantly. Don't stop. Then speak to him only in Shakespearean quotes. And if he tries to answer you, press your finger to his lips and say in a Russian accent, 'Hush, my love. The only sound I want to hear from you is your sighs of ecstasy...'"

I roll my eyes and thumb my phone awake. "Never mind. I forgot you were psychotic."

Josie throws her hands up. "I can't win with you!"

"I don't think we're playing the same game."

I swipe through Jason Connor's social media, again. His pinned post is I'm the #CelebrityCrush Yo! followed by tags of the rest of the *Lost Star* cast. I don't see anything recent from him. But people are still responding to that old post, tagging him, asking questions. There's even a comment about us. About me.

"Wait a second..." I pinch my screen and zoom in.

> Hey @thefunnyJason, what's up with your swoony celebrity crusher? Seems like low-hanging fruit, that one.

Josie peers over my shoulder. "What a douche."

"Eh," I say dismissively. "People are stupid."

"Did Jason reply?"

"I doubt it. He never replies to anything. Oh crap, he did!" I tap and read it out loud. "*I prefer my fruit from the top of the tree.* What? What's that supposed to mean?"

But at the same time, something inside my chest cracks

open. Jason Connor pretty much just told the whole world I'm not good enough for him.

"He didn't mean anything by it," Josie says. "He was just trying to be funny."

"It wasn't funny."

"I know." Josie flings a throw pillow across the room like a weapon. "That's why I'm going to have to kill him."

"He didn't even like the photos I tagged him in!" I whine. "He responds to that nardhead, and he doesn't even like my photos? He hasn't followed me back, either! Maybe he *is* a jerk!"

Another pillow slices the air. "And after I kill him, I'm going to make him apologize to you."

I ball my hands into fists tight enough for my fingernails to leave marks. How stupid am I? Imagining Jason Connor was flirting with me when he has Margarita Ayala waiting in the wings? What kind of an idiot thinks she has a chance with Jason Connor just because he throws on a smile and gives her a hug? He's got a closetful of those smiles at home. And for a guy like him, a hug is meaningless, especially when it's just for some swoony, sappy loser fan like me.

I kick at an abandoned sock on the floor. "At least I don't have to worry about him finding out about that scene I put in the book, because now I don't even care!"

"She doesn't even care," Josie, my real-life backup singer, echoes.

"He probably doesn't care, either. He's probably forgotten it even happened."

"He's forgotten completely."

"You know what? If Jill says I should walk all over Jason Connor to further my career, I'll walk all over him. I'll *trudge* all over him!" I illustrate this by stomping on the sock.

Josie clucks her tongue as she puts an arm around me. "I told you those Jason Connor memes were going to lead you to hell."

"It's going to be angry yoga tomorrow," I mutter.

"Yes! I love angry yoga."

"It's not something to be celebrated."

"Boo! I hate angry yoga."

"You're lying. You love it."

"You know I do. You know what else?"

"What?"

"When you go back to LA, you shouldn't even pack. You should buy yourself a whole new wardrobe on Rodeo Drive."

I drop my head on her shoulder. "Finally, some decent advice out of the bossy sidekick."

She kisses the top of my head. "I love you, too."

Chapter 6

If anyone doesn't feel like ripping somebody's head off, they should leave now.

VLOG, *RANDOM YOGA POSES*, APRIL 18

EMMY: Good morning, everyone! It's time for *Random Yoga Poses* with me, Emmy Ellison. Today we're going to do Virabhadrasana 2, also known as Warrior 2. This is a great pose for when you feel like you want to beat the crap out of someone, but *A*, you live in a civilized society and *B*, your frustration is kind of unfocused and might potentially get you picked up by a roving police cruiser...

But a little history first. The pose is named for a mythological Hindu warrior that I know you don't care about. All you need to know is that he had a thousand arms, flaming hair and eyes, and wore a necklace of skulls—and that makes him the best. So here we go. Feet wide apart. Leaning deeply into the lunge. This is a great hip-opening stretch because having closed hips leads you to doing and saying stupid things and feeling like a fool in front of people you want to impress, and I don't want that happening to any of you. You may not even know what a moron you are until some random stranger posts about it online. Arms up and out, one pointing fiercely in front of you and one pointing fiercely behind you. Look out over that front arm like your enemy is in your sights and you're going to blast him or her or them with your deadly yoga skills. Maybe your enemy is your own stupid thoughts and expectations that got out of control and now need to be pummeled into submission. Oh wait, we have someone on the live chat!

@namaste4ever says, *Peace and love to you, Emmy. I can feel that you need it today.* Stop trying to make me cry, @namaste4ever. I don't need that kind of negativity in my life. We're doing angry yoga, and if anyone doesn't feel like ripping somebody's head off, they should leave now. The rest of us are getting our Warrior 2 on. Okay, so as I get back into position, I want to tell you another reason why I picked Warrior 2 besides the flames and skulls, which were the major selling points initially. Warrior 2 helps with concentration. As you fix your razor-sharp gaze ahead, your mind will become clearer, and you'll be able to focus on whatever you want to manifest. Whether it's good or bad, or not necessarily bad but definitely not something to be proud of, you can manifest it. Okay, let's do this, people. Flames! Skulls! A thousand arms! (I can't believe I left that out as a selling point.) Go!

"I didn't say it was bad. It wasn't bad. It was…Ohio."

I roll my eyes and focus on the game. Kansas City didn't run the ball. They passed it. Incomplete. Second down.

She plucks at my sleeve. "Why do you still wear that horrible shirt? I've bought you nicer things."

Finally, I look her in the face. Perfect makeup. Designer earrings. Raven hair tamed by product and care and perhaps a blood sacrifice or two. We're so different. Always have been. I don't know what we were ever thinking.

"What is it you want, Margarita? Seriously. I'm paying attention."

She blinks, and I almost get a glimpse of something behind the hard-as-nails facade. Fear? Insecurity? Her red lips part, and she sucks in a breath, hesitating. I wait, but she doesn't follow it up.

"Really?" I shake my head. "You barge in here to what? Get my attention and then not say anything? What is this, a Charlie Puth song?"

Her gaze goes bitter. "I just thought we might spend some time together as a family. We *are* a family, you know."

She won't say it, but I can read between the lines. When Margarita got pregnant, she expected me to propose. Her family expected it, too. I thought about it, figuring it would be the right thing to do for the baby, but then Dad got sicker, and all the problems between Margarita and me got even bigger, and once Dad was gone, the only thing I was interested in was an exit door, not marriage.

Maybe I should feel guiltier about that, but I don't know how marrying Margarita would've fixed anything.

"Don't you ever think about meeting someone new? Falling in love? Being happy?" Even as I say them, the words kind of

Chapter 7

I'm not sure what could suck more.

Jason

MARGARITA SLAMS THE front door on her way in, and I look up from the NFL Network, where I'm watching an old game I missed during the season. Mattie's curly head is on my lap as he naps beside me on the couch with Possessed Baby tucked under his arm. His doll creeps the hell out of me with its wide, staring eyes and a yawing mouth that promises to suck out your soul in the middle of the night, but his mom got it for him, and he loves the plastic nightmare, so what's a dad to do?

She slaps her oversize purse on the kitchen counter, just like she used to when she lived here. It's like she owns the place, but she doesn't. She has her own place. This one is mine.

"Why are you here so early?" I ask. "You're not supposed to pick up Mattie till five."

"I have an engagement, so I'll bring him back to you for the evening."

I hate everything about that sentence. How she says "engagement" instead of telling me what she's really doing. And the way she makes it sound like she's doing me a favor by letting me see my kid. It's true I only get him every other weekend, per court order—my own fault for being "unstable"—but her acting all magnanimous about giving me more time with Mattie makes me want to punch the wall and disappear at the same time.

"What time will you be back to pick him up?"

"I'll just stay at your place tonight."

She squeezes onto the couch on the other side of me. I scoot as close to Mattie as I can without disturbing him and try to get back into the game. It's 10–3, Cincinnati in the lead over the Chiefs, and they're in position to score again. It isn't long before I feel Margarita's fingernails caress my arm under the sleeve of my retro Boomer Esiason football jersey.

"Not now." I pull my arm away and rub off the tickly sensations. "The Bengals are winning."

Her pout hides the flecks of flint behind her eyes, but I know better. "I know what's up with you. It's that celebrity crush girl from *The Terica Show*. You haven't been the same since."

I grab the bowl of blue corn tortilla chips off the coffee table and plunge my hand into it. "You're imagining things."

"So, where'd you do it? Greenroom at Terica's studio? The car? I know that's a favorite of yours. Airport bathroom before she flew back to—where is she from anyway?"

I'm too riled up to eat the chips. "I didn't do anything with her. She's a nice person, and I was trying to be nice."

"Fine. We won't talk about her. We can talk about us instead." Her fingernail is on the side of my neck now, but I don't know if she means to seduce me with it or slice open my carotid artery.

"Can I please just watch the game?"

She harrumphs and leans back against the couch cushions. For a minute, we sit in silence, but I can't concentrate. What down is it? Who has the ball? What freaking sport is this anyway?

"You know," she says, "if you were just trying to be nice, you're misleading that poor woman. After all, Jason Connor is her celebrity crush. She's going to read into everything you do."

I drop the bowl of chips back onto the table. Cincinnati must have blown it because the Chiefs have the ball, and the score is the same. It's first down. They're gonna run it, I'm guessing.

"Jason, are you listening to me?"

"I'm trying not to!"

Mattie stirs at my shout and turns over. I take the opportunity to haul him onto my lap so I can move farther away from Margarita's body pressed against my side.

She groans. "I hate this stupid sport."

"Then leave and come get Mattie in the morning."

"I'll stay. I've stayed with you through worse."

And there she goes. But I won't engage. If I don't engage, maybe she'll get bored. Go into another room. Go out to her car. Go to hell.

Fat chance.

Thirty seconds don't pass before she's back at it. "This reminds me of the early days when we used to visit your family. Sunday afternoons with the football game on TV. Your dad cooking outside. Your mom with the pitcher of mimosas. Your brother and his wife and their entourage of sticky little children…"

"They're foster parents, what do you want?"

choke in my throat. Margarita and I have been through so much together. And I know I hurt her. If I hadn't hurt her so badly, she probably wouldn't be the way she is.

Her laugh manages to sound both cruel and sad at the same time. Her cool hand caresses my chin. "Oh, *Jay*-son." She draws out the first syllable, long and Latin for me. Margarita Power Move Numero Uno. "It's not too late for us. Things could still work out." Her words are breathy, her mouth close to mine.

I jerk my chin away. This was a mistake. I don't want to mislead her. "Things aren't ever going to work out, Margarita. Things between us just don't work, period."

She drops the face, the exaggerated accent, everything, like a guillotine. "Well, they could, if you really wanted them to. We owe it to Mattie."

"It's not about what I want," I say.

"It's always about what you want! Besides, who do you think is going to love a total asshole like you? Untrustworthy. Selfish. Immature. Face it, I'm the only woman willing to put up with you for more than sex. But at least I know what I'm getting. And what I'm not."

Fiery anger and shame swirl in my chest, but maybe she's right. Maybe if I wanted it more, we could be a happy family. Although, no matter how many times my brain tries to process those words, they don't compute.

"The sex is good, though, isn't it?" She leans in, and I wince as her teeth nip across my neck.

This isn't love. This is planting a flag in soil. This is claiming. Besides, I'm pretty sure she's seeing someone else.

"What's your engagement tonight?"

Her straight black hair flies back as she sits up. Her lip lifts in a snarl. "None of your business."

"Then why are you acting like we're still together?"

"If you like having Matthew two weekends a month, we're together."

A stone expands in my throat. "What's that supposed to mean?"

"Nothing." She comes in again with her hot breath on my neck. "It's an appointment, that's all."

So *appointment* is the new euphemism for *date*?

I lean away from her. "I'm not as dumb as I look, remember?"

She dredges up a smile. "Did you know I've accepted the lead role in that celebrity crush movie, opposite you?"

I recognize Margarita Power Move Number Four: Change the Subject. I'm not happy about the casting, but it is what it is. "Yeah, Miles told me. Whatever, fine. Are you really gonna use Mattie as a pawn in all this? That's a real shit move, Margarita."

"Oh, you're one to talk about shit moves."

I ignore that. "The judge isn't going to change our custody arrangement just because we've split." It comes out sounding more like a question than a statement.

"You do whatever you have to, Jason. Although I believe *lack of a stable home life* was the judge's number one complaint about you. Besides, it's not all bad, is it? We have our moments." Her eyes are soft, dark, imploring. Her hand finds my thigh and begins to creep up. My insides feel like a bunch of kids running around with streamers, creating a wild, screaming tangle. My heart is the kid sitting in the corner, head on his knees.

God, what is she doing to me? Whatever we have, I don't really believe she wants it, either. It feels like some kind of punishment. For me. For her. For all three of us. And now I have to make a movie with her—a rom-com. I'm not sure what could suck more.

I brush her hand away. "Fine, you can stay the night, but I'm sleeping in the guest room."

She folds her hands in her lap, looking hurt. "I need you right now, Jason. Okay? Mattie needs you. We're your family. Isn't that enough?"

Enough for what? I want to ask, but I want the conversation to end more than I want answers. Is it my imagination, or is her bottom lip trembling? Is she acting? Margarita's been nominated for two Oscars, so it's possible. I've never been nominated for any, for the record.

Just then Mattie stirs on my lap. "Mami!" he cries, diving into her arms. He says something to her, but it's in Spanish, so I don't understand.

"What did he say?"

"He wants chicken nuggets."

I thought I might have heard *hambre* in there somewhere. "Are you hungry?" I ask him. "Hungry?"

He nods but doesn't try to say it. Here's another thing that kills me: bilingual kids often have delayed speech, and because Margarita speaks to him only in Spanish, most of the time I don't even understand him. Again, my fault, and I'm trying to learn. But it only makes me feel more like an outsider.

I can't believe Margarita would threaten to take away even the little bit of time I have with Mattie.

I repeat *hungry* a few more times, trying to get him to say it back.

Margarita sighs. "Leave him alone."

"Well, excuse me for wanting to communicate with my son."

She looks up toward the ceiling in a way I interpret to mean *this isn't worth my time* and stands up, hiking Mattie onto her hip. Possessed Baby's dead gaze is right at my eye level. I try not to recoil.

"I'll bring him back at five," she says, heels clicking across the tiled floor. "You can feed him dinner."

"Great."

"Bye, Daddy!" Mattie grins and waves.

"Bye, buddy!" I wave back.

Margarita swipes her purse from the kitchen counter, and the two of them disappear out the front door. I stare over the back of the couch at the place where they stood a moment ago while, in the background, a stadium full of people cheers.

Maybe Margarita is right. Maybe this messed-up relationship is the best I can hope for. Maybe I don't deserve anything better. Maybe I never will.

Completely checked out from the game, I pick up my phone. There's a text from Cameron, my agent.

Cameron: I hate this promo tour idea with the author chick! You guys were way too chummy on The Terica Show. It's gonna look bad.

I shake my head before replying.

Jason: Give me some credit, Cam. It's no big deal. Besides, a nice, sweet romance film will be good for my image. And BTW everyone else thought the whole hug thing was cute.

Cameron: They don't know you like I do. And they don't know Lost Star is on the line.

I blow out a lungful of air.

Jason: I haven't done anything. I don't get what you're so worried about.

She texts back the picture of the woman's hand on my butt from the autograph signing.

Jason: I didn't do anything with her.

Cameron: Well, people assume you did.

Jason: Well, I can't help that.

Cameron: (…)

Oh boy, the dreaded three dots. I buckle in for Cameronegedden. It's usually over quickly.

Cameron: Listen Jason. I'm telling you right now, if you screw this up, I'm out. I can't do this anymore. I've had about eight aneurysms since I took you on, and if you blow this, nobody else is going to want you either. You'll be relegated to porn flicks and HPV commercials!

Geez. Cameron! I type my reply.

Jason: I won't let you down. Stop worrying.

My agent deploys a battalion of emojis—crying face, mad face, eggplant, cat, skull and crossbones. I can't help but laugh. I don't know why she's overreacting. It's just a silly little promo tour for a silly little rom-com. Besides, Emmy's not like that. She could've made a move on me after the show, but she didn't. In fact, I wonder what she's been up to lately?

I pull up her website. I haven't been on here since I bought her book, and truth be told, I've been really busy with work and haven't read any more of it. I scan the links to vlogs and blogs, her TikTok account, Instagram, and whatnot. The thing that catches my attention is *Dolphin Tells Your Fortune.* That seems ambitious.

I tap the link, feeling a tiny zing of excitement. A vlog comes up. The video is from today. Just posted this morning. I press PLAY.

EMMY: Good morning, everyone, and thanks for tuning in to *Dolphin Tells Your Fortune.* I'm Emmy Ellison, and today is Sunday, May fifth. It's 8:22 a.m. Eastern Daylight Time, and Echo has graced us with her presence today. Echo, thank you for that. Say hi to your fans. Don't be one of those celebrities who's too cool for the selfie. That's it. Keep bumping the board. You know I love that. Yep, spray me, too. That's not rude at all.

Okay, for those of you just discovering us, welcome to my stand-up paddleboard where all the dolphin-related magic happens! We're happy to have you with us on *Dolphin Tells Your Fortune,* sponsored by Wok This Way. Wok This Way has three convenient locations: Port Richey, Tampa, and Clearwater. Okay, so the way this works is three different fortunes are hidden in the buoys you see floating out here in the beautiful Gulf of Mexico, and, yes, the buoys are really just amputated hunks of pool noodle. Echo will choose one, and that will be the fortune of the day. While we wait, let's take a look at what's coming through on the live chat.

@ChadAnimalLvr asks, *Isn't what you're doing illegal?* Gosh, well, Chad, thanks for joining us, and that's a great question. I'm not allowed to feed or touch wild dolphins, which I haven't done. Echo is actually a release from Mammal Dreams Aquatic Park, and she loves to flex her skills, so, no, what I'm doing is not illegal. If you want to know more, I invite you to visit the Florida Fish and Wildlife website.

Moving on . . . Oh, look! Echo has settled on one of the fortunes! Come on, Echo, bring it on over. That's it, girl! Aw! Listen to that chatter. I can never stay mad at you. Oh, you're gonna keep spraying me, huh? Maybe I can stay mad at you after all.

All right, folks, let's dig out the little baggie and break open that fortune cookie. *Dolphin Tells Your Fortune* says that your fortune for today is . . . Stop spraying, Echo. I mean it! Your fortune for today is *a shooting star is just a rock that is finally getting its moment to shine.* Wow, she sure got that one from the deep end. So there you have it, folks. Have you ever felt like you're nothing more than a rock hurtling through your life? Not even important enough to have a name, like Halley's Comet or Pluto or . . . Asteroid Belt? Well, don't despair, because the message today is you'll get your day to shine. It might take plunging through the stratosphere and a fiery death to make it happen, but your moment will come, and it will be beautiful. That's all for today from *Dolphin Tells Your Fortune.* Tune in again tomorrow—weather and dolphin permitting—for another daily fortune. Remember, Wok This Way is open seven days a week from 11:00 a.m. to 10:00 p.m. Find them online at www.wokthisway.com. And don't forget to subscribe and share. Bye, all!

God, Echo, stop spraying me! I swear—

The video cuts out. I take an inventory of what I noticed: athletic, golden-skinned body in a long-sleeved rash guard and red bikini bottom; that tiny mole on the bottom of her left eyelid; lilting yet gravelly Zooey Deschanel voice; sense of humor. It's supposedly passé to tan like that these days, but I have to admit the whole *Blue Lagoon* thing is working for me. Plus, I love red.

I drop the phone like a hot poker. Holy hells, maybe I'm in trouble after all.

Nah. Cam's just getting to me. Miles and Margarita, too. I got this.

Jason Connor is the king of his domain.

@ChadAnimalLvr asks, *Isn't what you're doing illegal?* Gosh, well, Chad, thanks for joining us, and that's a great question. I'm not allowed to feed or touch wild dolphins, which I haven't done. Echo is actually a release from Mammal Dreams Aquatic Park, and she loves to flex her skills, so, no, what I'm doing is not illegal. If you want to know more, I invite you to visit the Florida Fish and Wildlife website.

Moving on... Oh, look! Echo has settled on one of the fortunes! Come on, Echo, bring it on over. That's it, girl! Aw! Listen to that chatter. I can never stay mad at you. Oh, you're gonna keep spraying me, huh? Maybe I can stay mad at you after all.

All right, folks, let's dig out the little baggie and break open that fortune cookie. *Dolphin Tells Your Fortune* says that your fortune for today is... Stop spraying, Echo. I mean it! Your fortune for today is *a shooting star is just a rock that is finally getting its moment to shine.* Wow, she sure got that one from the deep end. So there you have it, folks. Have you ever felt like you're nothing more than a rock hurtling through your life? Not even important enough to have a name, like Halley's Comet or Pluto or... Asteroid Belt? Well, don't despair, because the message today is you'll get your day to shine. It might take plunging through the stratosphere and a fiery death to make it happen, but your moment will come, and it will be beautiful. That's all for today from *Dolphin Tells Your Fortune.* Tune in again tomorrow—weather and dolphin permitting—for another daily fortune. Remember, Wok This Way is open seven days a week from 11:00 a.m. to 10:00 p.m. Find

them online at www.wokthisway.com. And don't forget to subscribe and share. Bye, all!

God, Echo, stop spraying me! I swear—

The video cuts out. I take an inventory of what I noticed: athletic, golden-skinned body in a long-sleeved rash guard and red bikini bottom; that tiny mole on the bottom of her left eyelid; lilting yet gravelly Zooey Deschanel voice; sense of humor. It's supposedly passé to tan like that these days, but I have to admit the whole *Blue Lagoon* thing is working for me. Plus, I love red.

I drop the phone like a hot poker. Holy hells, maybe I'm in trouble after all.

Nah. Cam's just getting to me. Miles and Margarita, too. I got this.

Jason Connor is the king of his domain.

Chapter 8

Kill it on-screen, reach your dream.

FRESH LEAF BOOK CLUB, NEW YORK CITY, JULY 16

BEVERLY: Good morning, everyone! I'm Beverly Shipley with Fresh Leaf Book Club, New York City's premier source of publishing news and all the gossip. Today, I'm speaking with Emmy Ellison, author of the cheeky, fun romantic comedy *Hashtag Celebrity Crush*, which currently sits at number seven on the *New York Times* bestseller list. It's got everything you could possibly want in a romance novel—lots of pining, hot people in bathing suits, witty banter, and a heroine you can get behind. And, of course, we all know that the celebrity crush in the novel is based on none other than *Lost Star Dance Troupe* superstar Jason Connor.

EMMY: Inspired by.

BEVERLY: Oh, excuse me, *inspired by.* Emmy, how is the book tour going?

EMMY: It's been great, Beverly. We've been heading up the East Coast all summer, hitting the major cities. Most of the time more than one person shows up for the book signings. [*laughs*] Just kidding. I have to admit my hand is getting sore.

BEVERLY: So, the movie is being filmed as we speak. Jason Connor is playing the love interest. Seems appropriate. And the leading lady is his on-again, off-again partner, Margarita Ayala. Are you happy with those picks?

EMMY: Well, of course Jason has to play Gage, that goes without saying. And Margarita is so beautiful. I'm sure they'll bring the characters to life.

BEVERLY: Did you have any input in adapting the screenplay?

EMMY: Unfortunately, the director, Miles Gauthier, insisted on total creative control, so in a nutshell, no.

BEVERLY: Is that a problem?

EMMY: No, of course not! Did I make it sound like it was a problem? I didn't mean to make it sound like it was a problem.

BEVERLY: You're headed back out to LA at the end of this month, right?

EMMY: Yes, Beverly. As filming wraps up, I'll be combining my West Coast book tour with a big photo shoot playing off the whole celebrity crush thing. Almost like a mini–promo tour.

BEVERLY: How exciting! You'll get to spend some more time with Jason Connor. That hug on *The Terica Show* looked very warm. Maybe you'll get another.

EMMY: It was a great hug, Beverly. And he's a great guy. A class act.

BEVERLY: I'm sure. Let's talk about some of your other work. Anything coming down the pike?

EMMY: I've got another manuscript on submission, but no bites yet. I'm hoping, if *Hashtag Celebrity Crush* continues to do well, I might get an offer.

BEVERLY: Is it another rom-com?

EMMY: No, it's a massive space opera called *Prototype Yellow*. A ragtag team of space explorers learn the secrets of the universe, including the fact that they're fated to destroy it. I'd really love to see that in print.

BEVERLY: That's really different.

EMMY: Part of the problem, I'm sure.

BEVERLY: But a successful movie can be a game changer. You know what they say, *Kill it on-screen, reach your dream.* What would you say Emmy Ellison's dream is?

EMMY: [*laughs*] Hmm, Beverly, I don't know, exactly. Maybe reaching number one on the *New York Times* bestseller list? Gosh, that makes me sound like an inglorious narcissist, doesn't it? Maybe getting to do that hugging contest Sean O'Sullivan promised me on *The Terica Show.*

BEVERLY: Well, Emmy, good luck. We're all rooting for you. You won't forget us, will you?

EMMY: Never, Beverly.

Chapter 9

I've never been so thankful to have bought
Tic Tacs at an airport.

Emmy

THIS TIME WHEN I arrive in Cali, I've got the upper hand because they've given me a stylist. His name is Val, and the first thing I think when I see him is that Cinna from *The Hunger Games* had a baby with the TV show *Cupcake Wars*. I don't say that on my blog, though. I just use the word *fabulous*.

It's 10:00 a.m. Pacific time, and that means I'm already starving for lunch. The good news is, I don't have to buy a whole new wardrobe on Rodeo Drive, because Val picked out all my clothes, and they are AH-mazing.

"Our statement," Val says, looking a bit like the mushroom from *Alice in Wonderland* in his wide, lacy collar, "is going to be…" He squints at me appraisingly. "Butter!"

"Butter?"

"Yes. Rich, heavy foods and luxury and things with a sheen."

I don't quite know how to take that. I've been known to moisturize, but I thought that was a good thing. I certainly hope the whole "rich foods" theme isn't a hint for me to cut my portion sizes.

The photo shoot for *Vanity Fair* is on the Waldorf Astoria Beverly Hills pool deck. The hotel has an artsy, minimalist feel that I'm totally digging. Peyton would have hated it because the pool doesn't have five waterslides. Kids in Florida are spoiled rotten.

Thankfully, I don't have to wear a swimsuit. Apparently, "butter" to Val translates into a summery, raspberry-colored MISA sundress, high-heeled sandals I can barely walk in, and lots of gold eye shadow. As he paints my face, Val pokes my forehead with a long, skinny finger. "We need to get you Botox here and here."

"No Botox!" I slap his finger away. "I already spent two hours at your aesthetician's, and I'm pretty sure my human rights were violated."

It takes an hour to do my hair, but when he's done, I look like I could land six shampoo commercials. The downside is that by the time I stagger onto the pool deck on Val's arm, I'm hungry enough to eat a dinosaur.

"Do you have a chip pack or something?" I ask him.

His voice deepens. "Don't you even talk about food in my clothes."

Wow. Turns out there's a teaspoon of Samuel L. Jackson extract in those cupcakes.

Jason is late, but nobody seems to care. We all just wait. I check my phone. There's another text from Jill reminding me that "sex sells" and to "make those photos steamy, girl. We want to sell books!" When Jason finally shows up, they whisk him away and return him in a long-sleeved dark blue shirt, white pants, and bare feet.

"How come he gets to go barefoot?" I hiss at Val.

"Because you're short."

"I'm not *that* short."

When Jason makes his way onto the pool deck, I'm less bold.

"Hi," he says, his smile loose and disarming. They've put some more curl in his hair, effectively turning my entire vascular system into a wave pool. The shirt is tight and starched over his chest, tapering at the waist. I don't dare look any lower.

"Hi," I reply. I'm still mad at him over that "low-hanging fruit" comment and the fact that it's been months since we were on *The Terica Show* together and he hasn't liked even one of my posts, but I'm not going to be rude about it. Besides, my face is probably screaming like a stinking traitor how attracted to him I am.

"You look nice. I like the dress."

"You look nice, too. I like the…" I wave my arms at him vaguely. "Everything." Geez, as a writer, I should have more mastery over language.

We're ushered into position before the conversation can go any further, and thank God and Tom Hanks for that. I quickly discover that the plan for this celebrity crush photo shoot is for him to look all nonchalant and uninterested and for me to look like a lovesick washcloth. The photographer, an Asian woman with a clipped accent whose smile appears to have been surgically removed, points at me. "Put your hands like you are crawling up him, trying to get his attention."

I want to ask if she's serious, but I have to assume she knows what she's doing. I lay a hand on Jason's rock-hard chest, and immediately my face flushes. My other hand winds up on his abs, and when they flex under his shirt, I yank it away like I've been bitten by a rattlesnake. Jason doesn't do anything to make it easier for me. He just stares off into the distance.

I tilt my head and go for my best pining face, all the while adjusting my hands, trying to find a place for them that doesn't make me look like a drunk stripper desperate for an extra fifty bucks. Ten minutes later, I still haven't managed it. I should be enjoying this, but it feels awkward and wrong and, frankly, degrading. I don't know if it's pride or garden-variety self-respect, but I just can't do this.

"I'm sorry." I cease my pawing. "Can't we, like, just stand next to each other? Like normal people?"

The photographer turns to her assistant. "Oh God, she's difficult."

"I'm not difficult!"

But apparently, I'm difficult, because no one but me says otherwise.

The photographer waves a finger at me. "Okay, fine. Turn to each other. Put your arms around his neck."

Well, well, well, apparently being difficult works.

I've never been so thankful to have bought Tic Tacs at an airport. My face is two inches away from Jason's as they adjust our bodies, my heart thumping like a piston. I catch a whiff of his citrus-musk cologne amid all the chlorine molecules in the air, and I'm hyper-aware of his hands on my waist, although they kind of feel like they're just doing what they're told. I'm supposed to gaze longingly at him, but I can feel my face doing twitchy things.

It's just a photo shoot, Emmy. You can do this.

But everything is weird squared, and I feel like I'm made of right angles. I don't know if I can make this math problem look sexy enough to sell books. I'm just not cut out for this, and everyone here knows it, including Jason Connor. Especially Jason Connor.

But he's *right here.* In my arms. It'd be different if any of this were real. Even a little bit.

"Relax!" Val growls from behind me.

"Yeah, that's helpful!" I shout over my shoulder. The camera clicks as I do it. That'll be a keeper.

Jason sighs and squints but doesn't say anything. I'm screwing this up big-time. Later today, I have a book signing, which is something I can do. But this?

The next pose is even worse. They have me draped across his lap like a blanket. I should be ultra-turned-on, but the way they want me to hold my head is killing my neck, and Jason keeps shifting his hip where my elbow digs into it. I catch a glimpse of my face in the preview window of the digital camera, and it's truly horrifying. The following pose doesn't work, either. We're supposed to be lounging together by the pool, but it looks like we're waiting out a fire drill.

The photographer calls a break, and I find a table inside where I crack open my laptop, Val's sandals in a pile at my feet. I spend a few minutes deciding I'll go ahead and blog about this gawful photo shoot. I'm not too proud for that. I'm deep into the fifth paragraph of carnage when the smell of salami cuts into my creativity. Jason is standing in front of me, munching on a sub.

"What are you working on?"

Immediately, I transform into Bruce from *Finding Nemo.* "Do they have food for us?"

He shakes his head. "Models don't eat. I went on a sandwich

run." In his preppy clothes, he looks like a grown-up frat boy, casual and unbreakable. He holds the sub out to me. "Want a bite? Bread's a no-no for me anyway. Ends up right here." He points to his nonexistent love handles.

"Yes!" I reach across the table for the sub. He watches as I take a bite. Then another. Then a third. He doesn't move. It's very Christian Slater of him.

"Hey," he says on the fourth bite, "I'm still hungry, too, you know."

But it's so good, and I haven't eaten in ages. Plus, he deserves a little payback for being such an ass to me. And for never liking my social media posts. Or following me.

My chair grates against the floor as I stand up, still chewing, and get into position.

His eyebrows go up. "Are you—are you stealing my sandwich?" His voice cracks, but this time he's doing it on purpose, for effect.

"No." I stifle a smile and back up one step toward the glass doors leading to the pool deck.

"You *are* stealing my sandwich!"

"No, I'm not."

He takes a step toward me, a vampire smile on his face, and I take one back to match it. Another bite disappears. From the hallway behind Jason, Val is headed our way, flat iron in hand—I can only assume he's about to beat me to death with it for eating in his dress. Jason takes two steps toward me, fast, and that's my cue. Sandwich in hand, I turn and run.

"Oh no, you don't!" he shouts, but oh yes, I do—right through the tinted doors and across the pool deck. I knock a plastic chair over behind me to slow his chase.

Around the pool we go, but he's faster than me, and I'm

running out of furniture to toss into his path. Sunning itself on the surface of the water is a light blue inner tube with a bottom. Just when he's about to catch up with me, I panic and take a flying leap into it. Now I'm stuffing Jason Connor's sandwich into my face while skimming away from him across the pool. He puts on the brakes just in time to avoid ending up in the water.

He shakes his head at me, but he's smiling. So much for paybacks. He's loving this.

"Jump in after her!" the photographer shouts.

We both turn to her in confusion. She's wearing an insane, unnatural smile and bouncing up and down in her designer sneakers as she lifts the camera to her face.

Jason's open mouth snaps shut, and, without protest, he peels the navy shirt over his head in one movement, exposing all the muscles in his bare torso. He dives in wearing only the white pants, sending waves erupting across the surface. I crouch down low inside the inner tube, my dress forming a nest around me. He pops up, one hand seizing the edge of my floatie, bending it with threatening force.

"Fine, fine, you can have some!" I hold out the sandwich as a peace offering. He rises up like a sea monster for a bite. I feed him the rest of the sub, and it's not easy in a pool. There's a little dot of mustard on the corner of his mouth. Without thinking, I wipe it away with my thumb. His tongue flicks to that spot and lingers, eyes on me. For a second, I forget how to breathe.

Damn it, Emmy! Don't read into it!

Meanwhile, Val is glaring at me, and cameras are going off all around us. Now that the sandwich is gone, neither one of us seems to know what to do.

"Knock her into the water!" the photographer shouts. This lady obviously hates me.

"Please don't," I beg Jason. "I gave you back your sandwich."

He makes a gesture like it's out of his hands, but I can see him stifling a grin. "I have to do what they tell me to."

I open my mouth to rebut, but he leans hard on one side of the floatie, upending it and sending me tumbling over his shoulder into the water. Even though it's summer, the water is freezing! When I break the surface, my teeth are chattering, and I'm pretty sure I look like the dead girl from *The Ring*. Beside me, Jason treads water, his face transitioning back and forth between smug and apologetic.

"Are you mad?" he asks.

I part my *Ring* bangs. "I was already mad."

"I know." He adds sheepishly, "Flames and skulls?"

"You saw that?"

"Hashtag *Random Yoga Poses* showed up in my feed. *Recommended for you.*"

I smirk. "*Hashtag* it's just *Random Yoga Poses.*"

"*Hashtag* okay then."

"*Hashtag* get it right next time."

"*Hashtag* I will."

I'm starting to warm up in the water. I peek around his broad shoulders and see the cameras waiting.

Make those photos steamy, girl!

I can't believe I'm doing it, but I swim toward him. Jason Connor is right here, soaking wet, practically asking to be used for my own benefit. If my fans want sexy Cinderella, they're going to get it—*Little Mermaid*–style.

I dive down and swim under him, blowing bubbles teasingly. When I surface, I'm right behind him, and I mean *right behind him*. He turns in surprise. My hands are hidden under the water, but I know he can feel them on his bare lats. If I look him in the eyes, I'm going to blush, so I don't. Then his hands are on either side of my face, tilting it up. I blink into his aquamarine eyes. The cameras are clicking so fast they sound like insects.

"You're making this so hard," he whispers.

I don't know what he means. His thumb caresses my jawline. Underwater, my hands play along his washboard stomach, more than is necessary when the cameras can't even see them, but I can't stop myself. Our legs bang together as we tread water. Even these small touches kick off all kinds of reactions in my body. Jason is staring into my eyes with a hungry intensity. His hands shift to my waist, holding me in place, a reminder that he can move my body as he pleases, and I imagine what that might be like.

Holy heck, I didn't expect him to lean into this so much! All my red lights are flashing. The alarms are blaring. If I don't adjust course, my ship is going to crash, and hard. But maybe it's worth it. He's totally out of my league, obviously, though if he likes what he sees, there's a chance I could have *something* with him. Something meaningless and temporary, but something, nonetheless. Maybe that would be good enough. Now that I'm older and wiser, if I don't cling to any delusions or expectations, maybe my heart could survive it. Bulletproof people aren't afraid of a gunfight, right?

"Don't move! Don't move! It's brilliant!" the photographer cries.

I blink in the shards of sunlight glinting off the pool's surface. Jason is holding the shot like we've been told to. His face looks just like it did in that scene I love so much, the heartbreaking "Whoever cares most gets to win" scene. God, he's so good at this. I almost believe it's for me and not the cameras.

Maybe I'm making a mistake, playing him for book sales.

Maybe I didn't imagine our chemistry during *The Terica Show*.

Oh, Emmy, don't be stupid. You and Hollywood know each other better than that. Fool me once, shame on you. Fool me twice— you're probably Jason Connor. That or a Wham! song.

But I have books to sell and my dreams to recapture. Jason Connor is the conduit. I can do this!

His chest muscles are rock-hard under my palms. I wrap a leg around one of his for leverage and rise up so our mouths are only an inch apart. He doesn't fight it. In fact, he pulls me to him, and the fact that there's only one thin layer of wet cotton between me and his smoking-hot everything fuels my boldness. I lift my gaze from his slightly parted lips to those sea-glass eyes, and *oh Lord, have mercy!* With his arms cinched tight around me and that ravenous gaze, my warp drive's already at ten and about to overload.

I can't do this.

Jason is just acting, and I'm supposed to be acting, too. Except I'm not. No matter what I tell myself, this isn't just a marketing stunt, and I don't know how to stop feeling this way. Call me difficult, but this bulletproof stuff doesn't come easy for me, and right now I can't pretend anymore.

I push away, fill my mouth with water, and spit it at him. Playfully, I hope. His face transforms into confusion. I lunge away, but a hand closes around my ankle, dragging me back. Great. I've pissed him off. I wince and steel myself for paybacks.

"It's okay." He releases my ankle and holds his hands up in surrender. His eyes are soft, like maybe he gets it. "But let's give them some more shots. I have an idea."

His hand searches for mine under the water. I let him take it, melting at the reality that *Jason Connor is holding my hand!* He pulls me to a place where we can both reach bottom. When he spins around to face me again, I'm so far gone I'll do whatever he suggests. I'll say yes to anything.

He grins. "Chicken fight?"

I wasn't expecting that. I look around in case another couple has mysteriously appeared in the water. "There's nobody to fight."

He shrugs and does the nonchalant face. "We'll just pretend there is."

I don't know what he's up to, but why not? It's certainly less stressful than staring into his eyes and lying to myself that I don't feel anything. I watch his face disappear inch by inch under the water. For a moment, I'm all alone. Then his head and shoulders are pressing upward between my thighs, a sensation that awakens all kinds of interesting feelings I don't need to dissect right now, and I'm lifted up. When his head breaks the surface, the skirt of my dress covers his face.

He squints up at me as I stuff the folds of fabric behind his head and lock my legs. "Wow, you're a clencher, aren't you?"

"Two-time New Port Richey High School chicken fight champion at your service."

The cameras are snapping away, but there's not really anywhere to go from here.

"Were you a cheerleader in high school, too?" he asks.

"No, why?"

"Can you stand up?"

"Maybe."

"Try."

Nobody ever said I'm not up for a challenge. I brace myself on his hands and work my foot onto his shoulder. It takes a few yoga-balancing techniques, but I get the second foot in place and begin to straighten my legs as our hands fight to steady us.

"I'm letting go!" he warns as I take the weight off his palms. My arms pinwheel as he seizes my ankles, but we don't last. With a scream, I'm in the water again. When I pop up, he's got the biggest, realest smile I've ever seen on him in person. "That was awesome! We almost had it!"

"Angry yoga is good for your balance."

"Flames! Skulls!" He flashes his fierce face.

"A thousand arms!" I flash mine.

"I can't believe you left that out as a selling point."

"Right?"

"Come on. Let's try again."

We try a few more times, and it's a total disaster, except for the last time, when I manage to stand up for a full one-one-thousand count.

"And the crowd goes wild!" he roars through the megaphone of his hands.

I'm laughing so hard I'm half-drowning. We've drifted into the deep end again, and my toes don't even graze the pool bottom here. Somehow, without my realizing it, my arms have found their way around his shoulders, letting him hold me up. It happens instinctively, and I'm surprised to find that, instead of putting on another face, he's just looking at me, completely neutrally, letting it happen. I meet his gaze. For a moment that feels longer than it could possibly be, we don't try to do anything, don't try to be anything, don't even try to look like anything. It's oddly comfortable. Natural. Wonderful.

"Jason, look over here," the photographer says. "Difficult Girl, don't move."

Even though she's just cut short the best moment of my life, I do as she says. I stare at his profile as he does the smolder for the

camera. My eyes trace a drop of water meandering from a crease in his forehead, around his eyebrow, and down his dripping sideburn. On a whim, I trace the same path with my finger. Why not? I'll never get the chance again.

"Gorgeous!" the photographer cries. "We have what we need."

Val appears at the pool steps with a towel, and Jason gives me a little push in that direction. The pressure of his hand on my hip lingers even after I rise, soaking wet, out of the water.

I pad across the pool deck, wrapping the enormous towel around me, and peek at the computer monitor. Even though I'm "difficult" (or maybe because I am), the assistant scrolls through the thumbnails for me. A lot of the photos sparkle with diamonds of water spray, and my hair is a mess, but at least I don't look like a lovesick washcloth. I'm proud and a little shocked at how sexy some of the shots are. I guess Ariel got the job done after all. Although, come to think of it, things didn't work out that great for Ariel.

But I'm not some naive sixteen-year-old with a crab for a sidekick. I see Hollywood for what it is—a real-life *Hunger Games* where you either take down or get taken down. And I'm not going down this time.

There's one picture that sticks with me, though, even after Jason and I exchange a shy goodbye and I surrender myself to Val to be transformed for this evening's book signing in San Diego. The photo is of us in the pool, my arms around his neck. I'm looking out at a blurry, whitewashed LA skyline, but Jason is looking at me.

I can't get it out of my head as Val tugs at the knots in my hair and glops makeup remover under my eyes, redoing his work, slowly, with care, like a great artist creating a masterpiece from a lump of clay.

I can't help thinking Jason's looking at me like I'm the most beautiful thing in the world.

And it almost doesn't look like he's acting at all.

Chapter 10

Mascarpone-and-strawberries-on-toast proper.

Jason

IT'S ANOTHER DAY on the wires, and I'm waiting for the guys on the ground to get their shit together so I can do my part of the scene. To kill time, I twist my body from side to side, crossing the wires so they spin me back the other way. Kayla, hanging beside me in her Ruby costume, sticks out a foot and tries to help, but even with grunts and struggles, she can't reach.

"Thanks anyway, L'il Bit."

"Dance with me!" She punches her arms to the choreography of the scene for our season finale, which we'll be taping tomorrow.

"Work it, work it," I chant, diving into the arm motions with her.

We bop around for a few minutes until Hannah, the first AD, shouts up to us. "Jason Number Two, Kayla, you're on."

Game faces firmly in place, Kayla and I assume our positions. When the take starts, we tap our shoulders to supposedly engage our thrusters. All the CGI will be added later, so instead of life-size puppets being manipulated in front of a green wall, we'll look like a grown man and a supposed teenager—Kayla's actually twenty-two—flying through the ravaged badlands of a planet three galaxies away. Max, my rigger, lands me hard so I can crumple on the floor and look injured. Kayla shouts my name as she soars past.

"Leave me behind!" I yell hoarsely. Then I groan and gasp like I imagine I would if I'd really plummeted to a rocky exoplanet's surface at fifty miles per hour in only a leather jacket and extremely tight pants. Then I flip onto my back and blink a few times before closing my eyes and letting my chin fall heavily to the side.

"Cut!" Hannah says. "All right. Let's run it again."

We do a couple more takes until it's perfect. When Hannah calls the wrap, Jason Ramirez walks over and offers me a hand up.

"Saw your photo shoot in *Vanity Fair* today." His perfectly groomed eyebrows rise in what I'm guessing is admiration.

I swim my arms as Max launches me off my feet again. "Is it good?"

"Oh, it's good!" Sean says, appearing at Ramirez's shoulder. "*Fifty Shades of Baywatch* good. Something going on with you and Hashtag Girl? I didn't see room for Jesus between the two of you."

His words dredge up a familiar dread. "Nothing's going on. She's cute, but...What exactly are you guys talking about?"

Sean smirks. "Classic string-along then?" He exchanges a glance with Ramirez. "Poor girl."

"Wait, what?"

I'm trapped in my harness, so I can't follow them as they walk away, leaving me hanging—*literally.* "Guys, what are you talking about?" I call after them. They keep walking. I shake my head as I dangle. "What the heck are they talking about?"

Amanda slaps a magazine against my eggplant-colored chest. "See for yourself."

I shake the magazine open and find our spread. Holy cow, it's not what I expected at all.

The first two pages are filled with close-ups of Emmy and me practically on top of each other in the pool. In one shot, we're gazing into each other's eyes, our lips soft and parted, like we can't wait to taste each other. In another, her golden eyes are ablaze with the threat of a mermaid siren ready to drag her unsuspecting sailor down to his pleasure-soaked doom, and I look totally game for it. Flipping through the pages, I'm shocked to find every single photo is laden with so much sexual innuendo that, although I was there, and I know what did and didn't happen, I'm not sure my story would hold up in court. This doesn't look like an innocent crush at all. Not even close.

But, damn, we look good.

It's too sexy. Shit! Miles is going to blow a gasket. Not to mention the showrunners. What happened to the cheerleader pictures? I suggested those on purpose to lighten things up. They didn't use even one.

"Goin' up," Max says.

On the jolty ascent, I toss the magazine onto the set piece where I'll be landing. I roll my neck and shake my hands and arms out. It was only a photo shoot. It's not like I did anything wrong. Right?

"Sup," I say to Andrew as I'm lifted beside him ten feet in the air. I tug at the harness digging into my groin. Across the way, Sean is getting hooked into his rig. In this scene, he'll fly past me, and I'll duck out of the way just in time. This is one of my favorite parts of the job—the physical stuff. I love the dancing, too—not to mention my castmates and being Hadron. Frankly, I love everything about this gig. Losing my contract would be devastating. Even thinking about it sends cold fingers of dread into my gut.

Tomorrow is the last day of taping for the season. If the network fires me, it could be the very last day I ever come to work here. Not that that's going to happen. They love me here! I'm good at what I do. And I haven't given them any reason to decide I'm a terrible influence on the youth of today. Not lately, anyway. Unless you count that photo shoot, which is way hotter than it needed to be. Even my friends think I'm either seducing Emmy or stringing her along.

How about just doing my job? How about acting, which is, hello, what I get paid for? Maybe she's a good actor, too. Maybe we're just really good at acting. God, I don't even know anymore. I should've pulled back, damn it! But she's sexy and fun and I felt...things. I tried not to. I'm a guy, what do you want?

I adjust my harness again because things are getting even more pinchy in there.

What if I *am* seducing her? No, I don't think so. But if I'm not seducing her, it must mean I'm stringing her along. No, I don't think so, either.

I give up. Whatever. *Shake it off, Jason Number Two. You're okay. You're really a good guy, deep down. Waaaay deep down. Somewhere.*

Sean is finally rigged up, and we run the scene. First, Andrew and I fly down and "land" on the mountainside. Then Sean zooms toward us, and I wait until the very last second before lunging away—except I'm so busy trying to figure out if I'm a terrible person or not that I cut it too close. His foot clips me, and I go down hard. When Hannah calls, "Cut," I'm still curled up, rubbing the ball of fire that is my shoulder.

"You're supposed to get out of the way, Snack!" Sean calls from his landing spot down below.

I wince and sit up as the pain dulls to a throb. "I'm okay. We can reshoot it."

Hannah's dark-rimmed glasses pop out from behind the monitor. "No, I like it. We'll keep it. You need the medic, Jason?"

"Nope. All good, boss." I give her a thumbs-up and hang my legs over the green ledge for the long wait until my next scene. Plenty of time for healing. And for worrying. "Hey." I rub my shoulder as I call down to the closest crew member. "Toss me my phone, will you? Thanks."

I catch it and thumb it on. I wonder if Emmy has seen the spread yet. She's been on her California book tour the last week. I haven't friended her on social media because it's a bad idea to do that with fans, but she's at the top of my search list.

Looks like she posted some pool pictures her stylist took during the shoot. They aren't steamy ones. In fact, we're laughing and splashing, and I don't see one fireable offense in the mix.

"Look!" I hold out the phone as Amanda lands beside me on the ledge. "I told you it wasn't all *9½ Weeks*."

"Mm-hmm." She lowers herself shoulder to shoulder with me, legs dangling alongside mine.

"If I share these, do you think it will make me look like less of a scoundrel?"

Amanda's black-lipsticked laugh is a little ugly, and with her Maelstrom makeup on, her words come across as particularly ruthless. "You'd look like less of a scoundrel if Margarita was out of the picture. That's all I'm going to say."

I stare at the green all around us, the cast and crew working down below, the hustle and bustle of taping an action TV show—my life. "We haven't been together in months, and, when she does stay at the house, I sleep in the guest room. I think it's already over, honestly."

"What you *think* doesn't matter. You need to make it official. And clear. For everyone's sake."

My chest tightens. "But Mattie..."

"Mattie will be fine. I promise."

"She'll never let me see him."

"That's not her call. A judge makes that call, remember? Don't let her bully you."

I rub my shoulder some more; it feels like Sean left his toe in there. Amanda's words leave a bruise behind, too. "We've been together so long. I can't imagine things any other way."

Amanda pats my knee. "You deserve to be happy, *Snack*."

I wilt in mock self-deprecation. "Not you, too."

"It's a cute nickname. And there's someone out there for you. I know it. But you're not gonna be free until you cut Margarita loose. It's time."

"Amanda!" Hannah shouts from below.

"Oop! I'm up. See ya." She slaps my knee hard before getting to her feet so the crew can launch her across the set like a dark green leather rocket.

Do I really think Margarita would cut me out of our son's life if I ended things for good? Margarita is a good mother, but I know she enjoys the guilt-free time she gets when Mattie's with me and not a babysitter. And if I pulled the proverbial bandage off, what would really change for Mattie? Not much, probably. He's still young. Maybe now is the time for a fresh start. If I can demonstrate a healthy, stable lifestyle, even if Margarita's not a part of it, there'd be no grounds for cutting my time with him. Maybe I could even get shared custody. Fifty percent of my son's life could be spent with me. Just the two of us. And with the right person, it could be the three of us.

Maybe Amanda's right. Maybe I do deserve to be happy.

I swipe back through the photos Emmy posted. My favorite is one where she's half out of the water, trying to stand up on my shoulders, and I'm dodging her knee with my hair plastered all over my forehead. It's not a particularly flattering photo of either of us, but I remember really enjoying that moment.

I remember enjoying other moments, too—like the ones they published in the magazine. My gaze flicks over to it, lying ten feet away, face down and looking abused. I scooch to reach it but can't. I shift my position and reach out with my foot, but it's still too far. Trying a different tactic, I stand up, run toward it, and reach out, but I'm flung back by the wires and wind up bouncing.

"Going down," Max says.

"No, wait!"

The wires go slack, but I use the extra purchase to lunge toward the magazine and grab it. Victory!

As I'm lowered down, I flip to the photos again. Maybe they're not so sexy. Maybe I imagined it. I find the spread.

Nope. They're pretty sexy.

But we look good together. No denying it. She's beautiful and sensual, and seeing her in my arms brings back all the memories of that day. The way her muscles fought while she treaded water. Her finger tracing its way down my cheek. How she stole my sandwich and then fed it to me.

I turn the magazine clockwise, hoping it's less incriminating at that angle. Nope—turning it horizontal makes it even worse. I stifle the smile that bubbles up, too late, because Miles's pointy-tipped red Corthays suddenly appear inches away from my dangling, black Velcro space boots.

"I see you didn't listen to a word I said."

I slap the magazine shut like a teenage boy caught with a *Playboy* and frown in faux sincerity. "Why, Miles, whatever are you talking about?" The British accent is unintentional.

He shakes his head. "I can't keep bailing you out, Jason. You're supposed to be a family guy on a family show." He gestures to the magazine. "You look like a gigolo."

"Well, you know," I hem and haw. "That was the photographer's idea."

He snatches the magazine out of my hand and flips through several pages before finding a photo and shoving it in front of my face. "Was it the photographer's idea to make your celebrity crusher fall in love with you? Look at her!"

I scoff. "She's not in love with me. She's actually kind of mad at me, I think."

"I don't trust her, either. She might be obsessed with you. There are details in that book—"

"It's not like I'm hard to research, Miles," I cut him off, annoyed.

He narrows his eyes at me. "Have you read it?"

"Of course I've read it. It's fine!" It's only a partial lie. I've read about eighty pages or so. But I know Emmy's not obsessed with me. She's great.

Miles stabs a finger between Emmy's bedroom eyes. "This

girl is bad news for you. If I were any other director, I'd love the buzz for the movie, but I'm not just any director. I'm your friend. This movie's a one-off. *Lost Star* is your bread and butter. You don't need to be risking that. She's not worth it. No woman is."

Poor jaded Miles. I hope I never get like that. "There's nothing between us, I promise. There's nothing between me and anybody right now, not even Margarita. I'm ending it with her."

"You've said that before."

"This time I mean it. Things haven't been good for a long time, and I need to be able to live my life without everyone thinking I'm a cheating jerk."

"You are a cheating jerk."

"I *was* a cheating jerk. Now I'm just a jerk."

Miles's gaze softens. "I can't tell you what to do with your life, and, for the record, we both know you're not really a jerk."

In my mind, I add the word *son* in front of that sentence. In my mind, I replay it in my dad's voice. "What's so wrong with me showing Emmy a good time, anyway?"

Miles's left eyebrow goes up.

"Not *that* way. You know what I mean. Would it be better if I blew her off completely? I'm her celebrity crush. What would I look like then? Some arrogant, self-absorbed asshole. She deserves better than that."

Miles sighs so hard that the ends of his mustache tremble. My words chisel a hole in my own wall, too. Emmy does deserve more than the games I'm playing with her. Flirting with her on *The Terica Show*, then ignoring her. Acting all hot and cold at the photo shoot. Not that I meant to play games. That was never my intention. But, as usual, my intentions don't mean shit.

What are my intentions anyway? Maybe to prove that Jason Connor can be a good guy? That I'm not the cad the talking heads make me out to be? That I can be Hadron in real life—the funny, nice one who deserves a funny, nice girlfriend? A girlfriend who feeds him sandwiches and wipes mustard off his face. I was really hoping she'd lick it off her finger.

The grin slides across my face before I can stop it. When Miles sees it, he shakes his head as if I've just driven his point home.

"Wait! No, Miles, seriously. I'm gonna end it with Margarita. And then I'm gonna be America's most honorable celebrity crush. Have a little faith, how 'bout it?" I unleash the charming face and crank that sucker up to ten. Even grumpy, straight men aren't entirely immune.

"Whatever, Jason," he grunts, but I can see in his face that I've won. "How's that shoulder?"

I roll it around in its socket. "Solid."

"Good. You ready for tomorrow?"

"When have I ever *not* been ready for a huge honking dance number?" Now the million-dollar smile comes out to play. I do the running man in the air since I'm still not actually touching the ground. Finish it with a dab.

Miles grins, and I'm thinking I've made a nice fat deposit into our good vibes bank account, when he suddenly sobers. "One more thing, Connor. If you're going to end it with Margarita, make sure everyone knows it. You've got to make it clear you're unattached before you get involved with anyone else." He rolls up the magazine and stuffs it in his back pocket. "And for God's sake, keep it professional with the author. Can you do that?"

"Sir, yes, sir!" I salute as he turns to go. I can do that. Of course I can. The photo shoot and interviews are done, and I don't think Emmy and I have any more events together until the premiere in December. She's got a few more book signings, but I don't need to be there. Easy peasy. It won't even take any willpower.

As Miles retreats, Sean approaches. He's already in his street clothes, a baby-blue velour tracksuit. Immediately, he throws a haymaker into my sore shoulder.

"Ouch! What was that for?"

"You'll live." Sean looks across all the heads in the room as if he owns the place, as if all of this is his domain. It's his signature move. It's really impressive how he does that. "Your crusher girl still in town?"

"Yup," I reply cheerfully.

"Bring her to the cast party at my house tomorrow, after the final taping."

"Why would I do that?"

"Because I said so. That's an order from High Command." He flashes his alpha grin, the one that explains why he's the captain and the rest of us are all button-pushing monkeys.

He drops into fighting stance, and I mirror him, ready to defend. "I don't think that's a good idea."

"If you don't, I will." He drops the pretense and pulls out his phone. "What's her number?"

My plan to avoid Emmy unravels before my eyes. Why does he care so much about her coming? Is he really that annoyed that she picked me over him?

"I'm not giving you her number," I say in a voice that tries to be authoritative and comes out petulant instead. I don't have her number anyway, but I don't tell him that.

Sean looks up from his iPhone. "So you're bringing her then?"

I can't let Sean bring Emmy to that party. If anybody's a cad, he is. Besides, I'm her celebrity crush. That's my job. And if he brings her, I won't be able to avoid her anyway, so what's the difference?

"I'll invite her." This time my authoritative tone comes out sounding defeated instead.

"Great!" His mouth grins, though his eyes don't. "See you tomorrow, Snack." He delivers another smack to my shoulder. Geez.

"There's nothing going on between us!" I call after him as he saunters away. "And I'm not stringing her along!"

"Bring her or I will!" He waggles his phone in the air without looking back.

Shit.

Well, first things first. Amanda and Miles are right. I need to end things with Margarita, once and for all. Still dangling on the wires, I pull out my phone and text the mother of my son.

Jason: I need to talk to you. Let's have dinner. You pick the restaurant.

I pause, delete the last sentence, and then replace it.

Jason: Maple Block Meat Co. on Sepulveda. 7PM.

There. I feel more take-charge already.

Next, I call and make a reservation using my real name. That'll ensure the paparazzi are there to document it. Get the headline Miles is so concerned about. I feel kind of dirty doing it this way, but Miles is right. If people are going to stop judging me, they need to know I'm freed up. Then I can do things the right way. Although with whom, I don't know, since Emmy's on my "no fly" list. She's not a real candidate anyway, living so far away.

But I'm committed to taking her to Sean's party at least. I'll pretend I'm Hugh Jackman taking his celebrity crusher to a party. Professional. Proper. Mascarpone-and-strawberries-on-toast proper.

I can't text Emmy because I don't have her phone number, but maybe I can direct message her through one of our social media apps. Except when I do it, I see her DMs are closed. I check out the "contact me" page on her website and find a book tour schedule. According to it, she's at an indie bookstore in Manhattan Beach right now. What if I surprised her? Just to invite her to the party, nothing more.

My eyes glaze over as I imagine how that might go cinematically. The camera zooms from a wide-angle view of the bookstore to Emmy, seated at her designated book-signing area. She looks up from the table, pen in hand, and sees that it's me. The close-up camera catches her face breaking into a huge smile as she drops the pen. She steps first onto the chair and then the tabletop. I run up just in time to catch her as she dives off the table and into my arms.

The fantasy summons a wave of feeling that I'm sure isn't in my best interests to explore. What the heck am I doing?

It's only a party. Then she'll fly home. *Professional. Proper.* Surely I can do that.

I look up and realize I'm the only one still strapped into a harness. The rest of the cast is long gone, and there isn't a crew member in sight.

"Hey!" I call out. "I'm still here. Hello? Max? Miles? Hello?"

Chapter 11

Don't they want to exploit us for their entertainment?

Jason

WHEN THE CREW finally sets me free, I change into my street clothes and settle into the Alfa's warm, leather cocoon, blasting my *Bon Jovi and Friends* playlist. Somehow, Jack Johnson got in there (who knew they were friends?), but I don't kick him out because there's an ocean view on Manhattan Avenue, and his music is fitting. Sing it, Jack!

At the bookstore, there's a line for the folding table where Emmy is signing autographs. As I step into the space, which smells pleasantly of book glue and coffee, an employee offers me something small and sandwich-shaped on a tray. I decline politely and pull my ball cap farther down on my head. I could probably march right up and get her attention, but that seems a bit entitled.

I'm not too good to wait in line like everyone else. I pull out my phone, noting that Margarita hasn't replied to my text. Grrr. I'd really like to get this over with. We're deep into the filming of *#CelebrityCrush*, and I'm sure she'll need at least one night to process the breakup so it doesn't affect our on-screen chemistry.

Aw, who am I kidding? This is Margarita we're talking about. I want to get this over with for me.

The line moves along slowly, orderly. The book community is so civilized. No one even looks closely enough to recognize me. They're like hummingbirds, making low noises to each other and sipping nectar from the tiny paper cups the staff passes around. I accept a cup off a tray with a nod. Red wine. Probably a cabernet sauvignon. Not bad. Twenty minutes later, Margarita still hasn't texted back, and it's my turn to meet the author.

"Hi." I wave Forrest Gump–style.

She doesn't climb over the table and leap into my arms, but her face lights up, and I immediately feel like five million bucks. "Jason! What are you doing here? Did I miss something? Was I supposed to be somewhere?"

"Nope." I lean on the table. "I needed to talk to you, and your DMs are closed."

"Yeah. I had to shut all that down. I started getting..." She clears her throat. "Anatomy lessons."

"Ew." I grimace.

"So, what did you need to talk to me about?"

"You're wearing glasses." I point at the pink frames that swoop up at the edges.

"Val," she explains, pushing back from the table so I can see the rest of her outfit—a body-hugging magenta sweater that I like very much and navy slacks. "They're just plain glass."

"I like it. It has a *media specialist by day, superhero by night* vibe."

She smiles that smile that's just a tiny bit naughty, and I don't need the magazine to remind me of our pool shoot. Her hands on me underwater, touching me way more than the occasion called for. The way her eyes lit up like tiny suns. How her body responded when I touched her.

"Ummm, Jason, we should keep the line moving. What can I do for you?"

I jump. "Right! Sean's having a cast party at his house tomorrow. Would you like to come?" I pause. Then, against my better judgment, I add, "With me?"

Her eyes light up again. They're like desert glass. "I would love that."

"The whole cast will be there."

"I'd love to."

"It's going to be a lot of fun."

"Jason, I already said yes!"

The humming noises behind me grow louder and less civilized. "Maybe we should exchange numbers so we can coordinate?"

She nods and takes my phone. She deftly enters her information, her tanned fingers dancing across the screen. Her phone chimes as it receives my text, and she tucks it away again.

"Do you have a book for her to sign?" the little old lady behind me asks.

I don my most polite smile. "No, sorry, ma'am. I'll get out of the way."

"It's rude to show up to a book signing without buying a book."

"Oh, I didn't know that." Great, now I've just offended the

book community. Can't wait to read that grammatically correct headline. "I'll take one book."

Emmy looks confused. "I thought you already had the book."

"I do."

"Don't buy another book, Jason. I'll sign yours tomorrow."

Meanwhile, the buzzing around me has gotten steadily louder. Someone says, "Are you Jason Connor?"

"I better get out of here," I whisper to Emmy over the head of the little old lady getting her book signed. "I don't want to be recognized."

"See you tomorrow…" She gives me a mischievous smile and then raises her voice to shout, "*Jason Connor!*"

She did that on purpose, although I have to admit it was funny. No fewer than twenty selfies later, I escape to my car. Margarita still hasn't gotten back to me. I turn down Jack Johnson's "Banana Pancakes" and dial her up. It goes to voicemail like she's rejected the call. *Damn it, Margarita.* The reservation is in an hour. I call her again. Same thing.

Jack's breezy optimism is starting to grate on me, so I skip ahead to Guns N' Roses. Where would Margarita be? It's hard to know for sure, but come to think of it, she used to have drinks with the girls Thursday nights at this martini bar near our house. My house, I mean. I head there. Sure enough, after I walk the three blocks from my parking space to the Forty Winks, I catch a glimpse of her through the window at a high-top table with a pair of women, looking as elegant and untouchable as a priceless vase. When I yank open the door and approach them, Margarita's expression makes me feel like I'm a tornado ripping through the neighborhood. I pull the cap off my head and run my fingers through my hair.

"Jason?" She says my name the same way a person might say, *Why are you touching my things?*

"I've been trying to get a hold of you."

She uncrosses her legs and then crosses them in the other direction, Margarita Power Move Number Six. "Can't you see I'm busy?"

"Hi, Jason." One of her companions flits her fingers at me over her martini glass.

"Hi…" I don't remember her name.

"Piper," she supplies.

"Hi, Piper." I give her a half-hearted wave.

"You didn't even clean yourself up?" Margarita asks me.

"I just came from the *Lost Star* set." I wipe a hand across my eyes. It comes back black. "Listen, Margarita, I need to talk to you. I made us dinner reservations."

"We just got here." This one I do recognize—it's Janice from book club.

"Hi, Janice. How's book club going?" I ask.

"Well, thank you. We're reading a very interesting novel right now." She smiles coyly. "It's called *Hashtag Celebrity Crush.*"

All three women giggle, although it's not really a giggle. Giggles are cute. This is more like a scraping of one serrated knife against another.

"Margarita, I'm sure your friends won't mind if you have to leave a little early."

She executes Power Move Number Three—the one where she stretches her neck slowly in a complete circle, like she's warming up for an exercise class. It's a move that says, *I don't hurry for anybody.*

"Whatever you have to say, Jason, why don't you just say it now, so no one has to be inconvenienced?"

She isn't going to make this easy. Of course she isn't. I lower my voice. "I don't think you want me to do this here, in front of your friends."

I think I see a flash of something—fear? anger? disgust?—before she turns her attention to her cocktail napkin, purple-tipped fingers smoothing it flat. "Then I suggest you wait for a better time. Or…" There's daring in her glare now. "Just come out with it."

I don't want to do this here. Not like this. It's supposed to be a private thing. Well, a private thing that's documented by paparazzi. It's not supposed to be in front of her friends with no cameras. "Margarita, can't we just go have dinner and a discussion?"

"About what? Your next shortsighted decision? You've never needed to workshop those with me before. Say whatever you have to say. Just make sure it isn't something you'll regret."

Her unveiled threat is like the prick of a dagger against vulnerable organs, but I remember Amanda's pep talk. Margarita doesn't have the legal power to withhold Mattie from me, and without that, she's got nothing.

I try out Sean's move, looking around the place like I own it. I know it's not achieving the effect I want because I'm actually looking for something. I'm looking for some asshole with a camera to document this. And there's none.

"Well?" Her smile is slithery. She thinks she's won. But I deserve to be happy, and that starts with getting out of this burning house once and for all.

"Fine." I project my voice across the room. "It's over, Margarita!"

Her lips press together, and she shakes her head the tiniest bit, as if she can't believe I've called her bluff. Well, what do you know? I sunk an arrow. But no one even glances our way.

"I said, it's over, Margarita!" I repeat in an equally booming baritone.

Margarita turns her back to me and reaches for her collins glass. There's a desperation in the motion, like the glass is the closest thing to a hole she can crawl into. "Stop it, Jason. You're embarrassing yourself."

"It's really over this time!" I announce even more boldly as her friends widen their eyes at one another, probably wondering if they should step in. "We're done! We're really, one hundred percent done!"

Now a few patrons are looking my way. Good. No phones out, though. No video. What's wrong with these people? We're celebrities! Don't they want to exploit us for their entertainment?

"Just go, Jason." Margarita spits the words over her shoulder. "I know you probably have Little Miss Sun Damage waiting in the Alfa."

The color red taints everything I see. That comment was just plain mean, and there's no reason for her to bring Emmy into this. This has nothing to do with her. And if it does, so what?

"Like you haven't been seeing other people?" I snarl.

She spins on her stool. "Oh? Are we keeping score now? Because you and I both know what that tally sheet looks like."

It's the same old argument, but something's different. Margarita and I have broken up a bunch of times before. Neither one of us ever gave the other much pushback.

"Why are you fighting this?" I ask. "You've hardly come around at all in the last couple of months. We're clearly not in a relationship. This just makes sense."

Her nostrils flare as she doubles down. "I need you to stop talking right now, Jason. I'm here with my friends, and all of this"—she waggles a hand in my general direction—"can wait."

I feel the teeth grind in my jaw as she turns back to the table. She can't just switch me off like a TV set. This is happening, whether she likes it or not. I scan the crowd again, but everyone's attention is back on their dates, on their drinks. So, there's no one here to document my dumping of Margarita Ayala? Who needs 'em? I'll do it myself.

The phone dances off one...two...three of my fingers as I juggle it into position. I tap selfie mode and hold it out in front of me with my ex and her friends fluttering like overpriced pet store birds in the background.

"This is Jason Connor, and I'm telling the world right now, I'm breaking up with Margarita Ayala! I don't love her! She doesn't love me! It's over. It's done. For good! And it couldn't happen to a nicer person!" I hit STOP. Then, before I can overthink it, I post it.

There. It's done. I feel satisfied and a little breathless, like after I have to do one of my own stunts.

"Wow," Janice from book club mutters. "I thought you were trying to convince everyone you're not an asshole."

I expect Margarita to get all smug and threaten me some more, but instead her face has crumpled in a way that unnerves me. Immediately, she gets control of it before turning back to the table with languid confidence, a queenly dismissal of an annoying subject. But I know a Margarita cover-up when I see one.

She's hurt. I've hurt her.

I don't get it. I didn't break up with Margarita as much as state the obvious fact that we were already broken up; it's just that neither one of us bothered to read the memo. She's got to see it that way, too. How could she not? Now this whole thing has backfired on me. Making our split official was supposed to help my image, free up a slot where someone else would be allowed to go. *Have you seen Jason Connor lately? He's single now, and he's been behaving himself. I hope good things happen for him.* Instead, after that video goes viral (and it will), the media will be adding *verbally abusive boyfriend and dumb enough to advertise it on social media* to my list of offenses. Damn it.

"I didn't mean for this to happen this way," I say to the back of Margarita's head, or maybe to myself. She ignores me. Still, I stand there. "I'll see you at the studio tomorrow," I add.

"Goodbye, Jason," Janice from book club says with a death glare.

The short drive home features plenty of yelled lyrics and drums. By the time I get there, there's mayhem online, mostly hate posts against me. Every curse word I learned since third grade—and some brand-new ones I've just made up—shoot from my mouth. I've really effed this whole thing up. The network is going to hate it.

I wrestle up a bottle of Jim Beam and pour three fingers' worth over ice before plopping down in the den. Possessed Baby is sitting in the middle of the floor, probably summoning a demon. I swear that thing gets up and moves around by itself. But there's nobody else here to cuddle, so I pick her up and hold her against my body.

"What'll it be, Spawn of Satan?" I ask her, clicking the TV on. "*90 Day Fiancé* or that nice gentleman with the tigers?" Her glazed eyes and black mouth gape at me. I know she'll want the greater of the two evils. "*90 Day Fiancé* it is!"

I guess I just wanna see people with worse decision-making skills than me.

Chapter 12

Jason Connor, died from YouTube.

Emmy

"HE DID WHAT? Hang on."

The hotel bed squeaks as I plop cross-legged onto it. I minimize the screen with Peyton's face and pull up YouTube. Oh snap! Peyton wasn't exaggerating. There's a video, and it's bad. Really bad. It's so painful to watch that I'm not sure if I'm looking at a video or having an attack of appendicitis.

He broke up with Margarita Ayala! Why would he do that? Why now? And on social media?

"Did you see it?" Peyton's voice sounds young and high-pitched and a million miles away, which it might as well be.

"I see it. Oh, honey, the comments!"

"I know. Did you see what @SnarkierthanU said?"

I did, and it's not something a preteen should be reading. I switch back to her screen and change the subject. "What did you do today?"

"Mom!" Peyton sticks her face right up in the phone's camera. "We do *not* have time for small talk. If Jason Connor is as cool IRL as you say he is, you have to help him. He looks like a total douchebag."

I cringe. "Where did you hear that word? Do you even know what that means?"

"Tía Josie, and no. But I know it's bad."

My gaze wanders to the window of my Manhattan Beach hotel room. It's a decent hotel, but not fancy. Typical book tour accommodations. I have a view of the pool deck, at least.

"I don't know if I can help him, sweetie."

Peyton groans. "You have to! I can't have my friends thinking my mom is in love with a douchebag. It's embarrassing!"

"Stop saying 'douchebag.' And I'm not in love with him."

"Mom, I know you." She does. The last twelve years, we've pretty much grown up together. "Tell me you'll fix this. Please?"

"Fine." I sigh. "I'll fix it."

"Great! Thank you! I love you! You're the best! Wanna do a quick TikTok?" She tilts her head to the side in that cute way of hers.

"Always!"

"'Can't Touch This'?"

"You bet."

She gets the music going while I slide off the bed to my feet. When it starts, we launch into what's basically a really fast Macarena with a drumroll and a John Travolta ending. It's so fun that it instantly makes me happier. Anybody who is down on TikTok isn't doing it right, and that's my expert opinion.

"Good night, baby. Tell Josie I love her and thank her for taking such good care of you." Normally, Peyton would be staying with my parents, but my mom joined this cruising club, and the two of them are currently floating somewhere off the coast of Greece.

"I will."

We say goodbye, and a wave of loneliness floods through me. This is the longest I've ever been away from Peyton, and although I know she's not a baby anymore and she's as safe with Josie as she is with me, the sheer distance between us feels like it's too much. Not just the physical distance, either. The distance between these two worlds. New Port Richey, Florida, versus Hollywood, California. Books and beaches and kid stuff versus glamour and glitz, photo shoots, and interviews. Is it wrong that I want both?

I sigh and browse through more of the comments on Jason's post. They're scathing. I consider calling him, but how freaking presumptuous is that? When he asked to exchange numbers today, he didn't invite me to call him anytime I felt like it.

But he gave me his phone number and broke up with Margarita Ayala on the same day.

Stop it, Emmy! You're a fool to think this has anything to do with you!

Although that's what people are going to think, aren't they, after our *Vanity Fair* photo shoot? That spread was sizzling hot. Jill's text read something like: OMG you KILLED it, Emmy. More of that! In fact, I'm number five on the *New York Times* bestseller list now.

I browse my book's hashtag, and sure enough, there's a crap ton of buzz from my fans, mostly *Go, girl* tweets and swooning over the *Vanity Fair* photos. Since none of the photos Val snapped for me turned out like that, I'm chalking it up to the magic of Photoshop. Thank you, Photoshop, for validating me. When this is all over, I can stare at those photos and pretend I really had something with Jason Connor.

But he invited me to a cast party tomorrow! I'll get a chance to meet the entire *Lost Star* crew, hang out with them—it's way more than I imagined getting to do this trip. Why would he do that? He was so standoffish at the photo shoot. At least he was at first.

What if the breakup with Margarita did have to do with me? What if…?

No, Emmy, don't go there. You'll just be setting yourself up to be made a fool of again.

My swimsuit is hanging over the bathroom door, and I yank it down. There's a really nice hot tub here inside a gazebo that nobody ever uses but me. A bottle of pinot grigio is chilling in my ice bucket, courtesy of Val, who treats me like my life is a L'Oréal Because You're Worth It commercial. I hired him out of my own pocket after the last event. I had to put his fee on a credit card since the royalty checks haven't started flowing yet, but Val helps keep me from looking like a mediocre social media influencer who's trying desperately not to look like a mediocre social media influencer. That's priceless.

I'll just go simmer in 103-degree water and see if I can figure out how to help Jason Connor with his online presence. Social media is fickle. He can recover from this.

His loss is my gain, of course. The more he makes the news, the more I do, too, by association, but I made Peyton a promise. Besides, I don't want to see him get canceled, poor guy. He doesn't deserve that.

I pad across the pool deck and into the gazebo with my phone and a large Solo cup full of wine. Feet in the water, I pull up his contact info. One tap would call him. It's such an audacious idea. Calling Jason Connor on the phone. Like we're friends or something. Like we could ever be more.

My phone is in my hands, his number on the screen. I'm bulletproof, right?

No, that's a lie. I'm far, far from it.

Before I can stop myself, I tap CALL.

It rings twice.

"Hello?"

My heart jumps into my throat, but like *Lost Star* season two, episode one taught us, time goes in only one direction, and it's too late to take anything back now. "Jason, it's Emmy."

"Oh, hi. I thought that might be you." He coughs. Ice tinkles in a glass. A TV drones in the background. "What's up?"

"I'm sitting in the hot tub at the hotel." For frack's sake, what is wrong with me? I might as well have said, *I'm lying naked in bed.*

"Hang on a minute."

The video call request comes through, and I tap ACCEPT. Suddenly, Jason Connor is there, on my phone screen, like it's something normal. There are dark circles under his Gulf of Mexico eyes, but they still blow a crater in my moon.

"I'm on my third episode of *90 Day Fiancé*," he says.

"Ouch."

"It's been a rough night."

"I saw that." I sink all the way into the water. I wonder how I look on his end. Probably with mascara smeared under my eyes, Val's flat iron work frizzed by steam from the tub. Whatever. I can't worry about that right now. He's in a bad place. "Do you want to talk about it?"

"What's to say? I'm an idiot." The background flops behind him, and the TV sound disappears. I'm guessing he's lying on a sofa in his house. It's strange to see him this way, just looking normal. Not dressed up or made up or "on."

"Everybody's an idiot sometimes. You haven't cornered the market on that."

He laughs dryly and takes a sip of his drink. "Maybe you don't know this because, if you did, I wouldn't be your 'hashtag celebrity crush,' but I have a bit of an image problem."

I balance my phone against my rolled-up towel so I can kick my legs behind me in the tub. "I know it. I just don't care about things like that."

"Things like what?"

"Things people want me to see. I care more about how things really are."

His brow furrows. "How do you know the difference?"

I dip my head back and wet my hair. I can tell he's lying down now, holding the phone above him. Somehow it makes our conversation feel singularly intimate. For a minute, I forget I'm talking to movie star Jason Connor. I'm just talking to Jason.

"There's more to you than what we all see in the interviews and film clips and paparazzi photos," I say. "All your mistakes aside, you're a good person."

He rubs his forehead and winces. "Then why do I continue to make one terrible decision after another?" His voice cracks, and not for effect.

My heart lurches. "You don't always. You did something really amazing today."

He sniffs. "What was that?"

"You came all the way to Manhattan Beach and waited in line to invite me to a party."

I love the half smile that fills up my screen. It's one I haven't seen before in memes. It's just for me. "I did have to wait, like, twenty whole minutes."

"See?" I grin back at him. "And you gave selfies to my fans, which was really sweet. By the way, I can help you with your social media image, if you want. It's what I do for a living."

"Really? How would you do that?"

I shrug. "It's easy. We just post stuff that makes you look awesome rather than the stuff you post that makes you look like a jackass."

"But the jackassedness comes naturally."

"That's where I come in." I'm about to throw a few ideas at him, when I notice something. "Oh crap!"

His face on the screen looks truly concerned. "What's wrong?"

"I wore my Fitbit into the Jacuzzi." I peel it off and press the buttons. Sure enough, it's toast. "That was dumb." I throw it aside. "See, I told you you haven't cornered the market on stupid."

"What's the dumbest thing you've ever done?"

The question comes out of nowhere, and it sounds important, like the way I answer it matters. If I give him something shallow, I'll lose the precarious trust we're building. I take a deep breath. Even though I feel guilty saying it, I tell him the truth. "Getting pregnant at nineteen."

"You're a mom." He says it without judgment.

I nod. "Peyton's twelve. Don't get me wrong, she's the person I love most, and I'm grateful to have her, but she's the reason I left LA. She's why I gave up on my dreams."

"What were your dreams?"

I hesitate. It's the same question Beverly Shipley asked me in my Fresh Leaf Book Club interview back in New York, and I'm still not quite sure how to answer it. "You know, what *you* have."

"You mean having everything I do and say scrutinized?"

"I mean the good parts. Like *Lost Star*. I've always wanted to be part of something like that."

"Why did you have to give it up?"

I flip around in the tub and hold the phone over the bubbling water. "I couldn't raise a baby on my own. Not at that age. Not that far from my support system and while I was going to school."

He hesitates before going for it—the million-dollar question. "What about her father?"

I don't know how much I'm willing to tell him. "It's just the two of us." As it turns out, not much.

"He didn't want to be a part of her life?"

"Guess not."

That's a lie. I don't know if Rhett Castle would have wanted to be a part of Peyton's life. I never gave him the chance. Luckily, Jason doesn't press.

"The dumbest thing I've ever done is get arrested for fighting. I was drunk. I was with this woman."

My dashboard lights up like a '90s rave. Oh to the crap. I read that police report. It's the one I found.

"Her husband found out and came to take her home."

I nod in acknowledgment at his image in the phone. This is all terribly wrong. I should interrupt him. Tell him I know. That I read the police report. That I put something like it in the book, and I'm sorry.

But I can't bring myself to. I just sit there, frozen.

"It was stupid of me to fight him. I don't even remember why I did it, but I do remember a lot about that night." His eyes go glassy. "The seedy pool hall outside of Cincinnati—the Friendly Saloon, I think it was called. The pretty woman in a low-cut top plastered to my side. The front door swings open, and this Steve Carell–looking guy crosses the floor with his shirttails out, headed right for us, and he says angrily, 'Let's go, whatever-her-name-was,' and she says nastily, 'Go home, you're just jealous,' and I say idiotically, 'Do you want to take this outside?' Apparently, he did."

He lifts off the couch long enough to take another sip of whatever he's drinking. I don't move. I don't say a word. This is so personal. When I read this on a screen years ago, it didn't feel this personal.

"Eventually, the cops showed up. They took my stuff and threw me in a cell reeking of vomit. To this day, I don't understand how it happened, why I did it."

Still, I say nothing. I am like a person with a gun to her head. Nothing I do is guaranteed to save me.

"Maybe I was just drunk," he muses. "Maybe I was itching to use some of the martial arts skills they'd taught us for the show. Outside, after I'd turned this guy's face into a cube steak, it was surreal. I remember marveling at how much my hand hurt. The red and blue police lights turning the sidewalk into a disco. The guy's blue sedan double-parked in front of the bar. And the worst part?" He pauses for a long moment, as if rallying the confidence to finish. "Their kid. Their kid watching it all through the car window."

I cringe. That detail wasn't in the police report. His eyes are squeezed shut, like maybe if he closes them hard enough, he won't have to see it replaying in his mind. His sigh is a long, loud crackle through my phone speaker.

"So, what do you think, Emmy? That story makes my epic breakup with Margarita look like *America's Funniest Home Videos*, doesn't it?"

"Maybe he was abusive?" I say half-heartedly.

Jason's voice is far away and soft. "Nope, I don't think so. He just loved her. He just really loved her. And I didn't."

My chest constricts like an imploding star. This thing I have done—putting that scene in the book—is even worse than I suspected. What I thought was just a police report of a young guy's stupid, testosterone-filled mistake is Jason's biggest shame, eating away at him. I wove that painful memory into a story and put it out there for everyone to see. When he discovers what I've done, he'll hate me.

But how could he not know? They're almost done filming the movie.

He snickers. "I bet my epitaph is going to read *Jason Connor, died from YouTube.*"

I manage a small laugh. Even without my Fitbit on, I can tell my heart rate is over a hundred beats per minute and rising. "Jason?"

"Hmmm?"

My voice shakes. "Have you finished reading *Hashtag Celebrity Crush?*"

He makes an awkward emoji face, the one that's basically a cylinder of gritted teeth. "I haven't finished it. But I will. I promise—"

"Forget about that. What about the screenplay? Have you read that?"

"We didn't have time for a big table read. And I only read the scenes for the next day. It's kind of my process. TV actor thing."

A little noise of relief bursts out of me. It's not too late. There's a chance I can fix this. "You know, in the time I've been here, I've only gotten to see one day of filming. I'd really like to see some more."

The sentence is 100 percent true, but I feel like a liar saying it when my real intention is to corner Miles Gauthier, grab him by the lapels, and beg him to cut the bar scene.

Jason's shoulders relax. "Of course! Why didn't you say so before? Come to the set tomorrow. You can be my guest. Here, I'll text you the address." The video pauses as he switches apps. When he comes back, his eyelids close and stay that way for too many seconds—long, sexy blinks. I'm not beside him, but for a moment, I imagine I am. Instead of me in a hotel Jacuzzi and him on his couch, I see myself stretched out beside him on cool white sheets, able to reach out and smooth a runaway curl on his forehead, slide my hands under his shirt, open his mouth with mine. No secrets between us. No betrayals. All my feelings reciprocated. I pretend it's something that could actually happen.

It's getting far too hot in the tub. I stand up to cool off. When I check my phone again, his eyes are open, watching the water stream off my bare middle.

I lift the phone to face level. "I should let you sleep."

"What? I'm wide awake." His eyes are fighting the pull of sleep. It's adorable, and gorgeous, and killing me. I don't know if I'll be able to pull any of this off—talking Miles into nixing the bar scene, fixing Jason's social media presence, and keeping him from reading the rest of the book, all the while playing vixen for the rest of the world and wrangling my own feelings. But I have to try.

"Hey, Jason," I bark, spurring him awake. "I think your epitaph's going to read *Jason Connor, died of mustard.* There was an insane amount of mustard on that sandwich."

His smile is slow and sleepy and only half there. "I love mustard. Can I pick you up for the party?"

Jason Connor picking me up in a fancy car for a celebrity party? Yes, please! "I'd love that."

Dipping his chin down, he looks up and says, "Okay." It's the meme. He did it on purpose.

He sees that I recognize it. I'm grinning too hard to hide it. "Good night, Jason Connor."

"Wait, wait, before you go..." His lips fill up the screen of my phone, and he makes a smooching noise. He's given his phone a sloppy kiss. "That's for you, Emmy Ellison, for choosing me."

A warm zinging sensation flutters over me, like I imagine it feels when your spaceship is scanned by aliens with one of those humming sweeps of blue light. "I'll always choose you, Jason Connor."

Chapter 13

That's gotta hurt, I don't care who you are.

CELEBRITY STRAIGHT TALK, AUGUST 4

AMIL: Have you heard? Our boy Jason Connor has spawned a new hashtag. He's such a trendsetter! Hello, all. This is Amil Nair with *Celebrity Straight Talk*, coming at you, as always, with my secret weapon, Isla Wallace.

ISLA: Hi-la, it's Isla!

AMIL: So, Isla, you're going to have to take the lead on this segment because my therapist has banned me from all depressing subjects, like war, climate change, and Jason Connor.

ISLA: No problem, Amil. You know I'm always here for you. Jason Connor is the genesis for the recently trending How Not To Break Up hashtag. It comes after he filmed himself ending his relationship with costar and longtime partner, Margarita Ayala, and *posting it online*. That was a real penis move.

AMIL: What was he thinking, Isla?

ISLA: He obviously wasn't, Amil. Because you just don't do that. Hence the hashtag. He's taking a beating for it on social media, too.

AMIL: Isla, you know I'd stop my own heart if Jason Connor was doing CPR training, but I must say, he's really made a donkey butt of himself with this stunt.

ISLA: The mother of your child deserves more respect than that, even if she is seeing some producer on the side.

AMIL: That's a rumor, but agreed. She took it pretty well, though.

ISLA: She appeared to, but, Amil, that's gotta hurt, I don't care who you are.

AMIL: Truth be told, Jason looked a little unhinged in the video, don't you think, Isla?

ISLA: I didn't want to be the one to say it, but I agree. The hinges were definitely hanging off the door.

AMIL: Did he seem rushed to you?

ISLA: Yes! Like he couldn't wait to get it over with.

AMIL: It begs the question. Could there be someone else?

ISLA: You mean someone like that author, Emmy Ellison? The one he did the steamy *Vanity Fair* spread with?

AMIL: Her? No way, Isla. There's nothing going on there.

ISLA: Are you sure? There were a few photos in that magazine where I was pretty certain there was something going on under the surface. Literally.

AMIL: Here's the question you have to ask yourself, Isla: Would *you* dump Margarita Ayala for some nobody romance author from nowheresville?

ISLA: Uh, no, Amil, I wouldn't.

AMIL: I rest my case.

ISLA: But Jason might.

AMIL: Actually, you're right. He's done crazier things.

ISLA: So, here's the real question, Amil. Are we going to forgive Jason Connor this time?

AMIL: Jesus tells us to forgive everyone, Isla. Especially fools and tax collectors. And Jason Connor is definitely a fool.

ISLA: [*laughs*]

AMIL: [*laughs*]

ISLA: I'd still collect his tax, though.

AMIL: Oh, me, too. I'd raise his bracket.

ISLA: File his extension.

AMIL: Handle his arrears.

ISLA: [*laughs*]

AMIL: [*laughs*]

ISLA: Who knew taxes could be so much fun?

Chapter 14

Please God and Tom Hanks, just...no.

Emmy

THE LA TRAFFIC is a horror show, so I arrive late to the lot. I try to look like I know where I'm going as I navigate the fake street cafés and walkways between sets. I dodge a courier laden with bagel bags and give a wide berth to a gaggle of extras screaming and running from a guy holding a sign over his head that reads MONSTER.

Jason said it was Stage 10. I swivel my head in all directions, searching for numbers. The longer it takes me to find the studio, the greater the chance Jason will find out about the bar scene. I know Miles wants "complete creative control," but nothing's off the table as far as I'm concerned: begging, pleading...my next-born child. Hugging my hoodie close around me in the cool morning air, I flag down a nice golf cart driver who finally points me in the right direction.

I slip in the back door and blink in the dimness. At the front of the room, the crew is working on lighting and moving props around. The director's chair and all the other chairs around it sit empty. They haven't started filming yet. I'm not too late.

I think I spy Jason's brown curls for a moment before they disappear behind a false wall. He phone-kissed me last night! Granted, he'd been drinking, but I don't think it was the alcohol doing the kissing. I think it was more. But before I can celebrate, I've got to take care of this problem.

To the right is some seating with a decent view of the action. To the left is a folding table with a gorgeous spread of food. My stomach makes a long, low rumble, reminding me I was in such a rush this morning that I skipped the free breakfast at my hotel. I didn't even pick up one of their addictive little cinnamon buns on the way out.

"Tourists aren't allowed in here." A tall, frowning woman with a headset surprises me.

"Oh, hi!" I say brightly. "I'm Emmy Ellison, the author of the book. Jason said I could come watch the filming today."

"Yeah, okay." Recognition flickers in her eyes. "You can sit over there." She points to the lonely faction of chairs in the shadows.

"Any chance I could see Miles Gauthier for a minute?" I hold out my finger and thumb about half an inch apart to show her just how little time I need.

"I doubt it," she says over her shoulder as she walks away.

So it's not going to be easy. That's okay. I just need an excuse to hang around the director's chair so I can waylay him. I head for the buffet.

One of the things I love about California is the prevalence of avocado toast, and today doesn't disappoint. As I stack two hard little green-smothered toasts onto a paper plate, I glance over my shoulder, hoping to catch a glimpse of Miles. No such luck. I pop a piece of pineapple into my mouth and grab a Fiji water. As I loiter with my food, something catches my eye—a booklet of papers with its spine broken sprawled on a chair just a few feet in front of me. It's a script! Nobody seems to care much about it at the moment, so I'm guessing it's okay if I take a peek. I can see for myself whether or not there's a reason to panic.

Balancing my plate in one hand, I lean forward and reach for it with the other. A second before I can grab it, one of the actors swipes it up. I stretch out my arms and force a yawn. "Whoa, that's a good stretch! Boy, I'm stiff! I should go to the spa or something. Get a massage. Or do some...goat yoga."

He doesn't even look at me. I scan the room for more orphaned scripts lying around, but, alas, no success. I take another bite of my avocado toast instead and look for Miles. Jason is on set now, talking with one of the cast members. His face is drawn, and his body language is all weird and limp. In fact, he looks kind of upset. A part of me wants to be totally inappropriate, barge up there, and make sure he's okay, but then I spot *him*! Miles Gauthier. At the buffet table.

He's perusing the danishes. Damn it, I should've waited to go for the food. Frickin' story of my life. I shove the rest of the avocado toast into my mouth and push through the chairs to the table where Miles stands with his back to me. Even though I chew as fast as I can, my cheeks are bulging when he turns to me, and my mouth is too full to say a word.

I make a tight-lipped smile, sign *eat* with my hand, and give him the thumbs-up. So lame! I turn away and chew furiously, finally managing to gulp it down, but when I turn back, he's already heading to his seat.

"Mr. Gauthier!" I croak, but it's too late.

I'm planning on the best trajectory to tackle him, when he says, "We ready to run the bar scene?" Instantly, my blood turns to Waldorf Astoria pool water.

Oh no. Oh no, no, no, no.

The actors find their places, and I don't take my eyes off the set as I slink across the room and sink into my chair. This is it. This is the dreaded scene. How did I not notice it earlier? The pool table. The beer mugs. The spaghetti straps and Daisy Dukes on the female actors. It's the flashback scene where Gage beats up his girlfriend's husband. It's really too late. No wonder Jason looks so unhappy.

I can imagine how it all went down. Early this morning, he read the lines, preparing for work. It was probably confusing for him because he just told me the story last night. He probably thought, *Is this déjà vu or something?* And then he probably realized, *Oh my God, she knew all along. She let me tell her this story, this horribly painful story, and all this time it was already in her book.*

A sour taste overwhelms my palate. I want to hug myself, but I don't deserve it, so instead I grasp the chair seat and force myself to watch as someone pinches last-minute pomade into Jason's hair. He looks sexy as all get-out in a white tee, jeans, and cowboy boots. My body still remembers the feel of his arms around it. My heart remembers the intimacy of last night's conversation. Tears jump into my eyes. Whatever this could have become, it's all over now. I'm pretty sure he's never going to speak to me again.

What kind of a person does what I did? I guess back when I wrote that scene, I wasn't thinking of him. I was just thinking of myself.

I wipe a hand across my eyes. He doesn't deserve this. They're still prepping, so I might as well use the time. I said I would help Jason with his social media presence. I'm pretty sure that deal's off, but at least I can defend him.

I pull out my phone and navigate to his breakup video. There are nasty comments and plenty of them. Some are awful toward him, and some are awful toward Margarita or me. People can be real trolls. I log in to one of my fake accounts and respond to as many of them as I can. I defend him. And I defend her, too. Their business is nobody else's. It's not even mine, and I'm his friend.

At least I almost was.

Then, as a comment on the video itself, I type:

> Are you seriously going to suggest there's a GOOD way to break up with someone? The last time I broke up with someone it was at his sister's wedding. I caught the bouquet. He was happy about it. I wasn't. There's #NoGoodWay. Leave them both alone. #HowNotToBreakUp

"All right, let's run it," Miles says.

I force myself to watch, my heart breaking as Jason sets up his pool shot and a beautiful brunette cheers him on. The crack of the cue ball against a stripe rings through the room. The door bursts open, just like in his story. I wait for whoever is playing the unfortunate husband to enter—the guy Jason is going to have to fake punch as he's forced to reenact the moment he's most ashamed of.

My stomach clenches as I drop my face into my hands. I can't watch. I just can't. Then Jason's voice rings out. "Nora!"

Wait. That's not right.

I look up. It's Margarita standing in the doorway. She crosses the set and says, "I knew I'd find you here."

This isn't right at all! I sit up straight, my heart ping-ponging through all the different sectors of my body. There's more dialogue I don't catch. Then suddenly, Duran Duran's "Rio" is blasting over speakers. Jason does a total *Grease* move, riding a chair to the floor, and everyone sidles into place for a huge dance number. Suddenly, people are everywhere—on top of the pool table, perched on bar stools, swinging and being swung, tossing and being tossed.

Oh. My. God. Miles turned my book into a musical...to Duran Duran! It's genius. It's insanity. It's a thing of beauty.

My open mouth is wide enough to catch a murder hornet. My brain is exploding into tiny, happy bits of confetti as each song clip melts into the next and the bar set transforms into *Footloose* meets TikTok meets all my wildest Simon Le Bon dreams. They run the dance like twenty times, no kidding, while my shock slowly wears off. By the time Miles calls, "That's a wrap!" I've pretty much got it memorized myself.

"We'll take a break." Miles's voice carries across the room.

I check my phone. It's almost one o'clock. When I look up, Jason has disappeared again. Is he not going to talk to me at all? Although, a couple of hours ago, I was convinced he'd never talk to me again.

The buffet is being rejuvenated with sandwiches and fruit by a pair of caterers in purple polos. I'm just making a move to check out the facelift it received when the scent of jasmine and vanilla overwhelms me. I turn, and startle to find Margarita standing there in Nora's white shorts and yellow halter top. I check to see if she's come to talk to someone behind me.

"You must be Emmy," she says.

"H-hi." I run my suddenly sweaty palms down the front of my jeans. Frickity frack, she's even more beautiful in person. Half a foot taller than me. Straight, shiny black hair with the ends lopped off just at her pointy shoulders. Body with curves in all the right places. I feel like one of those orange-hued 1970s photos next to a high-res digital image. "It's so great to meet you, Margarita."

"Jason has told me a lot about you."

Even though she's technically my competition, I start fangirling. Hard. "You were amazing out there. Thank you for bringing this book to life. It's a dream come true for me. The dance scene was... There are no words!"

Her eyes flick up and down me, like she's an android and I'm a crate that has mysteriously appeared in the airlock. "Are you enjoying yourself in LA?"

"Yes," I say quickly.

"I'm sure Jason is helping you feel welcome."

I don't know what I'm supposed to say to that. "He is." Surely that can't get me in too much trouble. "I was just headed to the buffet. Do you want to come with me?"

Margarita's lips press together in a grimace, either like that was a terrible idea or like the whole idea of eating is abhorrent. She doesn't even bother answering me. "If you get bored here later, I think they're filming the *Little House on the Prairie* remake just across the way. It was nice to meet you."

She walks back to the set, her hips rocking sensually even though nobody but me is watching her go. It takes me a minute to decipher her insult. The *Little House on the Prairie* reference is her way of calling me small potatoes. It stings, although I can't blame her for being in a bad mood. She did just get dumped.

Still, despite everything, I really want Margarita to like me.

I've lost my appetite for the buffet, and even during the break, Jason doesn't come looking for me. Finally, he appears on set again, and I watch him interacting with Margarita. Miles says something about shooting a few close-up scenes in the bar, easing into his chair with his refilled coffee tumbler. The crew pushes a large camera up to the pool table.

Even though they supposedly broke up last night, Margarita reaches up to pick lint off the collar of Jason's T-shirt as he's talking to one of the crew. When he notices it's her, he peels her hand off but doesn't let go right away. Instead, he holds it for a second before letting it fall.

This is all too weird and uncomfortable and confusing. I should just go.

I start to get up just as Miles calls for action, and about three seconds in, all the weird uncomfortableness and confusion gets ratcheted up to twenty when I realize what scene this is. It's a kissing scene. And not just any kissing scene. It's the scene where Gage and Nora finally get to unleash all the burgeoning sexual tension that's been building between them. It's not in the same place I wrote it, but I'd recognize it anywhere.

Oh no. Please God and Tom Hanks, just...*no.*

My face and neck grow hot as Margarita hops up on the pool table, long legs dangling. She tears Jason's shirt off and throws it to the floor like it's on fire and about to kill him. He does the same to hers. I sink into my chair, trying to disappear into the collar of my hoodie as their mouths lock in a deep, hungry, shirtless kiss that seems to go on forever. Then he lays her down on the pool table and climbs up, pinning her with his body. As he devours her in delicious, slow-motion kisses, one hand reaching for his belt buckle, I'm caught in the awkward and excruciating place of being totally turned on while at the same time roiling with jealousy. When Jason's pants hit the floor, I audibly whimper.

Holy freaking mother of pearl. I should have gone for low heat. Young adult. *Sweet Valley High*. Amish romance, even.

"Cut!" Miles calls out.

Thank God and Tom Hanks that's over. But then they do the whole thing again, and it's worse for me the second time because I know what's coming. *Little House on the Prairie* is sounding better and better.

"Jason," Miles says, "on this next take, grab her breast when you go in for that kiss."

I shoot out of my chair, tripping over my own feet on my way to the exit. I shove the back door open into the bright outside, blinking my vision into focus just in time to see a tour tram barreling my way. I dive clear and try to remember how to get back to the parking lot, zigzagging this way and that through the false streets, my head swimming.

I don't know why I'm so upset. Jason's just doing his job. It's not like he's with Margarita. It's not like he's with *me*, either!

Plus, he was with her for real until yesterday. The only thing that's changed in twenty-four hours is me getting stupid ideas in my head. Ideas that he might really want me. That I might have a chance against the likes of Margarita.

Tears sting the backs of my eyes, but if I let them fall, I'll never be able to respect myself again. Where the hell is the exit to this maze of lies? My foot strikes the Spanish tile at the edge of a fountain and down I go, just like a dystopian government at the end of a YA film. Right before my palms meet concrete, two strong arms catch me. For a split second I dare to dream, but Jason doesn't wear Chanel. I crane my neck.

"Val?" I squeak.

He's got more blue eye shadow on than all my mother's '80s photos combined. His tight, shiny, long-sleeved shirt makes him look like he's about to meet the other cyclists at the starting line for the Tour de France.

I wince at his fingers digging into my armpits as he sets me on my feet again. "How did you know I was here?" I ask. "Do you have a tracker on me?"

He steers me in the opposite direction from where I was heading. "Precious, you shared your calendar with me, remember? And I see you're attending a cast party tonight, which is not something we're prepared for, so I am taking you shopping."

My voice comes out kind of whiny. "Are you taking me to Rodeo Drive?"

Val stares straight ahead. "I will take you to Paris if I have to."

A warm feeling spreads through my chest, and my shoulders straighten. We march out of the set area into the street, faces forward and purposeful, two people who know where they're going and what they're doing.

"Do I remind you of Laura Ingalls?" I ask him.

He scoffs. "Laura Ingalls wishes."

Chapter 15

Total world domination.

Emmy

FIVE HOURS LATER, Val peels a lock of hair from my head and wraps it around the shaft of the curling iron while I dip my fingers into a single-serve bag of Cheetos. My new outfit hangs from the bathroom doorway, a turquoise and light blue jumpsuit that is kind of like the navy Target jumpsuit I already own but with some extra zeros on the price tag. Outside the hotel window, two children make a beeline for the pool while their mother follows behind more slowly. A comfortable quiet fills the room.

"Do you style anybody else but me?" I ask, tossing the chip bag in the trash and licking my fingers.

"Right now, you are my only tribute, Katniss Everdeen."

My head swivels toward him. "I think of you as my Cinna!"

"May the odds be ever in your favor." He spins it back around. "Where are you from? I thought I detected a bit of an English accent earlier."

"I've been watching *Downton Abbey*. What do you think?"

"Elegant, yet condescending. I think you've nailed it."

A warm, wavy tendril of hair falls against my cheek. Something about it makes me feel like I'm in a safe place. With a safe person. "Val, do you think somebody like me could ever compete with Margarita Ayala?"

He pauses and catches my eye in the mirror. "My mother used to tell me, 'Child, don't swim where your feet don't touch.'"

"Wow, that accent went from London to Mississippi real quick."

"Georgia," Val corrects. "And I never shared that particular opinion with her. Although, if you're to win Jason Connor away from that Latina lovely, you're gonna need a little Botox here." A finger comes at my face.

I swat it away, giggling. "I said no Botox!"

"Why do you want him so badly, anyway?" Val asks, getting back to work.

"Who doesn't want him? He's perfect."

"Nobody's perfect, lass."

I study the stains on the ceiling while Val applies concealer under my eyes. "I felt like we had a connection once or twice. We have fun together. And he's starting to open up to me more. But I don't know for sure."

"If you want the man in your bed, I'm pretty sure you can get the man in your bed."

"I know that." A mascara wand thickens my lashes. Shimmery powder makes my skin sparkle.

"So, if that's not enough, here's a question to ask yourself: What do you want to get out of this?"

I stifle a scowl. I wish people would stop asking me that—what I want, what my dreams are. The truth is I don't really know. I want my youth back. I want my bright, shiny future ahead of me, the one that got swallowed up by a huge mistake and thirteen years of hiding from it. I want Jason to feel something for me that comes from above the waistline. I want...

"I want to sell lots of books," I say.

Val's derisive laugh tells me he's not impressed.

I try again. "I want to be famous."

He blows in my face, sending powder particles scattering. "I would say that's done."

"I want to be famous-*er?*"

He scoffs. "Come on, girl, dig deep. What is it you're really after?"

I didn't realize Val was supposed to be my therapist as well as my stylist. I press my bare toes into the hotel carpet, and that night thirteen years ago blinks to life again in my brain. Another hotel room. Another party. Another smoky eye like the one in the mirror, only younger, more naive.

Can I call you a cab? Rhett asked afterward, standing in the doorway looking all Billy Zane in his rumpled shirt and boxers.

Aren't we going to talk about the screenplay?

You know what? I don't want to string you along, honey. Your screenplay isn't going to be made into a movie. It's just not. You're not at that level. You're small potatoes. It's not bad. It's just not...special. Forget it. Hollywood's not for everyone. What was your name again?

I blink up at Val. "What I really want is to belong here. But I don't know if I'm cut out for it."

"Hmm." He nods. "Katniss Everdeen didn't think she was cut out to launch a revolution. She just showed up, and look what happened."

"But Katniss was badass."

"Katniss had skills and knew how to use them. You do, too. The difference between you is, she had a reason to win: survival. And, eventually, taking down the Capitol to protect the people she loved."

I see Rhett's smug face in my mind's eye, and this time I feel anger, not shame. Val's right. I'm good at what I do. Why shouldn't there be a place for me here? I might be from District 11, but Jason obviously has some interest in me. Maybe he prefers a fierce, bow-and-arrow-wielding, imperfect heroine to a splashy, made-up, Capitol-bred princess like Margarita.

Katniss got the guy *and* the glory. Maybe I can, too.

My heart rate spikes, and I check my wrist, forgetting I ruined my Fitbit last night in the hot tub. Could I win Jason Connor's heart for real? I mean, he's taking me to this cast party, not Margarita. What if I didn't have to fake a Cinderella story because it really was a Cinderella story? But if I get my hopes up, and I'm wrong…

"I don't need to take down the Capitol, Val. I just need it not to crush me to bits."

His purple contact lenses bore into me, giving him a wise cyborg-ish vibe. "Nobody's crushing my tribute to bits unless she lets them. Have a look."

He steps aside, and I see my full face. My lips part. I hardly recognize myself. Val has transformed me into a movie star, all my best features enhanced. My lips are full and pink and pouty. My eyes, sultry and mysterious. My skin is golden and radiant. Every wavy lock of my hair is flawlessly in place. If I saw myself walk into a room, I would turn my own head.

"Do you think Jason Connor's going to be thinking about Margarita Ayala with you on his arm tonight?"

I squint my perfect eyes. "Who is Margarita Ayala?"

Val laughs. "That's my girl." He starts packing away his implements. "And what are we going to use our newfound superpowers to accomplish tonight?"

Turning my face left and right, I appraise myself from every angle. I don't look like a redshirt today. I don't feel like one, either. Maybe Val is right. Book sales are going well. My social media stats have never been higher. I'm in *Vanity Fair*, for crying out loud. In fact, for the first time, I feel like I could have it all—fame, fortune, even Jason Connor.

My face splits into an evil smile. "Total world domination."

Val laughs, and it's the first time I've heard that noise, which is 100 percent Samuel L. Jackson.

"Just kidding. Maybe I'll focus on helping Jason with his social media mess and see where that goes."

Val's pencil-line eyebrows go up. "Interesting."

"I'd like to see what it feels like to be with Jason Connor without a side agenda. It seems like something Katniss might do, you know, on her way to kicking ass and taking names." I squirm in my chair because I'm not being totally honest with Val. I haven't told him about that awful bar scene. It's not in the script, but it's still in the book.

Val reaches for my new jumpsuit and holds it out for me. "Just don't spill anything while you're at it, or I'll go Black President Snow on your ass. Got it?"

I hold out a finger for the hanger. "No promises."

Chapter 16

What would Hugh Jackman do?

Jason

I SHUT MY car door and saunter into the pool area of Emmy's hotel. As I cross the deck, I spot the gazebo with the hot tub in it, where Emmy was last night during our phone call. Red bikini bottom. White bikini top. Hair wet. Belly button dripping.

I clear my throat as I approach the door to room 136, shove one hand into the pocket of my gray athleisure pants, and rap on the door with the other. When she opens it, I have to fight to keep my jaw clamped shut.

I thought I loved red, but Emmy in turquoise is a whole other story. With her golden skin and shimmery blond highlights, she's what the Caribbean Sea would look like if it were sexy and single.

"Hi," I say, swallowing hard. I don't want to gush, but there's no reason not to compliment her. "You look amazing."

"Thank you."

I catch a whiff of coconut, and suddenly I'm drunk on piña coladas and getting caught in the rain. I hold out an elbow for her. On the one hand, I can't wipe the smile off my face, but on the other hand, I need to keep it professional. Surely taking a girl to a party is proper, right? Except, when she looks this good, it feels like it's not.

What would Hugh Jackman do? He'd open the door for her. I know that much. We'll start there.

As I pull open the Alfa's door, she spots *#CelebrityCrush* on the passenger seat. I left it there so she could see that, yes, even though it's taking me forever, I *am* actually reading it, just like I said I would.

"You promised to autograph that for me," I remind her, falling into the driver's seat. "Hey, you just lost my page! And you didn't sign it."

"I don't have a pen." She doesn't seem too apologetic as she relocates the book to the back. It almost looks like she's shoving it under the passenger seat.

AC/DC fills the car as I hop onto the 405, and we're both so quiet I'm wondering if I'm missing something important. Then I realize that this is the first time we've been together that hasn't been booked and organized and scripted. Emmy's hands tap nervously on her turquoise knees, and I'm inappropriately happy to see that they're still bare of nail polish. I start wandering down a rabbit hole where those sexy hands are running themselves across my stomach again...

Nope, nope, nope. Stop, Jason. Bad Jason. Get back to professional. Speaking of professional...I turn the stereo down.

"So, hey, have you thought any more about that social media stuff we talked about last night?" The traffic is better than it should be on a Friday evening. It's a friggin' miracle we're moving at all, honestly. I check my mirrors and accidentally cut someone off getting into the fast lane. Sorry, dude.

"Oh, yeah." Her hands stop their drumming. "I posted something yesterday at the filming."

The filming? Does she mean…? I open my mouth but no words come out.

"You know. The *Hashtag Celebrity Crush* filming."

I feel like a tool. Did I invite her?

"You invited me, remember?"

"It's coming back to me now."

"You forgot."

"I forgot." Shit, I suck. I toss her my best puppy dog eyes. "I'm sorry. Filming is kind of intense, and with *Lost Star* still taping, life's been a whirlwind. Can you forgive me?"

It's true—my life has been consumed by work these last few months. And doing a movie is different from a TV show. Set changing all the time. Different people to work with. So many takes. There's a huge level of stress.

She looks out the window. "There's nothing to forgive. You were working."

I'll take that as a yes. "So what did you think?"

"I love that Miles turned it into a musical."

"It's good, isn't it?"

"Yeah, it is." She shimmies from side to side and waves her arms to the choreographed moves.

"You learned it? Hold up!" I call up the playlist on my stereo and jump in one-handed so I can keep driving. I sing and half dance along to the series of Duran Duran song clips while

Emmy struggles to keep up. I call out cues to help her with the transitions.

"Hands up! Push, push. The wave! The wave! Now we're gonna do that whole thing again, but faster."

Her moves are loose and carefree, and when she adds facial expressions, I find my smile stretching even wider. I ham it up extra *extra*, trying to score a giggle. By the time the song is done, we're both laughing. It seems to have cracked whatever ice had formed over us.

"So, you want to hear about my social media ideas for you?" She twists in her seat and leans against the side door, facing me with her golden-hazel eyes shining.

"Absolutely I do! I'm on the edge of my seat."

She holds her hands out, ready to launch into her vision. "We're going to appeal emotionally to your fans. They always want to know more about you. They want to interact with you. They want to feel like they have some sort of connection with you. We're going to give them that."

"Okay..."

"You love to dance, so we can do TikToks. We can do some behind-the-scenes vlogs from *Lost Star* and *Hashtag Celebrity Crush*. We can even do some stuff with the both of us where they can live vicariously through me. We're gonna give them the Jason Connor everybody loves—the funny, cute, charming, boy-next-door Jason—talking to them and with them wherever they are!"

I shoot her a sideways grin. "Do you really think I'm cute and charming? You don't have to answer that. But for real, are you sure that's enough to cancel the fallout from Breakupgate?"

"Oh, your friends are going to help with that tonight. At least I'm counting on it. The *Lost Star* cast are your friends, right?"

I scrunch my face in mock disbelief that she's even asking me this. "Of course they are! Why wouldn't they be?"

"Good, then it'll be cake."

Her confident smile eclipses the scenery bouncing by in the window behind her. I can tell she's in her element with all this stuff, and I feel like maybe, with this beautiful siren reining in my social media stupidity, everything is going to be okay.

"So how much is this campaign going to cost me?" I ask.

She makes a scoffing noise.

"No, seriously. I can afford to pay a social media marketer, and I'm hiring you. So how much do you charge?"

Her lips twist to the side. "I'm supposed to fly back home tomorrow morning, but if we're going to do this, I'll need to extend my trip. How about two days in LA? All expenses paid."

"That's it?"

She nods. "That's enough."

"Deal." I hold out a hand, and we shake on it.

I'm pretty sure our handshake lasts a beat longer than is normal, although I can't prove it. But I'm not supposed to be flirting with her. It's not my fault she's so fun and beautiful that I can't help myself. Speaking of not being able to help myself...

"Oh, I almost forgot!" The car swerves as I reach behind me where a small silver gift bag rests. I toss it onto her lap.

"You got me a present?"

I put on my nonchalant face. "Just a little something. No big deal."

She digs into the tiny bag. "I hope it's a puppy."

I stifle a laugh and then switch to mock-apologetic mode. "If I'd known you wanted a puppy, I'd have gotten you a puppy..."

"It's a new Fitbit!" She shakes off the tissue paper.

"It's actually a smartwatch." I point to the packaging. "It

tracks your heart rate, blood pressure, oxygen sats, menstrual cycle…"

She nods, brow furrowed. "Are you concerned that I might not be tracking my menstrual cycle?"

I was just rattling off what I remembered reading, but now I realize it's weird. "I, uh, yeah, well—" I search for a joke that doesn't suggest I see myself being in any way involved with her menstrual cycle.

She lets me off the hook. "It's okay. I love it. Thank you."

Before I know what's happening, she plants a quick kiss on my cheek.

I still feel the pressure of her lips as I pull onto Sunset Boulevard. Something is alive in my chest that feels like it's been dead for way too long. I'm starting to wonder if this whole keeping-it-professional thing is just a way to torture myself. Nevertheless, I pull up behind Ramirez's BMW and hurry around to open Emmy's door for her, just like Hugh Jackman would do. Her eyes shine as she gazes up at Sean's enormous mansion.

"You ready?"

She holds my arm in a tight grip as we enter through the towering doors, cross the opulent foyer, and pass the twin spiral staircases. Through the archway to the left, crew members are chatting in Sean's large and well-loved kitchen. Through the archway to the right, beautiful people crowd around a wide stone fireplace. But I lead her straight through the living room to the patio, where the action always is.

Sean has high-end lounge chairs and papasans sprawled about so the whole place looks like his own private Skybar. The patio heaters glow orange under their sun hats. String lights trace a fairy path out to the ultra-mod pool and waterfall spa. Andrew is at the baby grand, as usual, playing show tunes. It sounds like

he's on *Oklahoma!*, the second Broadway show in his usual repertoire, which means our timing is good.

"Snaaaack!" Sean feigns an exaggerated run at me. I let go of
Emmy so she doesn't get hit by the shrapnel of his hug, which is
really just an excuse to give me a noogie.

"Hello again, Miss Ellison." He takes Emmy's hand and
kisses it with the flair of a Victorian gentleman, a match for his
steampunk-inspired ruffled necktie, silk waistcoat with no shirt
under it, and tall, shiny boots. "Make yourself at home." He
points out all the important areas to Emmy, including the three
bars. "You gonna get this vision of a woman a drink, Snack?"
His attention catches on something over my shoulder. "Oops, my
buddy Idris just showed up. Gotta go!"

I give Emmy a tight-lipped grin. "Would you like a drink?"

"I'd love one." Her smile is ear to ear. Sean has that effect on
people.

Mount Ramirez spins on his stool as we approach the bar.
Emmy's eyebrows go up when she sees who it is.

"Sorry, man, but we kind of hit your car on the way in," I
joke, bumping fists.

"It was my fault." Emmy holds out her hand. "I distracted
him. Nice to see you again."

Ramirez shakes her hand. "Likewise. I'm sorry to say this,
but if Connor hit my car, there won't be any more hugs because
I'm going to break both his arms."

"Ha ha," I fake laugh. Then I add, "Just so we're clear, I didn't
really hit your car. Please don't hurt me."

Amanda appears out of nowhere and hugs me from behind.
"Jason Number Two! You're here!"

I hand Emmy a glass of wine and introduce them. "Why am

I always Jason Number Two?" I ask. "I've been wondering this for a while."

"Because I always score the highest on the 'Who Is Your Favorite Jason?' polls," Ramirez says. He knocks back the rest of his drink and nods to the bartender for another.

"I find the whole numbering system demeaning," I say.

"Aww, poor baby." Amanda pats my cheek, squeezing between us and Ramirez for a refill on her screwdriver. "So, how are you enjoying LA?" she asks Emmy. "Seems like you guys are having fun."

"I love being back here," Emmy says.

"She's going to stay a few extra days," I add.

"Lovely." Amanda tugs my elbow not-gently. "Can I borrow Jason Guinness for a minute?"

I raise my glass to her naming convention.

Emmy smiles. "Of course! I'm sure Jason Rum and Coke will be fine company."

"I do know a few good jokes." Ramirez grins.

"I have one," I hear Emmy say as Amanda steers me away. "There's this bar on the top floor of a skyscraper..."

Once we're out of earshot, Amanda whirls on me. "Two words, Connor. *That video.*"

I do my cringey face, only for real. "Oh yeah. That."

"What were you thinking?" She pushes me down onto one of the loungers by the piano. Andrew is deep into "The Farmer and the Cowman."

"What? You were the one who told me to break up with Margarita."

"I know, but I didn't know you were going to do it on YouTube!"

I lean back against the cushions and groan. "Miles said to make it public. Otherwise I might get replaced with Zachary Tay."

"You mean *that* Zachary Tay?" I follow her gaze to, sure enough, Prince Reese himself, elbow propped on the piano, tumbler in hand.

I snarl. "I thought this was a cast party."

"You know Sean. Nothing can be small. Have you seen her since?"

"Who? Margarita? Yeah. We filmed the movie today, and she dropped Mattie off just before the babysitter came over."

"And she hasn't fed your celebrity crusher a poisoned apple yet?"

"I don't think so. I think she's finally accepted that it's time to move on."

Halle Berry arrives in my peripheral vision, and I get distracted because, secretly, she was my celebrity crush for my entire childhood.

Amanda grabs my chin and turns it back.

"Ouch! What was that for?"

"What's up with you and Author Chick anyway?"

"Nothing. Nothing's up with us." I peek at Emmy, who is filming Ramirez with her phone.

"You sure about that?" Amanda grabs for my chin again, but I karate block her.

"Yes." I shake my head. "No."

Amanda giggles, and it's a great giggle. I think half her roles were won with that giggle. I point to her glass. "How many of those have you had?"

Now Sean has joined Jason Ramirez and Emmy's little party. He's making big arm movements, tapping into his classical Shakespearean training as Emmy videos him.

"You can't keep your eyes off her," Amanda says, her *wow* face on. "Look at me!"

"Sorry. I don't know what's wrong with me." Seriously, what *is* wrong with me? I feel all jittery and hungry and electrified. Either my blood sugar is low or I like Emmy more than I realized.

"I want you to be happy, Jason, I do." Amanda frowns. "But you need to find someone you can have a real relationship with. Not a frolic."

"A frolic? What is that? Is that a Norwegian hat?"

"You know what I mean. A *frolic*. Something that has no staying power."

A Pacific breeze has arrived at the party, tickling the torchlight into flickers. It rattles the palm trees and mixes with the music and ambient conversation, awakening a melancholy déjà vu. How many times have I sat on this patio, hearing those same sounds? How many times with women? How many times alone?

"I wouldn't describe Emmy as a frolic."

"She lives on the other side of the country, Jason. *Hashtag Celebrity Crush* is going to come and go, and so is she. You need to find someone you can share a life with. Someone who will love you and Mattie for longer than *a few extra days*."

She's right, as usual. Emmy is leaving in two days. And how would that be any different from the one-night stands I've sworn off? I run a hand through my hair and sigh heavily. "Do we have to do this now?"

"I think we do." Amanda catches me glancing at Emmy again. "Geez, you're like a barracuda with a lure."

"Would it be the worst thing in the world if we had something, even something temporary?"

Amanda sucks on an ice cube from her glass. "Listen up, Jay. First of all, I like Emmy. I do. I think she's fun and talented, and I know having her around strokes your ego, and there's nothing wrong with that. But one of two things is happening here. One, she's hoping to get a chance at having a hot affair with her celebrity crush so she can tell all her girlfriends about it when she gets home, in which case you're back to being a player. Or two, she's got it in her head that her obsession with you is actual real feelings, and when it's all over, she's going to be brokenhearted, in which case you're going to look like the asshole who took advantage of her." She pauses. "And there's a third scenario—that you're just the ladder for her climb to the top."

Her words throw a blanket over any good feelings I had left. Is Emmy hoping we'll have a roll in the hay and then say our goodbyes? Does she want something more, something I can't give her? Or is she flat-out using me?

Margarita's voice resurrects itself in my brain. *Face it, I'm the only woman willing to put up with you for more than sex.*

"I just...I just really like her."

Amanda throws up her hands. "Whatever. I tried. I hope you know what you're doing."

"I assure you, I don't."

"Well, you better figure it out."

"That's pretty unlikely as well."

"I guess I'll just go make friends with Zachary Tay then, since we'll likely be working together." She pretends to look for him.

"Mean girl." I shoot her a hurt look before my gaze lingers past her toward the piano. Andrew's wife, Renee, has joined him, and they're singing together. There's an easiness and warmth around them that is palpable. Occasionally, she hits one of the high keys for him, and they share a smile.

Amanda follows my gaze. "Wow, Margarita has really done a number on you."

I'm thinking she's right. Actually, I know she's right.

"Listen." She shakes my shoulders back and forth in a one-armed embrace. "I'll help Emmy have fun tonight. You go talk to other people. Give yourself a little space. Keep it light. Easy-breezy. Stop at three drinks. You know. The basics."

Andrew trails his fingers across the piano keys in the pause between songs. "This one's for Jason Connor!" he announces. I wave and smile, acknowledging him and everyone else looking at me. It takes me a second to recognize the tune—"Desperado" by the Eagles.

I glance at Amanda. "Did you put him up to this?"

She's got her Maelstrom face on. It's ice. And knives. And laser beams. "We're your friends, Jason. We want what's best for you. And, selfishly, we don't want to lose you on the *Lost Star* team. Can you just, maybe, keep it in your pants at least until you sign next season's contract?"

"I love it when you get all ladylike."

She sputters a laugh, and an ice cube shoots out of her mouth and lands on my lap.

I flick it off. "Classy."

Emmy is now video-ing Zachary Tay by the pool. What is it with that guy and all the things I care about? I roll off the lounger to my feet and stumble once on my way to the piano. Singing along, I hold out a hand to Renee, who always reminds me of Meg Ryan in *Top Gun*, and gently lead her away from her husband and into my arms. I spin her slowly as I sing along to the mournful lyrics.

When the song ends, I hug Renee and give Andrew's shoulders a squeeze. There, that should count as mingling. Emmy's talking to the Chris trifecta now—Evans, Hemsworth, and Pratt. Holy cow, is there an *Avengers* reunion this week I wasn't aware of? I'm dying to know what she's up to. I grab another Guinness for me and a glass of pinot grigio for her on the way.

"Hey." I raise my beer to the Chrises as they smile and walk off. Emmy is busily tapping away on her phone. "Whatcha doing?"

"Just working on your PR campaign with the help of your friends."

I gesture in their direction with my glass. "I don't really know them that well. They're more Sean's friends."

"Oh." Emmy looks surprised. "Well, they're very nice."

"They didn't steal my title of celebrity crush while I was gone, did they?"

She accepts the wine and takes a sip. "Don't worry, Jason. They're in the stratosphere, but you…" She swallows and grins. "You're on the ISS."

A warmth flows over me, like there's a hot tub up here on the International Space Station.

Andrew has stopped playing the piano, his musical talents replaced by a rousing salsa beat. I start shimmying involuntarily, and that naughty smile of hers plays across her face as she glances down at my hips.

"Do you know how to dance salsa?" I ask her.

"I've danced to Marc Anthony once or twice, but the honest answer is no."

"Come on, I'll teach you." I hold out a hand.

She takes a step backward. "Isn't it hard?"

"Hard? Pssh!" I lunge forward and snag her hand before she can run away from me and jump into the pool again. Hauling her over to a clearing, I take her wine from her and set it beside my beer on a nearby high-top. "It's a one-two-three-skip beat. That's all you have to do. I'll lead, and as long as you keep your feet doing the right thing, you're okay."

It's a gross oversimplification but call me an optimist. Besides, I feel like I should earn the honor of being higher on her list than Captain America, Thor, and Star-Lord. My left hand holds hers loosely, and I press the other against the small of her back.

"Elbows out," I say softly. "First we'll do it side to side." She giggles as she copies my footwork, but, to her credit, she picks it up quickly. "That's it. One-two-three-skip, one-two-three-skip. You can tap your toe on the skip if you want. Just don't step on the skip." I flash her the fierce face. "*Never* step on the skip."

She falters. "I stepped on the skip!"

"Oh no! A planet just exploded! Just kidding, keep going. One-two-three-skip. You got it! Okay, now we're gonna do it front to back." She picks that up quickly, too, so I show her a few more moves. She's kind of wiggly for salsa, but it's like adding a shot of hot sauce to a Bloody Mary. Nothing wrong with some zip. She stumbles against me, and I relish the sensation of steadying her.

"Sorry," she whispers, hand pressed against my chest.

"No problemo," I whisper back. She doesn't pull away.

Maybe everyone is wrong about us. Maybe this thing I'm feeling is a good thing. Her fingers tickle the back of my neck. Her smoky-eyed gaze is sultry and dark and punctuated with desire. Her lips are so close I can hear her exhales. My blood rushes as I hold her against me, forgetting about the music, the dancing, professionalism, everything Amanda said to me only minutes ago. We're alone back here, relatively speaking, and every mutinous inch of me is urging me on as I run a thumb across her cheek.

She doesn't stop me. She's waiting for it. I see it in the way her eyelids flutter, in her held breath. I feel it in how her body moves against mine, subtly but unmistakably. The pull of her want is as strong as mine. We are a tide.

I lean in and meet her slightly open mouth with my own. She tastes like pinot grigio and smells like a coconut breeze, one that is carrying me far, far away from all my cares. In the shadowy landscaping, our kiss feels clandestine and forbidden, but at the same time, precious. Meaningful. When our lips part, there is fear in Emmy's eyes. Not fear of monsters or bodily harm. I know that look: it's fear of consequences.

"I'm sorry," I whisper, letting her go. "I should have asked first."

"No, it's fine. I was definitely giving you signals."

We glance around semi-discreetly, but no one seems to have noticed us. An impromptu chuckle escapes me, and she giggles in reply. We're acting like teenagers, and I love it. I feel like a teenager, edgy and fearless and free. Ready to grab Emmy by the hand so we can backpack across Europe, visit thousand-year-old churches, and kiss under balconies erupting with flowers. Not that I'm in a position to purchase Eurail tickets and disappear into the Swiss Alps, although I could get lost in Emmy's eyes, fiery and golden as the stars above.

I rescue our drinks from the nearby table and hand Emmy hers with a tight-lipped smile. "You sure that was okay?"

"It was more than okay. It was a dream come true—better than all the times I imagined it." She reaches for my hand, and our fingers tangle together for one electric second before reality sets in and I pull mine back.

"I'm not supposed to…" I glance around. "The network is threatening to let me go if I get any more bad press."

"Oh." She wraps both hands around her wineglass and brings it to her exquisite lips. "I did hear that. I'm sorry."

"I'm sorry, too! Because I really want to hold your hand right now." She looks at me over the rim of her glass, and it's the sexiest thing I've ever seen. "And I want to kiss you again. Right now." She bites her lip while smiling at the same time, and now I'm really going over the edge. "And then maybe again, a few minutes later, if you're on board. But I'm afraid if I do any of those things…" I wince. "I'm afraid it won't be good for me."

Her eyes go wide. "Have I gotten you in trouble?"

"Of course not!" I cut in quickly. "And, to be clear, I love that we kissed. I've been thinking about kissing you for a while now, or trying not to, ever since you fed me that sandwich in the pool. And then you called me and talked me down over the phone. When I'm with you, I can just be happy. You make me feel like someone who deserves to be happy."

Her chest rises as she takes a deep breath, inhaling my words along with the heady scent of jasmine. "You do deserve to be happy, Jason Connor. And you make me happy, too. Bringing me to this party, treating me like I'm a somebody even though I don't really fit in with this crowd." Her gaze flicks across the vast outdoor space and all its celebrity occupants. "You took the time to include me, and I appreciate that."

I want to tell her that she *is* a somebody. That she fits in just fine. Heck, all my friends love her. That she's not so different from everyone here. And I like that she seems like a girl who might watch a football game on a Sunday afternoon. Who might throw a ball with Mattie and me on the beach. But before I can say anything else, the screeching of whatever insane sound system Sean has rigged up out here slices through the night. The music shuts off abruptly, and his voice booms across the loungers and piano bar and pool deck, out into the manicured lawns and beyond.

"Attention! Attention, everyone! I believe the time is ripe to settle a score. A score that has raged since...March, I believe." He turns to Andrew. "Andrew, was it March? Yes, Andrew and I both agree it was March. A rivalry that must culminate tonight!"

The moment is lost. Instead of telling Emmy how great I think she is, I stand shoulder to shoulder with her, waiting like everyone else for the details of Sean's latest foolishness.

"What is it, you ask? What is this contest that has torn family and friends asunder? What injustice will be righted tonight, in this very patio area where I am standing, which is far enough away from the pool but central enough for everyone to see? Why, it's the epic hugging contest promised to us by Emmy Ellison on *The Terica Show*! Oh yes, Emmy, I see your eyes getting all wide like you didn't know this was coming. Back in March, Emmy claimed that Jason Connor gave the best hugs in Hollywood. Well, I've disputed that, and today we're going to find out the truth. Let's go! Up here! *Lost Star* men and Emmy Ellison. Right here! Right now!" His finger attacks the air each time he says "right."

I glance at Emmy and do my best *Quantum Leap* impression: "Oh boy."

Chapter 17

I don't know what just happened there, but I
don't think it was healthy.

Jason

EMMY AND I head toward Sean, and now I know why he wanted
her to come to his party so badly. The guy's got a real problem
with competition.

"I'm a shoo-in, right?" I whisper to Emmy as we navigate
tables and chairs and people.

"Oh no!" Sean booms into the mic before she can answer.
"Already Jason Connor is trying to influence the outcome of our
hugging contest. Emmy, are you a believer? If so, we're going to
get you to swear on a Bible. Tommy!" He points to Tom Holland,
who looks up in surprise from where he was minding his own
business on the abandoned piano bench. "Would you mind grabbing a Bible off the library shelf? I think there's a New American

Version there somewhere in between Dante's *Inferno* and *The Life-Changing Magic of Tidying Up*."

"No need for that!" Emmy abandons her wineglass and spins in a circle to address the convening throng. "It'll be an honest contest. The man who wins the title of best hugger will have to earn it. But I'll need someone to video it for me."

Kayla breaks from the crowd. "I got you!"

Great. My nerves prickle. Of course I want to hold on to this meaningless and ridiculous title, but I don't want to do anything dumb in the name of friendly competition. I managed to steal a kiss from Emmy without consequences, but if I do anything improper during the contest, the network won't like it. Plus, to be honest, I'm genuinely scared I can't win against these guys.

Sean lines everyone up—me, Ramirez, Andrew, and himself, with Emmy standing on a tile sunburst in the large, open area near the piano. Kayla gives the nod, and Sean launches into emcee mode.

"Hello, America and beyond! We're here today to prove once and for all who the best hugger is in the cast of *Lost Star Dance Troupe Saves the Universe*. It's been suggested that it's Jason Connor over there..." I raise my hand in a half-hearted wave. "But I challenge that notion! Emmy Ellison is here today to do the honors. She's promised us a fair fight, and we're going to hold her to that." Sean gives her a punishing look.

"So, who's going first?" Emmy asks brightly.

I don't want it to be me. Everyone knows going first is a bad idea.

"I'll go." Ramirez takes slow, deliberate steps in her direction. The brightness of his shirt amplifies the muscles of his upper body in the same way a room painted white looks larger than a wood-paneled den. The two of them standing next to each other look like a *Lord of the Rings* audition: orc and elf.

"We've got an eager beaver!" Sean says into the mic. "First up, Mount Ramirez. Let's see if this big lug doesn't crack her in two before the rest of us get a chance to compete."

"Ha ha," Ramirez says without humor. Then he just stands there.

Sean rolls his eyes. "Are you waiting for a trumpet? This isn't the Olympics."

"I'm just a little nervous, that's all," Ramirez says. "I mean, here's a beautiful woman that I don't even know—"

"Oh God," Sean interrupts him in disgust. "And now the flattery starts. Don't butter her up. Just hug her already, you big baby!"

Ramirez rolls his shoulders and flexes his hands. Next to him, Emmy stands open armed and expressionless, like a life-size, huggable mannequin. We watch in amusement as Jason Ramirez bends low, wraps all that muscle and sinew around her, and lifts her off the ground. Emmy makes a little squeal sound that I kind of like and am kind of jealous about at the same time. Camera in hand, Kayla moves around the perimeter, filming from all angles.

It's not a short hug. Maybe not as long as the one I gave her a few months ago, but long enough. I don't know if the same gimmick I used back then is going to work this time. Although why do I care anyway? It's a stupid contest. And if one of these guys steals the title, it just might take some pressure off me. Let somebody else be lit in Emmy's spotlight for a while.

"Whoa! Wow! She's back on her feet again," Sean says. "Looks like we don't need to call the paramedics after all."

Ramirez releases Emmy, first to her toes and then to the

soles of her platform shoes. He steps back, his expression more than a little cocky. Emmy mouths, "Whoa!" and gives him a big grin. The crowd laughs. I swallow hard.

"Well, that was a—"

Emmy snatches the mic from Sean before he can editorialize. "Okay, my impressions…So, Jason 'Mount' Ramirez made an unexpected yet savvy move with the whole under-the-arms approach. It not only lifted me off my feet—which I liked a lot—but also offered me the opportunity for some cheek-to-cheek action." She looks straight into the camera. "Ladies and gentlemen, it was smooth as a peach, in case you're wondering. The length was appropriate. I didn't recognize his cologne, but it had a very woodsy, manly smell. If I had to sum up this hug in one word, I would call it…" She taps her lips as though searching for the right word. "*Gallant.*"

"Yeah, but it didn't transport her to another dimension," I mutter.

"Well played, Ramirez." Sean gives him a firm handshake. "All right, I'm next!"

He hands off the microphone and leaps into the "ring." Wasting no time, he takes Emmy's hand and flings her one way, then the other, and then whips her, spinning, right into his arms, where he holds her for a long moment before dipping her down to the floor. When she's finally on her feet again, her cheeks are flushed pink and her eyes sparkle. To a smattering of applause, Sean releases her from his embrace slowly, her hand last of all.

"Oh my," Emmy says, accepting the microphone from Ramirez. "Okay. Give me a moment." She fans her face with her hand. "So that was definitely a hug to show a girl a good time. It was playful and seductive, with just the right amount of throwing me pleasantly off-balance while letting me know that he was never going to let me fall. It was definitely...*swoony*."

Sean nods to her with affectionate smugness and then leans into the mic. "And mine is the virile-yet-sensual scent of Clive Christian. She left that part out."

The audience laughs, and I'm starting to sweat a little. I know the big shots at this party don't care about this silly little contest, but Emmy will post it online, and it would suck to have Sean rub it in my face if I lost. Plus, I'm kind of jealous. I want Emmy to pick me again.

"Worried, Snack?" Sean comes shoulder to shoulder with me and bangs his teeth together. "You should be."

"Nope." I feign confidence. "I got my winning hug on deck right here. And I've added some special sauce to the recipe."

"That sounds...disgusting."

"You know what I mean."

He raises the mic, still glaring my way. "All right then, two left to go. Who's—"

"I'll go." Andrew jumps in before he can finish.

Sean presses the mic to his lips, and in a mock-serious tone says, "Andrew, did you get your wife's permission for this?"

Andrew turns to Renee, who is perched on a nearby lounger. "Honey? May I hug this young lady?"

"Win it, babe!" she shouts.

Andrew moseys up to the stage, and with no preamble, folds Emmy against him, and holds her for a long moment, rocking ever so slightly from side to side. There's no fanfare. In fact, it's the same kind of hug someone might give their niece. There are a few *awwww*s from the audience when he lets go.

Sean makes a gagging noise. "Okay, Emmy, let's hear what you thought about that lame hug."

"Wow." Emmy holds a hand over her heart. "Let me tell you, folks. That hug was so warm and so authentic. I didn't feel like we were in a contest at all. I felt like this man had real, true emotions toward me. Like he would let the zombies take him instead. I felt... loved."

Sean snatches the mic back. "Well, there you have it. Creepy uncle hug gets five stars. I don't know what just happened there, but I don't think it was healthy."

Andrew holds his glass up. "I'll give you one later, Sean."

"That's a big no thank you!" Sean makes an awkward face at the camera. Then he turns to me, his voice dropping a register. "And then there was one." We're nose to nose, Sean glaring into my face. He covers the microphone with his hand. "You got that bottle of special sauce shook up real good, Snack?"

"I do."

"Well then, let's see what you've got." He steps aside with a flourish.

I stroll up to the sunburst where Emmy waits, expectant and nervous, just like when I first met her on *The Terica Show*. A few *Go, Jason*s stand out from the normal sounds of conversation and laughter. I've made my decision. Screw it. I'm not letting these guys show me up. No way. No how. I'm going to give her that same long, warm hug I did last time, and this time there will actually be some feeling behind it. Then I'm going to whisper a few sweet nothings in her ear that will make her melt in my arms. I don't have the words ready, but I don't need to rehearse this, because how I feel is just going to come out when I open my mouth. I'm even kind of excited to hear what I have to say. And then... who knows? I won't kiss her again because that would be stupid, but... well, we'll just have to play it by ear.

I don't know what Emmy wants. I don't even know what I want. But right now, I have a contest to win.

I take both her hands in mine. "Bulletproof, right?"

"Yes." She barely breathes it.

I open my arms, and she falls into them. I wrap them around her and feel her body submit to mine. I close my eyes and count to five, breathing in the scent of coconut. As she relaxes even more against me, I tug her in closer. My hand slips into her hair, and I can't help squeezing a handful of its softness. She feels so good in my arms, so right. It doesn't feel like some stupid party game that'll soon be all over every celebrity blog and podcast. It feels like Christmas. Or slingshotting around the moon. Things I haven't felt in forever wash over me—excitement, hope, desire. Real desire, not just the kind that distracts. A want that runs so deep it tears you apart. I don't ever want to let go. Sliding my chin down into the cascade of her hair, I run my lips across the curl of her ear and whisper, "Emmy, I…"

And then something catches my eye, and I freeze. Miles Gauthier is here in his Baby Yoda T-shirt, jeans, and expensive shoes, standing with two of the showrunners from *Lost Star*. Where did they come from? They're watching us with interest.

Miles's stare says, *Really, Jason? Really?*

My eyes say, *But I broke up with Margarita, and I made it public, just like you said.*

And his say, *I said keep it professional! Does that look professional?*

It's like someone has thrown the switch on my main breaker. All the good feelings are gone, and I realize how bad this looks. Hugh Jackman would not be doing this—I'm pretty darn sure about that.

"Never mind," I whisper, pulling my hand out of Emmy's hair. It accidentally catches in her waves and tugs too hard.

"Ouch." Her hand flies to her head.

"Sorry." I wiggle my fingers to untangle them from her hair as my brain fights to interpret the body language of the showrunners. Does that foot shuffle say, *That's it. We're done with him for good?*

The crowd is murmuring. Sean is grinning. "Looks like our incumbent may have choked! But let's hear what the lady has to say, *after* she gets her hair untangled."

Emmy smooths her hair with an annoyed look and accepts the microphone. Miles glares at me, but the execs aren't reacting at all. Relief floods through me, then shame, and then acceptance of what an ass I am, with relief and shame mixed in—the Jason Connor grief journey.

"It wasn't as good as the last one," Emmy says into the mic.

With melodrama, I drop my forehead into my hand—my way of signaling to her that she can go ahead and blast me, no hard feelings.

She turns to the camera. "Yeah, it was a disappointment. Ended abruptly. Pulled my hair. There was a promise of pillow talk that would have truly elevated it, probably pretty darn high I'm guessing, but that fell flat. I think he wears Calvin Klein, but that's not enough to make up for what happened here tonight. All in all, I'm afraid Jason Connor has lost the title."

"Whoa!" Sean shouts. "A *crushing* defeat for our celebrity crush! Get it? *Crushing?*"

I continue to wallow in fake self-pity for the benefit of the camera, and Sean waits patiently so Kayla can capture plenty of footage of it. When all that carrying-on has settled down,

Sean asks the question: "So, Emmy. What's the verdict then? If Jason Connor isn't the best hugger in the *Lost Star* dance troupe, who is?"

Emmy taps her lips in that way she does when she's pretending to think. "Honestly, I have to go with Andrew."

"Yes!" Renee shrieks, jumping up from the lounger. "Yes! That's my man!" Andrew blows a kiss to his wife and takes a bow.

"Andrew?" Sean dons his liberally offended face.

"Andrew," Emmy confirms. "His felt the most real. And I liked his cologne best."

"Woody's Love Grenade." Andrew grins.

"So that's it then?" Sean grabs someone's napkin out of their hand, balls it up, and in fake fury throws it to the ground, where it falls lightly because it's a napkin. Then he kicks it.

Emmy takes her phone back from Kayla and finishes off her vlog with a few words. The crowd disperses with inappropriate comments and laughs. When all the dust and pain have settled, we just stand there. The look in Emmy's eyes makes me ache.

"I'm sorry," I say. "The showrunners are here. It threw me."

"It's fine." She scrutinizes the patio stones under our feet. "I understand."

I look over my shoulder to where Miles and his entourage are watching Anthony Mackie killing it at darts. I jerk a thumb in their direction. "I should go do some damage control, just in case."

"Okay." She nods. "I'll just upload some of these videos."

She's not making eye contact with me. Running off now seems like a shitty way to treat her after I kissed her and said all those things. But I can't ignore this potential problem. "You sure you're okay?"

She shrugs. "It's fine, Jason."

My arms hang at my sides. I want to take her hand, pull her to me, kiss her forehead, do something to show her how I really feel about her, but I can't. I guess the best thing I can do is get this over with. I trot backward. "I'll be right back. I'll be *so quick.*"

I turn and make my way over to Miles and the gang.

Chapter 18

#HowNotToBreakUp

AUGUST 4

JASON: Hey everyone, Mount Ramirez here. I've been asked to tell you about my best breakup, and honestly, I can't think of a breakup that went well. I guess maybe I'll talk about the time I broke up with this one girl in college. I thought I was being pretty cool about the whole thing. I took her out to dinner at a nice restaurant. We got through the whole dinner—steak. Right? I spent money on her. And during dessert I said, "I don't think we have a future together." It's a benign, nonjudgmental sentence, at least I thought so at the time. She burst into tears at the dinner table. The waitress gave me dirty looks until we left.

@JasonRamirez1022 #HowNotToBreakUp #NoGoodWay @thefunnyJason @MargaritAAA

SEAN: My best breakup? Oh my! So many to choose from! Oh, say my name first? They know who I am. Okay, fine. This is Sean O'Sullivan. I think my best breakup was just last week, come to think of it. We were in bed, that's all I'll say. It was afterward. We were eating cashews, and she said, "These are fatty nuts," and I said, "What did you say? It's over!" Thinking back, it might have all been a misunderstanding. @PutYourPantsSean #HowNotToBreakUp #NoGoodWay @thefunnyJason @MargaritAAA

KAYLA: Hi, I'm Kayla Williams. *Lost Star Dance Troupe Saves the Universe.* I think breaking up is easy. You just, like, ghost them. That way you don't have to have any uncomfortable conversations. I don't owe him anything. I mean, it was only six months of our life. I Venmoed him the money for the hoodie I kept. I don't know why we have to make such a big deal about it. Throwing Skittles at someone's window followed up by shouting and crying is…yikes, right? I don't know what his problem is. Seriously. @KayKayLaLa #HowNotToBreakUp #NoGoodWay @thefunnyJason @MargaritAAA

Chapter 19

I'm honestly starting to pity myself.

Emmy

AMANDA JOINS ME at a high-top table near the pool. I finish uploading one more social media post and tuck my phone into my purse.

"You okay?"

I force a smile. "Of course! Why wouldn't I be?"

She twists her perfectly lipsticked mouth to the side. "Jason bombed the contest. That probably wasn't in the plans, was it?" She adjusts the bodice of her skintight dress and takes a sip of her drink. The way she flicks her hair out of her face makes me think of a real L'Oréal Because You're Worth It commercial. Come to think of it, I think she starred in one or two.

"Oh, that's no big deal," I say, although inside I'm still reeling from the total bait and switch of that hug. The way he pulled me to him so tight…again. His hand in my hair. His breath in my ear. He was about to whisper something.

"I can tell it was a big deal." Amanda's brown eyes look like they don't take shit from anybody.

I sigh and lean back in my chair. She's a friend of Jason's. Maybe she has some insight, and maybe I can tease it out of her without admitting my own feelings. "I'm not stupid, you know. I know how Hollywood works."

She nods. "Okay. So you know you don't have a chance with him, right?"

That went in the opposite direction I expected it to. "I—I'm just here to sell books and promote the movie," I stammer.

Her smile is half pity, half razors. "Oh, Emmy, hon. I know he's hot. He's successful, he's charming. Everyone falls for him. You're not the first."

I'm sweating now, even in the cool evening air. "Did you?"

Her laugh is spontaneous and melodious. "Nah, Jason and I go too far back for that. But you have to understand. Jason's job is on the line. He can't afford a messy affair with a fan."

I pick at the mosaic tiles in the tabletop. "It was a hug, not an orgy."

Amanda gives me a knowing look. "Except it wasn't just a hug, was it?"

Shit, she can see right through me! I cross my arms over my chest. "It was a social media stunt, nothing more. And I didn't even put Sean up to it. I just capitalized on it."

Her eyes narrow. "You're good at that, huh?"

I don't know how Amanda and I suddenly became enemies, and I don't want to argue with her. But the only other choice is admitting how I really feel about Jason and having her laugh about it, either to my face or behind my back.

"Look, we both work in this business." I uncross my arms and hold the chair seat instead. "Although, I'll admit, with him, sometimes it's...confusing."

"I don't say this to hurt you." Amanda studies me. "But you know he has a son. You have a daughter, right? When you have kids, your relationships need to be stable."

I don't let myself squirm. "Did he say that?"

"Does he have to?"

Shame heats my cheeks. Great, now she's basically called me a bad mom. Of course I understand we have a responsibility to our kids, but I can't help the way I feel. Besides, we had one kiss. Aren't we at least allowed to figure things out before we start slapping labels on everything and judging it?

Still, I know she's right. This whole thing is more complicated than I'm giving it credit for. If it's even a *thing*, which I'm not sure it is.

Over Amanda's shoulder, I spot Jason crossing the patio toward us. I sit up tall.

He drops his elbows onto our table. "So, this is the gorgeous women's section! I've been looking for it all night."

Amanda slides off her seat and wrinkles her nose. "Tell me you've got better pickup lines than that."

He takes her place on the high-top chair. "Thanks for keeping my seat warm."

Amanda gives me a hard look. "No problem. Emmy and I were just finishing up a riveting conversation...about you."

"About me?" Jason looks over his shoulder at her, but she's already gone.

"She's lying. We were talking about...pie." I can't help but look at his mouth. *Jason Connor kissed me!* I want to scream it from the rooftops. And at the same time, it feels like a dirty little secret.

"Okay, well, I think I got everything smoothed over." He blows air out of his cheeks. "The showrunners were the last people I wanted to see that performance."

Performance. The word is like a dagger between my ribs. Suddenly, I feel like a *Westworld* android, getting hurt over and over again for other people's entertainment.

"I posted the videos from tonight." I paste on a smile. "They're taking off already."

His face lights up. "That's great!"

I take a deep breath. "I was thinking maybe I should just go home tomorrow after all."

His face transforms in confusion. "What? I thought we had a deal."

"Maybe it's not such a good idea. After what happened tonight." I run a finger over the rim of my wineglass, staring into the dregs.

"Emmy!" Jason takes both my hands in his across the table. "Don't let that stupid contest bother you. That was me. I panicked. The showrunners didn't even care. They know the whole thing's a publicity stunt."

I gaze into his eyes—two clear, indigo pools in the dim patio lighting. "The contest was a publicity stunt, but what about the rest of it? Won't it look bad for me to be hanging out with you, making videos all weekend?"

He pulls his hands away and takes a swig of his drink. "You'll be helping me fix my image. They'll be happy. As long as it doesn't look like we're having some sordid affair, it'll be fine."

I hate the word *affair*, and adding *sordid* in front of it makes it that much worse. What I feel for Jason Connor doesn't feel like a sordid anything. Is that how he sees us?

"The videos are doing well, Jason. Maybe I should just go home."

He looks around and then takes my hands again and presses them to his lips. "Please stay, Emmy. I want you to stay. I still need your help. And I want to make it up to you."

His hot breath on my fingers combined with the memory of that soft, slow, delicious kiss gnaws away at my righteous indignation. I don't want to become Jason Connor's latest disposable utensil, but he's lived in my heart forever, and he kissed me, and now he's asking me to stay. How can I say no?

He must sense my weakness. One side of his mouth curls up in the tiniest smile. "Whoever cares most gets to win, right?"

Damn it! He used my favorite line on me. That is cruel and unfair and 100 percent effective. Of course I will stay. I'll take whatever Jason Connor is willing to give me. It's not the same for him, but so what? This was always the deal, right? He was never going to feel about me the way I feel about him. Crushes are, by definition, one-sided, and here in Hollywood it's even worse.

I'm not nineteen anymore. I'm a grown-up, and we all know the hull gets thicker the longer you travel through the void. Bulletproof isn't something you are, it's something you become. I want more than he can give me, of course I do. I want him to feel the way I do. But I can do this. I can keep my emotions in check. Let him "make it up to me," whatever that looks like. *Dear God and Tom Hanks, Emmy, don't imagine what that looks like!*

I clear my throat. "Fine, I'll stay and finish the campaign."

"Thank you!" He releases my hands. His smile is genuine. Victorious. Unapologetic. He hasn't got a clue what he's doing to me. I'm honestly starting to pity myself.

I look around the patio. I don't feel like being here anymore. "I think I'll get an Uber back to the hotel." I stand up.

His chair scrapes on the pavers as he stands up, too. "Are you sure? The party's not over yet."

"I have to get up early. I need to change my flight in the morning, make arrangements for Peyton, and extend my hotel stay."

"I'll drive you."

"It's better if we don't leave together, don't you think?"

A muscle moves in his jaw. "I guess you're right."

"Thanks for bringing me tonight. I mean it." I give him a tight-lipped smile. "It was a dream come true."

His gorgeous brow furrows. "Of course."

I dig out my phone to order a ride, but he stops me. "I'll do it. It's the least I can do."

I watch the thick night air toss his curls around as he navigates the app. I rub my bare arms and marvel at how the moonlight gilds the classic angles of his gorgeous face, the relaxed curve of his neck and shoulders. God, he kills me. This whole thing is like a dream that I know I'll have to wake up from. It's torture. When he looks up from his phone with a melancholy smile, I think I might die of happiness and heartbreak at the same time.

"I'll call you in the morning," he says as I slide my purse over my shoulder.

What I want to say is, *Do I have a chance with you, Jason Connor? A real chance at you being mine? If we both wanted to, could we make it work?*

What I say is, "See you tomorrow."

Chapter 20

Body language! Proximity! Breath mints!

Emmy

I GET UP early the next morning to make arrangements for my extended stay. The mom guilt is real, but Peyton doesn't seem to mind because Josie is going to take her and her BFF to a waterpark. Josie is paying, and I'm grateful for that because my checking account is gasping for air. I've got to talk to Jill about when the royalties will start rolling in. It'll be nice when my income is steadier.

I reschedule my flight for the Sunday night red-eye. That will give Jason and me all day today and tomorrow to work on his social media presence. He video chats me as I'm about to call the front desk and move my checkout to Monday morning. "Hey there! I texted you my address. What time are you coming?"

He's as effortlessly handsome as ever, and I have to reroute power to my shields just to look at him through a screen. Meanwhile, all of Val's pixie dust from last night has worn off, and I'm plain old Emmy again, in jeans and a sloppy bun. Unfortunately, I can't afford a stylist 24/7.

"I don't know how long it'll take to Uber it to your place, but I can leave in the next fifteen minutes or so."

"It'll take over forty minutes up US-1 with traffic." Jason squints into the phone screen. "It'd be better if you were staying here in Santa Monica. Actually, I have four bedrooms in this house. Why don't you just stay here?"

If I had bothered to get a coffee this morning, I would have aspirated it. "Are you serious? You want me to stay with *you*? In your *house*?"

"It's no big deal. No one will know. Paparazzi don't come to your house—by law. Besides, I have my son this weekend. I only get him every other weekend…Hang on a sec." The phone jumps and sways, and I hear him talking to someone in the background. A moment later, he appears onscreen again, this time with a little boy's curly head next to his—an adorable, brown-eyed miniature version of him. "It'll be better if we cut out the travel time."

"Okay." I find myself smiling at the view of him holding his little boy. I've never seen this side of him. He and Margarita have taken care to keep their son out of the media.

"Okay, well, hurry over. We'll see you soon! Wave bye, Mattie!" The little boy's fingers curl in a shy wave.

"Bye." I wave back. I'm still staring at the screen long after it goes dark.

I finish my packing and get checked out. On the way to Jason's house, Jill calls. She's never called me on a Saturday before.

"Emmy!" she shrieks, like I've done something terrible. "What on earth happened?"

My pulse ticks up a beat. "What are you talking about?"

"That contest thing you posted! What happened with Jason?"

I glance out at the Pacific Ocean meandering alongside me, huge and cold and immovable. "Nothing happened. He just lost."

"Girl!" This time she sounds like I've done something asinine. "There's no room for that. You are number two on the *New York Times* bestseller list right now. Did you even realize that?"

I pop up in my seat, almost hitting my head on the car's ceiling. I've been so busy here in LA that I haven't even checked the week's numbers. "Oh my God! That's amazing! We'll go up even more after the movie launches, right?"

"Oh, hells no!" Now you'd think I'd done something criminal. "The premiere isn't until December. That's four months away. You've got to keep the magic going or we could lose all the momentum we've built."

"Okay..." I'm confused. "So, do you want me to do another book signing?"

"No, no, no! Forget all that. You need to play the celebrity crush angle harder, Emmy. No more contests where he loses. No more awkward displays like that whole hair thing. Uh-uh. Nobody exists but this guy. And you two are falling for each other. Big-time."

My stomach twists. "I feel like maybe it's enough. My fans are happy."

"Emmy, don't be so selfish," Jill says, and my face gets hot. "Every woman on the planet wants to be you right now. We don't get to do it, but you do! Why are you holding out on us?"

The driver looks at me in the rearview mirror. I duck down in the seat, take Jill off speaker, and press the phone to my ear. "Jill, he's a human being, not a line item in a marketing plan. What do you want me to do?"

"You're a beautiful adult woman! I shouldn't have to tell you. Body language! Proximity! Breath mints!"

Suddenly, I'm reminded of Ursula, the sea witch. At least I still have my voice. "He's trying to clean up his image, and I feel like this is getting in the way of that."

Jill makes an exasperated noise. "So we're going to miss out on hundreds of thousands of dollars in book sales *and* the number one slot on the *New York Times* bestseller list so Jason Connor can just screw up again with the next girl? Emmy, come on."

I can't believe what I'm hearing, and at the same time I can. This is how other people see him. Is Jill right? Am I being naive? Am I sacrificing for a selfish, spoiled man-boy who doesn't deserve it? Who doesn't even care about me?

Hundreds of thousands of dollars is a lot of money. But even worse, I don't want to miss my shot at getting back into Hollywood. I blew it in college over a guy. I don't want to make the same mistake.

I breathe out a long, slow yoga breath. "What do you want me to do? Specifically."

"Get something juicy for social. A kiss. Touching that's *not* scripted. A blog post about how good he is in bed would be nice."

"Ugh, Jill!"

"What? People need to know that it's possible."

"That what's possible—the height of tackiness?"

"For a movie star to fall in love with one of us! For Nora's story to be *our* story. A hope, Emmy. We just need a hope."

"I'll figure something out."

I hang up. I can't believe I'm number two on the *New York Times* bestseller list, and the movie isn't even out yet! I've got to keep the momentum going. But how do I make Jason look like a gentleman on his social media while planting the seeds of something else on mine?

I don't want to do anything incriminating, but I also can't throw away my opportunity. I'm not a Chosen One. The only way I'll break into the Hollywood scene is if I play all my angles. Dig in my footholds. Jill's right—I'm almost there. Now is not the time to chicken out. Once I hit number one on the bestseller list, maybe I can relax. But until then, it's Cali against me.

As far as Jason goes, Amanda straight up told me I've got no long-term prospects with him, and the way he acted during the hugging contest proves she's right. I've just got to keep my eyes on the prize. Jason will be a moment in time—just like Rhett was—and I won't lie to myself that it's more than that. Besides, I'm leaving in two days. My real life is all the way across the country. Not to mention that, eventually, Jason Connor is going to finish my book and hate me. Yeah, I keep forgetting that part.

The truth is I've got nothing to lose.

I turn my camera on selfie mode. Pinch my cheeks to give them some color. Purse my lips. I snap the photo and then send it to him with a message: On my way!

I can't wait, he texts back.

My insides swirl like the guts of every unfortunate redshirt headed into a dark cave on a lonely crash site with nothing but a retro-futuristic flashlight and a bad feeling. But I can do this. I know what I'm getting into, and the prize is so much bigger than a movie deal. I've *got* the movie deal. This time, the prize is knowing that Hollywood didn't beat me after all.

I can still carve out a place here for myself if I play the game right. I'm sorry if Jason Connor is one of the pieces I need to move, but he's playing his own game.

Whoever cares most gets to win, right?
In this case, the one who cares most is me.

I ring the doorbell of Jason's sprawling Spanish-style bungalow. He answers wearing sweatpants and a *Stranger Things* T-shirt with a frying pan in hand. I swear, this guy doesn't look bad ever.

"Come on in! I'm so glad you're here!" With his free hand, he drags my suitcase just inside the doorway. I follow his bare footsteps to a kitchen with distressed cabinets and lots of chrome. It smells like sausage. My stomach revs like a car engine.

He glances down at it. "You hungry?"

"Starving."

"Good. I made breakfast."

The kitchen offers a view into a sunken den with a TV where Mattie is watching cartoons and playing with toys on the floor. I ease myself onto a bar stool that bellies up to a breakfast nook and watch Jason cook. I can't help noticing how comfortable the vibe in here is. How normal and relaxed. Not what I imagined—but then again, what did I imagine? A disco ball? Twenty-four-hour bar? White tiger on a leash? At the same time, I feel kind of small wondering what he would think of my trailer. It's quaint and beachy and fun, but it's not this.

Then I imagine both of our little families here, together: Peyton playing on the floor with Mattie, me opening cabinets alongside Jason, knowing exactly where he keeps the plates. The thought is a dangerous pebble tossed into the water.

To distract myself, I gather up the pile of books on the counter in front of me and sort through them.

Brown Bear, Brown Bear, What Do You See? by Bill Martin Jr. and Eric Carle.

Where the Wild Things Are by Maurice Sendak.

On the bottom, #*CelebrityCrush* by Emmy Ellison.

My heart jumps in my chest. Page 101 is dog-eared. I already know the bar scene starts on page 213. He won't get to it until long after I've left, hopefully. When I look up, he's eyeing me with a sexy half smile.

"I'm loving it. I really am," he tells me.

I smooth out the folded triangle marking his page and close the book. "Seriously, you don't need to read it. You filmed the whole screenplay. I mean, why do you need to read the book?"

"Because you wrote it."

I can't stop the tide of feelings his words elicit. God, he's a charmer! Maybe I should just tell him about the scene. Ruin everything now, before...

Before what?

He turns back to the stove, his muscles tensing and relaxing under his T-shirt with each shift of weight. The sweatpants don't do his butt justice, but I admire it anyway. The curls on the back of his head are tantalizingly mussed. When he turns back toward me, our gazes meet, and I realize I'm biting my lip. I avert my eyes and curl my legs around the stool.

Maybe I could hide the book instead.

He drops a plate in front of me and tips what looks like a veggie omelet and two sausage links onto it. "Coffee? Orange juice?"

"All of it." I match his grin as he slides a fork my way. I feel both comfortable and completely out of place at the same time. I never pictured being at his house. With his kid. And him making me breakfast.

No, that's a lie. I did imagine the breakfast part.

My coffee and orange juice arrive with a small bowl of sugar, yellow and pink artificial sweetener packets, and oat milk on the side. He fills a second plate and drops onto the stool next to me. I take a bite of omelet, and three chews in, I think I've died and gone to vegetarian heaven. I push back from the counter, my eyes widening. "Is there goat cheese in here?"

He nods, his fork poised to dig into his own plate. "With tarragon, chives, and roasted red peppers. Do you like it?"

"Wait! Stop! Where's your phone?" I spot it before he says anything, dive for it, and then aim it at him. "Smile, Jason Connor! You're sharing this recipe with Instagram today. It'll be our first post in Operation Keanu Reeves. We're going to make you into somebody that everybody can't help but love!"

"Operation Keanu Reeves, huh? I like it."

He gives me a meme-worthy head tilt and a grin. I snap the picture. Somehow it transports me to backstage on *The Terica Show*, waiting in the shadows, bingeing on *Lost Star* memes, not even knowing he was there. Now I'm here. In his house. Plotting a social media campaign with him like we're two ex-browncoats running a job together. It's Jason Connor and me against the world.

Come to think of it, I haven't looked at one of his memes in days. I haven't needed to. All the expressions I love are right in front of me.

The TV in the den distracts me, breaking the spell. I glance at his son watching cartoons. "Isn't Mattie going to eat with us?"

"Oh, that kid only eats Cap'n Crunch for breakfast." Jason scoffs. It's the same scoff he does on TV. And it's adorable.

God, who am I kidding? I've fallen for him for real, and hard. If I'd ever convinced myself I could rein it in, I was a fool. I should have gotten on that plane this morning. Instead, here I am.

I make a production of doctoring my coffee with sugar and oat milk so I have a reason not to look at him. My bite of omelet is robotic. Beside me, Jason eats in silence, completely relaxed in his own space. I'm not going to come out of this whole. I just know it. Yet there's no way I'm walking away.

"You said you had a daughter, right? Peyton?" Jason asks me, spearing a sausage with his fork.

"Yes." He remembered her name. That's really nice.

Stop it, Emmy!

"You have a picture?"

"Sure." I fumble my phone out of my purse and open Snapchat, favored app of tween girls across the galaxy. I flick through the saved ones. Some are of her. Some are of me. Some are of the two of us together, puppy ears and all. Somehow looking at pictures of Peyton with Jason makes my stomach clench. Their universes don't intersect.

He studies her photo. "She's almost as beautiful as you."

I smile as warmth floods across my chest. "Would you like to meet her?" I hold my finger over the VIDEO CALL button.

One eyebrow goes up. "Of course. If you're okay with that."

"She'd never forgive me if I said no."

I tap the button, and Peyton picks up right away. "Hi, Mom!"

"Hey, nugget. Guess what? There's someone here who wants to meet you."

"Oh my God, oh my God, oh my God! It's Jason Connor, isn't it?" She squeals so loudly I have to bump the volume down.

Jason leans in. "Hi, Peyton. Thanks for making room in your schedule. I've been trying to set up this meeting for days."

Peyton fangirls hard, rattling off all the movies and TV shows she's seen Jason in and telling him how much she loved him in each of them.

Jason nods and chuckles his way through her monologue. "Thanks! Wow, some of those were…" He throws a heavy glance my way. "Not for kids."

"My mom covered my eyes for all those parts. But you were awesome in the rest!"

"So what about you?" he asks. "What do you like to do? Sports? Clubs?"

"TikTok!" she replies without hesitation. "The retro dances especially. Like the Renegade!"

Jason pops up from his seat with genuine excitement. "I actually know that one!" He props the phone against his coffee cup and launches into the moves with her. Joy floods through me as I watch them interact, but a thread of uneasiness weaves its way in a second later. This isn't right. It's one thing for me to risk my own heart, but I can't risk my daughter's.

At a natural pause in their conversation, I smile at Jason and reach for the phone. "It's time to go, honey," I say to Peyton.

Peyton shouts a goodbye to Jason and tells me she loves me.

"Love you back, nugget." I hang up.

"She's great," Jason says, forking up more eggs.

"I wish…" The words pop out of me before I can stop them.

He's fast. "You wish what?"

I can't say it…that I wish this was for more than a weekend, that he'd have a chance to get to know Peyton for real, and we could have an actual future. If I say it, I'll look like some naive, dumb fangirl who doesn't understand how the world works. I should understand how it works because I've fallen into this trap before. And this is Jason Connor, notorious lover boy. Let's face it, charm is his default. All the feelings in the room are mine.

"I wish…" My brain grapples. "I had some sour cream."

His brow crinkles. "Sour cream?"

I double down. "Yes, sour cream. It's great on omelets."

"I have sour cream."

Great. Now I have to ruin this amazing omelet with sour cream. While he's getting it, Mattie comes wandering into the room. When he sees me, he runs to his dad. Jason swings him up into his arms as he brings me the sour cream I don't even want.

"This is Emmy." Jason rubs Mattie's back as he hides his face in his dad's neck. "Do you want to say hi?"

"Hi, Mattie," I say, calculating how much sour cream I need to put on my plate to not look like a total psychopath. Mattie peeks at me, and his big brown eyes take on the same playful coyness I've seen in scene after scene of Jason's work. "Looks like he's got the Connor gift of expressions," I chuckle. "Lucky boy."

"Well, let's hope he didn't get the bad stuff." Jason swings him in the air until he giggles. "So, what's on the agenda today? You said something about TikToks?"

I'm busy smearing sour cream around on my plate so it looks like I ate some. "Yeah, so I see us recording three different Tik-Toks with some dance moves from *Lost Star* and *Hashtag Celebrity Crush*. And then maybe you can be a guest on my yoga vlog, if you don't mind. And I have, like, ten other ideas. If you have any ideas, we can do those, too. More is better. We'll just take off and nuke the entire site from orbit..."

Jason nods, tickling Mattie. "It's the only way to be sure."

Oh to the snap. He finished my favorite *Aliens* quote. I've been waiting my whole life for someone to do that.

He stares at me as I sit, frozen. "Is everything okay?"

"You Michael Biehned me," I finally say.

"You Sigourney Weavered me first."

I let my eyes play over him. Teasing smile. Child in arms. T-shirt clinging and draping in all the right places. The light from the kitchen window fuzzes all his edges, and I want to cross the room, grab his face, and kiss him long and slow and fearlessly. I want to ask him to forget everything else and to please, please be mine . . . totally and forever.

Mattie squirms out of his dad's arms and grabs my hand, dragging me off my stool. His timing is good. I'm done eating, the sour cream is sufficiently smeared, and I need a distraction big-time.

"Libro! Libro!" he shouts.

I recognize the word from what Josie has taught me. "You want me to read you a book?"

Jason nods. "Go ahead. That'll give me time to clean up. The babysitter's coming at ten. Then we can work."

I gather up the books on the counter and follow Mattie to the den, where I plop down on the sofa next to a truly awful-looking doll. While Mattie peruses the bookshelf, I glance toward the kitchen to make sure Jason isn't watching. Then I stuff *#CelebrityCrush* under the couch. Mattie hands me a Mo Willems classic, *The Pigeon Needs a Bath!* His warm, little body curls into mine as I open the book to the first page. Wow, it's been a long time since I've done this.

It's a fun book. It's so easy to do the voices and make him giggle, although I imagine Jason does it better. When I finish, the doorbell rings, and Jason lets the babysitter in. Mattie runs to her. I'm still in a blur, but it's a good blur. A dizzy, "just got off the Disney teacups in the Happiest Place on Earth" blur.

"Why don't I give you a quick tour, and you can tell me where you want to film?" Jason asks.

I shake off the fogginess and find him standing by the couch. I smile at how he calls taking videos with my phone "filming." His eyes drop to something beside me, and he grabs Mattie's doll.

"Sorry about that. Possessed Baby is hard to stomach before noon." He shoves it onto the bookshelf, facing the wall. "I honestly think it's haunted. It always shows up somewhere I don't expect, threatening me with its dead, empty eyes."

"That's a great way to sell me on sleeping here tonight." Too late, I realize I've set him up perfectly.

"I didn't know you needed an incentive."

He's deadpanned it, which somehow makes it worse. Now the ball's in my court. I scour my mind palace for a witty reply and come up empty. I laugh uncomfortably instead.

He scratches the back of his neck. "Tour?"

I jump up from the couch. "Absolutely!"

I'm introduced to Leah the babysitter, the dining room, and the three smaller bedrooms. Across the hall is the master bedroom, complete with a view of the pool and the ocean. It has a sprawling bed covered in a rumpled white duvet. I can't help but imagine waking up in that bed every morning and eating breakfast with that view. I'm being foolish and naive and cruel to myself, but I can't help it. I let myself imagine it. Like Jill said, people like us just need some hope.

I follow Jason as he pushes open a set of French doors, revealing the gorgeous pool deck with its keyhole alcoves, oversize wrought iron furniture, and stunning view of the Pacific Ocean.

"We'll do the TikToks out here," I say immediately.

He goes to find his phone while I haul a few chairs out of the way. When he returns, I'm all business.

Or *mostly* business. The blinking heart on my wrist is the only thing giving me away.

Chapter 21

#OperationKeanuReeves

AUGUST 5

@thefunnyJason: I may have lost the #CelebrityCrush hugging contest to @AndrewValentine, but I doubt he can beat my Goat Cheese Omelet with Chives and Roasted Red Peppers! It got five stars from the one person I served it to. #Recipes #VegetarianRecipes #EatYourVegetables

@thefunnyJason: Hey, everyone, who wants to dance? This first one is from *Lost Star Dance Troupe Saves the Universe*, except it's set to my favorite song when I was in tenth

grade—"Put Your Records On" by Corinne
Bailey Rae. And, no, that song's not just for
girls. #LSDTSTU #danceparty #LoveYaCorinne

JASON: Hey, everyone, this is Jason Connor, and this time
I'm joined by Emmy Ellison, author of *Hashtag Celebrity
Crush.* We're going to perform a dance from the movie,
which is coming out in theaters this December. The music
is a Duran Duran mash-up, circa 1982. We only spent
like three hours on this, so we'll try not to screw it up. Go
get your mom. Seriously, she's going to love this. Ouch,
Emmy! What was that for? We're the same age.

VLOG, *RANDOM YOGA POSES*

EMMY: Hi, all, and welcome back to *Random Yoga Poses.*
I'm Emmy Ellison, and joining us today is Jason Connor.
You probably know him. If you don't, you can just ignore
him. He's new to yoga, so I picked something really
advanced so he doesn't go telling all his friends at the
gym how easy yoga is and how it's not a real workout.
On the other hand, I don't want to have to take a trip to
the ER today, so why don't we just compromise and go
with Triangle Pose? Start by planting your feet just like
this—one pointing sideways, one pointing forward.
That's it. Good, Jason! You've got it. No, you're not done
yet. Now slide your arm down your front leg, all the way
down as far as you can go. But turn your body to the side
and keep your legs straight. I said keep your legs straight.

You're supposed to imagine you're being pressed between two panes of glass. Nope. Whoa, what's happening? You look like a Transformer. Okay, whatever. We'll call it a modification. Your other arm goes straight up to the loving and healing sky. Whoops, try not to fall over. Oh wow, somebody needs to work on their balance. Okay, why don't I just stand here and be like a wall for you to lean against so you don't fall? Wait, that's not working! Okay, it's sort of working. Are you made of sandbags? I'll just stand here holding you up with my two spindly arms for a count of thirty. See, yoga is a great workout! Thanks everyone for tuning in. See you next time on *Random Yoga Poses*. Oh, and don't forget to like and subscribe!

Chapter 22

Whoops, it's probably time to say something.

Jason

"LET'S TAKE A break," I beg from where I'm sprawled out on Emmy's yoga mat on the patio. "I think the triangle may have broken me."

"I can't believe you've never done yoga before, Jason Connor. What's wrong with you?" Emmy stands over me, tapping away on her phone. The wind is grabbing at her hair, blowing it in front of her face. She bats at it and huffs it out of her mouth. Amanda is right. I can't keep my eyes off her.

I only pretended I couldn't do the yoga. It was fun having her hold me up.

"Okay, that one's uploaded. I guess I can give you a break."

I loll on the ground. "What time is it? Midnight?"

She glances at the smartwatch I got her. "It's four fifty-seven in the afternoon."

Leah has Mattie in the pool. It feels so good just lying here, listening to the sounds of splashing water and his giggles. Emmy drops down cross-legged beside me on the mat. I squint up at her, and she scoots until her head blocks the sun for me.

"That's so much better, thank you." The pavers under me are warm, and my body relaxes, sleepy and content. I risk putting a hand on Emmy's bare knee. It's warm, too.

"We're getting good engagement." She swipes her finger across the surface of her phone like a madwoman and pretends not to notice my hand. "Lots of positive responses. And the How Not to Break Up hashtag is settling down, too."

"You're so good at this." I pat her knee because somehow I'm thinking that's less intimate than just letting my hand sit there. "I bet you're good at everything. Sing me something."

"Oh, I don't sing." She laughs.

I open one squinting eye. "What do you mean you don't sing? Everybody sings."

"I do sing, during shower concerts. And in the car. But I do it very badly."

"Shower concerts?" I lift up on my elbows. "How much is a ticket?"

Her phone goes face down on the yoga mat. "That's not happening." She starts to stand up, but I grab her hand, stopping her.

"No, don't go. Let's just sit here for a few minutes. I won't make you sing. I promise."

Our fingers are tangled together, and neither of us pulls them back. The wind has picked up, and the Pacific Ocean sighs a little louder than it did when we first came out here. Meanwhile,

Mattie and Leah are chattering away in the pool, accompanied by a cacophony of seagulls.

I sing the opening line to the first song that pops in my head, "Hopelessly Devoted to You" from *Grease*. It's part of Andrew's typical repertoire. She laughs at my *wah-wah-wah-wah-wahhhhh* rendition of a steel guitar and slips her hand free. I miss it already.

"So you're not a singer. What else aren't you good at?" I ask.

She thinks for a moment. "Making cakes in round pans. They always stick."

I sit up all the way. "There's a trick to that. You've got to grease them with butter and flour. Or use Baker's Joy spray. It has flour in it."

"Interesting." She pulls the rubber band out of her hair and re-tames her messy bun. She put on yoga clothes for our *Random Yoga Poses* shoot, and they accentuate every slope and curve of her body. "What about you?" she asks. "What are you bad at?"

"IQ tests."

She snorts.

I keep going. "Cold fusion. Keeping plants alive..."

"Anything on Pinterest," she interrupts.

"Girl, *same*," I say. "You're bad at disciplining dolphins."

"You suck at sweet nothings."

Oooh, sharp turn! "I thought we were past that."

"What made you think that?"

I deserve her mini-attack and am prepared to take the damage. "I'm sorry. They were going to be epic, by the way, my sweet nothings."

"Well, maybe you could try again later."

Whoa, sharp turn again! My mouth opens, but nothing comes out. Does this mean she's forgiven me? Are we doing this?

She gazes out at the pool. "Dating."

"Wh-what?" Is she reading my mind?

"You just did a meme." She grins. "I meant I'm terrible at dating."

"I'm terrible at dating, too."

"We should do a Venn diagram."

"I'm terrible at knowing what a Venn diagram is."

"It's circles that overlap when you share the same answers." Her eyes light up. "Oh my gosh, that would be a great vlog post! A Venn diagram of things we suck at. People could compare it to themselves and post in the comments."

"How did you suddenly make this about work?"

"I'm good at making things about work."

"You're good at being cute."

"You're good at being cute, too."

"We could put that in the Ben diagram," I say.

"Venn," she corrects. "And, yes, we could."

Her golden eyes lock on mine, and this is getting a little insane. All the appropriate pheromones are swirling around us like hairspray particles, but I'm a statue, and she doesn't move, either. It's a standoff. An impasse. A deadlock. I think about Amanda womansplaining me yesterday. Is Emmy hoping for a great story to tell her friends? Or is she hoping for something more? Because I can see in her eyes that she's hoping for something.

Honestly, I am, too. My insides are alive with excitement and hope and maybe even dragonflies. Being with Emmy feels easy and warm, like the stones under me. I don't have to be "on" or constantly apologize or worry that everything I do will be scrutinized. I can be myself.

Plus, Emmy's funny. I love that she's funny. And beautiful. And sexy. And has the hands of an Egyptian goddess... Whoops, it's probably time to say something.

"So, what's happening with your dolphin fortune-telling vlog while you're here?"

She takes a deep breath and visibly switches gears. "It's chaos. Millions of people, or seventeen at least, have no idea what's going to happen in their lives."

I suppress a chuckle and go for the straight man. "How do you live with yourself?"

She shrugs. "I applied for a clone, but I was denied. I don't know why. I promised to let her do fun things, too."

Did I mention how much I love the fact that she's funny? It makes me want to kiss that naughty little smile even more. I'm fully astride the disaster motorcycle now. Also, I'm pretty convinced Emmy isn't just hoping for a story she can brag about later—her cues are too subtle for that. And if she was just using me, she wouldn't be helping me clean up my image. Which means maybe she wants more. But what kind of more? She leaves tomorrow night on the red-eye. We won't see each other for months. She has a kid to think about, just like I do…but let's be honest here, we're both adults, and with all the sparks flying between us, there's no way this show isn't ending with an R rating.

God, I'm a terrible person, aren't I?

Although, if I like her, too, does that change things? Is there a way to be with Emmy that doesn't make me look like an oversexed opportunist and tank my career? And career aside, there's another big question here: If there is a way for us to be more than just a blip on each other's radars, have I got the chops? Or will I, as usual, end up disappointing everyone involved?

I don't care if I disappoint myself, but I don't want to hurt Emmy. I don't want to find out at her expense that I'm this broken thing that can never be fixed. I want to make her feel the way she makes me feel.

Emmy stands up, shattering my train of thought, which is probably for the best. "Come on. Let's go inside and do our Venn diagram. Do you have a whiteboard?"

I hold a hand out for her to pull me to my feet. I resist the urge to reverse it and yank her down on top of me. Besides, she's pretty strong for a wiry, little thing. Maybe she *is* one of those mermaids that drag sailors to the bottom of the sea and drown them.

Seeing her butt in those yoga pants as I follow her inside, I gotta admit, it wouldn't be a bad way to go.

Chapter 23

I'm sure you're great with all the pans.

EMMY ELLISON'S PERSONAL VLOG, AUGUST 5

EMMY: Hey, everybody, this is Emmy Ellison coming at you with my usual nonsense, and I don't know why you put up with it. But today is special. We're doing Venn diagrams with Jason Connor! Yay! So exciting! Oh, and here he is!

JASON: Hi, everyone!

EMMY: Hi, Jason. Welcome!

JASON: Thanks for having me.

EMMY: I love it when he's all formal. So, in case you don't know what a Venn diagram is...

JASON: I didn't know what it was...

EMMY: It's a couple of overlapping circles, and you can have three if you want. Just draw them like this, and the idea is that, if you have something in common with the person you're doing it with, you put it in the overlapping part of the circles. And if it's something that you don't share with that person, you put it just in your circle. You'll see how it works. So, the circle on the right is my circle...

JASON: And the circle on the left is mine.

EMMY: Easy as killing stormtroopers, right? Our first topic is Things We Suck At. Let me write that at the top of our whiteboard. Okay, we got a little head start on this earlier.

JASON: Emmy sucks at singing.

EMMY: I do. But Jason's a good singer. So we're writing that in only my section. Singing. Get it?

JASON: I think they've got it.

EMMY: Feel free to make your own Venn diagram to see if you suck at the same things we do. We established earlier that Jason sucks at keeping plants alive.

JASON: And cold fusion.

EMMY: Well, everybody sucks at cold fusion. That one doesn't count.

JASON: Why doesn't it count?

EMMY: Because it's impossible right now with our current level of technology. It's like saying you suck at time travel.

JASON: I do suck at time travel. Emmy sucks at baking.

EMMY: Just baking in round pans.

JASON: I'm great with round pans.

EMMY: I'm sure you're great with all the pans.

JASON: She sucks at anything on Pinterest.

EMMY: That is a true statement.

JASON: I do, too, so that one can go there.

EMMY: Awww! See that? We have something in common! Doesn't that make you feel closer to me?

JASON: Oddly, it does.

EMMY: Okay, what else?

JASON: You forgot cold fusion.

EMMY: Fine. I'll write down cold fusion.

JASON: See how she humors me?

EMMY: It's easier than the alternative. Jason, what else do you suck at?

JASON: Loading the dishwasher. I'm a disaster.

EMMY: I'm good at that. But I'm awful at getting splinters out. If my daughter gets a splinter, it's a medical emergency.

JASON: Yup. Put me down for that, too.

EMMY: Dishwasher... that goes in yours. Splinters, another thing we share.

JASON: We're both good at dancing.

EMMY: Yeah, but we're not doing what we're good at. We're doing what we're *not* good at.

JASON: We're not good at sucking at dancing.

EMMY: You're complicating this unnecessarily. Oh, we've got someone on the live chat. Let's see what they have to say! You read it, Jason.

JASON: Okay. @Shoopsaywhat says, *You two are adorable. When's the wedding?* [*fake laughs*] What am I supposed to say to that?

EMMY: The wedding's tomorrow. Sorry you're gonna miss it, Shoop.

JASON: You can't put that on the internet! Now people are gonna think we're getting married.

EMMY: My followers aren't idiots. They're just smart-asses. We're fine. I promise. Okay, why don't we try a different topic? Does anyone have an idea for a topic? Jason, will you reset the board for us?

JASON: Absolutely! It would be my pleasure!

EMMY: I love it when he gets eager. Okay, Shoop, are you the only one out there today? Did the zombic apocalypse happen, and we missed it? Shoop suggests Places You Want to . . . Oh no, we're not reading that. Shoop, shame on you!

JASON: The board is reset!

EMMY: That's great, Jason. Can I have the pen? Let's do bucket list items, all right? That's a safe topic. You go first.

JASON: I want to do indoor skydiving.

EMMY: Oh, that sounds fun! I'm gonna put me down for that as well.

JASON: I want to climb Mount Everest, too.

EMMY: That's a hard *no* for me. I don't do snow. I want to have tea with the queen.

JASON: I'd do that. I want to live forever.

EMMY: I want to live forever, too.

JASON: I want to have more kids.

EMMY: Wow, really?

JASON: Yup. For sure. I think it'd be great for Mattie to be a big brother. What about you?

EMMY: Umm…well…actually, yes. I'd like to have more kids.

JASON: Another one for our overlap. This is fun!

EMMY: I want to swim with dolphins.

JASON: I've done that. For *Hashtag Celebrity Crush*. It was awesome.

EMMY: I'm jealous. I want to not be jealous.

JASON: I'm thirsty. I want a glass of water.

EMMY: I want a glass of water with a slice of cucumber in it.

JASON: I want calamari.

EMMY: I want a pair of those earrings where it looks like they're going up the side of your ear.

JASON: Aren't we supposed to be writing these down? Here, I'll do it.

EMMY: I want a guy who writes things down for me so I don't have to.

JASON: You already have him. It's me. I'm right here.

EMMY: Well, I don't really *have* you.

JASON: For all intents and purposes, you have me. At least for right now, when you need someone to write things down for you.

EMMY: I always need someone to write things down for me. It's a constant need of mine.

JASON: Maybe you should want to not have to write so much stuff down.

EMMY: Yeah, put that down.

JASON: Okay. Our Ben chart is looking pretty full.

EMMY: Venn diagram, and you're right. I think we've done our job here. Share some of your Venn diagrams in the comments, and we'll post a collage tomorrow. This is Emmy Ellison with Jason Connor. Good night and thanks for joining us. Don't forget...like! Subscribe!

Chapter 24

What will Jason Connor make the news for next?

HARPER ROSE TALKS HOLLYWOOD, AUGUST 5

HARPER: Hi, everyone. This is Harper Rose from *Harper Rose Talks Hollywood* coming to you with the latest celebrity gossip, and boy, do I have a doozy for you today! It's about Jason Connor. Does that surprise you? It shouldn't. After displaying devastatingly poor judgment in dumping Margarita Ayala on social media last Thursday, he spent today appealing to his fans in a PR campaign orchestrated with his new friend—author, social influencer, and bad-hair-day poster child, Emmy Ellison. Gawd, Emmy, where was your stylist? Probably day drinking. I would be. Whether the two are doing anything else together besides work is anyone's guess, but,

I mean, come on now, who are we kidding? Highlights of the celebrity crusher and crushee's action-packed day together include a preview of dances from the upcoming film *Hashtag Celebrity Crush*—that was actually kind of fun—poorly executed yoga poses, and something called a Venn diagram. Check it out for yourself because I'm not explaining it here.

So, here's my take on this: They're together—definitely. They're keeping it on the down-low to avoid any scandal that might jeopardize Jason's role on *Lost Star Dance Troupe Saves the Universe*. But, knowing Jason Connor, he'll screw it up somehow. I've known Jason Connor for a long, long time, and he's ten pounds of trouble stuffed into a five-pound bag that already had two pounds of trouble in it. Still, their antics have been super popular with fans. They've had hundreds of thousands of views already and the posts have only been up for a few hours, so yay for you, Jason. I'm rooting for you, darling. Always.

As far as Emmy Ellison goes, don't feel too sorry for her when Jason breaks her heart. This whole celebrity crush thing has been great for her! I mean, when was the last time you heard me talking about a *writer*? She's playing her hand like a pro, selling truckloads of books, and I have to respect that. Her West Coast book tour's over, though, so, Emmy, please go back to Florida already and pick up a VO5 hot oil treatment on the way. Thanks.

Now, if you missed out on any of the social media blitz Jemmy has been doing—and, yes, you heard that term here first!—I've got links below to all of their posts. Enjoy it now because we won't see anything like this again until early December when the *Hashtag Celebrity Crush* promo tour kicks off.

All right, let's talk about today's poll! The question of the day is: What will Jason Connor make the news for next? *A*, epic fail involving Emmy Ellison; *B*, offending the yoga community; *C*, caught using plastic straws; or *D*, other—put your best one in the comments. I can't wait to read them! That's all for today on *Harper Rose Talks Hollywood*. Don't forget to stop and listen to the Rose!

Chapter 25

Permission to redo my submission for the hugging contest?

Emmy

IT'S BECOMING PRETTY obvious that Jason can cook. The salmon filets are on a maple plank on the grill outside, and I'm showing Mattie how to pop the stems off the fresh green beans. A mix of quinoa and heaven is simmering on the stove. And I'm barely holding it together.

"Oops! Just pinch off the top. *Solo esta parte.*" I rescue half a bean Mattie threw into the trash and show him the stem.

Leah has gone home, and it's just the three of us making dinner together. It would be fair to say I've fantasized about having dinner with Jason Connor at least two hundred times, but it was never like this, with his little boy on my lap, Jason going back and forth between the grill and the stove, and Alexa spinning a mix of Gipsy Kings and what Jason calls "Italian cooking music." He started with a playlist he called *Aerosmith, but Louder* but I put a stop to that.

I wonder what Peyton is doing right now? If she were here, what would she be doing? Popping beans with Mattie instead of me? Stuffing down preteen angst around the fact that I'm dating? Entertaining us all with her never-ending chatter? And how would Jason be with her? Could he, eventually, love my daughter?

But I'm being ridiculous. Peyton is super lovable. Of course Jason would fall in love with her! I'm 100 percent sure of it.

No, that's a lie. I've never trusted a man enough to let him try. I didn't even trust her own father.

"Okay, I think we're done!" The last bean is popped, and I set Mattie's feet on the floor and dump the contents of the colander into the steamer. The guitar music is going crazy, and it's got my head in a flurry along with the two glasses of wine I've had. As Jason blows through the kitchen and stirs the quinoa, he dances and sings along to the unintelligible Gipsy Kings lyrics. He grabs my hand and twirls me with a casual familiarity I'm not sure I've earned, even after spending all day with him.

I will say that I think I pulled off my goal of helping myself without hurting Jason. Nothing we posted today is even remotely sexy, but my fans are loving it and Jason's getting less hate. Besides, it was fun. A lot of fun.

Jason releases my hand and heads to the kitchen, giving me a chance to check my notifications. The likes continue ticking up, and we made *The Harper Rose Show*, which is sure to launch our posts even further.

Then I read a text from my agent:

Jill: The videos are fun, Emmy, but kind of blah. Give us something juicy, will you? First place is calling!

What? Hells no!

I delete the text and chase the rock in my throat with a gulp of wine.

I don't want to believe she's right, but Jill's been in this business way longer than I have. How much damage would it do if I just posted one photo? Something suggestive, but tasteful? Nineties-rom-com-level heat? Monet *Water Lilies*–level innuendo?

"Wash your hands, Mattie," Jason calls, sliding the filets onto plates. The quinoa is next. Then the steamed beans. Before I know it, I find myself snuggled into this little family for dinner. It's delicious in more ways than one. Mattie says something in Spanish—something to do with explosions, I think—and throws a steamed bean on the floor.

"Mattie, stop throwing your food, please," Jason says.

Another bean hits the floor. Then a third. Jason shoots me an apologetic look. "He always does this. I don't know how to handle it."

I reach over and try a trick that always worked with Peyton. One by one, I collect his beans and arrange them into letters spelling his name. "*¿Que dice eso?*" I point. "It says Mattie."

Mattie and Jason exchange the same shocked meme face. It's freaking adorable. Mattie picks up a bean from the letter *E* and eats it. Then another. And another.

"I'm afraid to make any sudden moves," Jason whispers, sitting frozen in his seat. "What witchcraft was that?"

I take a bite of salmon. "Presentation is everything."

When dinner is over, I offer to clean up the kitchen while Jason gets Mattie to bed. I load up the dishwasher expertly (one of my talents, according to our Venn diagram) and wipe the counters and table down with a fierceness that almost hides how nervous I am about what comes next. When the kid's asleep, what do the grown-ups do?

I finish my job and head out to the pool deck. The sun is a dark stripe of orange glowing on the horizon, and it's chilly enough that I have to go back inside for my hoodie—I'm used to Augusts that are hot and humid deep into the night. The warm water from the Jacuzzi swirls around my bare legs. It's not long before Jason appears at my side. He rolls up the cuffs of his pants, and his feet slip into the water next to mine.

"Is he down?" I ask.

"For the count. We're finally alone. Well—except for Possessed Baby." He shoots a glance at Mattie's doll lying on her side on a pool lounger.

The orange stripe disappears, heaved over the horizon by an explosion of stars. The sound of the ocean permeates every cell in my body. I'm alone with Jason Connor, on his patio, at his house, and the world is a tinderbox ready to ignite.

Jason's hand falls over mine where it clings to the edge of the Jacuzzi. I open my fingers and let his entwine them. I know that when I lift my head, he'll be there, ready. It's not a surprise. I know his past. I'll be just one more of many. Why do I want more than that? Who do I think I am?

When I raise my head, he's looking at me, waiting with that effortlessly gorgeous face I fell in love with through screens so many times. So what if this isn't perfect? So what if it's only for a weekend? I'm with Jason Connor. Isn't that enough?

This time I'm the one who leans in for the kiss.

My dashboard lights dance like the spinning stars above us. All my insides ignite with the slow movement of our mouths. He tastes like all my dreams come to life. I want so much for this to be more than a fling.

And if it isn't, I want it anyway.

I slip into the water, fully dressed, and a surprised laugh escapes him as I pull him in with me. Together we sink to our chests, enveloped by shockingly hot water. My body against his is too eager; it tells him too much. How desperately I want him. How much more this means to me than to him.

He takes off my smartwatch and sets it to the side, brushes the hair out of my face, and smiles in a move so tender that my brow furrows. He doesn't have to do that. He's already got me.

"Jason…"

His kiss cuts me off, soft and restrained. Under the water, I cling tightly to his shirt, like otherwise I might get dragged down to the bottom by my own demons. "What?" he whispers into my mouth.

"What were you going to say to me? During the contest?"

He stiffens and then pats my arms and pulls away. The disconnect is jarring. I can barely see his face in the dim light as he sinks down onto the hot tub seat.

"Emmy, I'm not a good guy. You know that, right?"

What the hells? I lower myself onto the seat across from him. Now we are just two people sitting, fully clothed, in a hot tub. "I don't think that's true."

"You don't understand. Everything I touch turns to shit. I don't want to drag you down with me."

Actually, everything Jason Connor has done since I've met him has helped propel me skyward. What he's saying sounds like an excuse. My heart gives a little shudder. "Do you...not want to be with me?"

"That's not it, of course not!" He shakes his head, studying me in a way that suddenly makes me self-conscious. "What do you want, Emmy Ellison? What is it you *really* want?"

It's that same question—the one I hate, the one I don't have a real answer to. Right now, I want Jason Connor to have the same feelings I do, to want me the way I want him, and not just for a night. I want the bar scene to be magically rewritten so I don't have it hanging over my head. I want to forget about bestseller lists and ad clicks and what might send the Twitterverse into its latest temper tantrum. And, more than all that, I want the world to fold up and then unfold itself in a way that lets me have it all: fame, fortune, glamour, glitz, cozy dinners, kid cuddles, and all the people I love in one place.

But I can't tell him any of that. Besides, Jason has something else going on right now, and I don't think it has to do with me at all. So I tell him a different truth. "I want to be here for you right now, whatever that looks like."

His face changes. I'm not sure I've seen this expression before. It's too raw and sad for memes. "You know I lied to you that night we were talking on the phone."

What? Another bait and switch? I'm not sure I can handle this. I try to control my expression. "You did?"

"I told you the dumbest thing I'd ever done was punching that guy in that bar. It's not. The dumbest thing I ever did was miss my son's birth."

My heart relaxes. If he needs to get something else off his chest, I can handle it. I can be there for him. I want to.

"It's okay," I say. "You can tell me."

He sighs. "I was with someone the day Margarita went into labor. I met her at one of Sean's parties. My phone fell between his couch cushions somehow. Turns out it's hard to receive phone calls when you don't have your phone. Margarita ended up with an emergency C-section, and I didn't even know it. I found out later that Mattie lay alone in an incubator at the nurses' station until Margarita woke up because there was no one there to hold him. Because *I* wasn't there to hold him."

He blinks and stares out at the blackness. "I was supposed to cut the cord. I'd watched all the YouTube videos. He was twelve hours old before I even knew he existed. I had to wake up first, right? Take some ibuprofen. Eat something. Figure out what happened to my phone. Care enough to drive over to Sean's and get it. I didn't even think about them, either one of them, all that time. That's the kind of guy I am." He laughs wryly. "Wanna like my page now?"

"But your dad had just died, right?" I ask softly.

He nods. "Yeah, that's true, but it's no excuse." He sniffs hard and runs the back of his hand across his nose. He manages to make even that look good. "I'll never forget what it felt like to read Margarita's texts from the night before. It was like my stomach was being shredded. *Jason, it's happening. Jason, come to the hospital quick. Jason, where are you? Jason, why aren't you answering your phone? Jason, something's wrong. Jason, they're taking me into surgery. Jason, I'm scared. What if the baby's not okay?* And then I think it was a bunch of 'eff yous' after that."

His voice cracks, and his eyes are glassy in the dim light. "People say newborns don't need much. Food. Warmth. Somewhere to sleep. If you don't bond with your baby right away, don't worry about it, they say. But at the hospital, he felt like a stranger in my arms. This tiny person, this little piece of me…Honestly, it felt like I was at work, on set, holding somebody else's baby. That's when some paparazzi posing as a parent snapped the picture in the 'Hey, buddy' meme. I'm not saying, 'Hey, buddy,' in that picture. My face doesn't look like that because I'm emotional at being a new dad. It looks like that because I screwed up, again, and I'm coming to terms with the fact that this child in my arms isn't going to have the wonderful father that I did. That meme shouldn't say, *Hey, buddy.* It should say, *Sorry, kid. You deserve better.*

He squints and pinches the skin between his brows with one hand. I reach for the other one. "I'll never use that meme again."

He forces a laugh. "Don't worry about it. It's par for the course, Emmy. I do something stupid, and the universe amplifies it."

I shake my head. "You're not being fair to yourself. I've watched you with your friends and your fans, all those kids from the fundraisers. You have the most generous heart and a fun-loving energy that's contagious. And as far as Mattie goes, Jason, you're a great dad! So you screwed up that first day. You've more than made up for it. It's clear how much you love Mattie, and he knows it."

His eyes are starting to look puffy. "I want to do right by him. I want to be the best version of myself. I just don't know if that's even possible. Everything I do turns out wrong. Even when I think I'm doing something right, it turns out wrong. It's like I'm cursed. Or clueless. Or just...an asshole who doesn't realize he's an asshole."

"You're not an asshole." I can't stand listening to him berate himself like this. The words spill out of me. "You want to talk about sucky parenting? I never told Peyton who her father is."

He blinks. "Wha-what?"

I nod, as shocked at my confession as he is. "Put that in the Venn diagram."

He leans forward, my hand captured in both of his. It's his turn to listen.

I take a deep breath. I can't believe I'm about to do this. "Peyton's dad is Rhett Castle, the director. Do you know him?"

"Of course I know Rhett Castle. He's the jerk who abandoned you guys?"

I grimace. "He didn't technically abandon us. He doesn't know. They don't know about each other."

His face crumples in confusion. "But you said…"

"I lied, too." I press my lips together. "I met him at a party when I was a student at UCLA. I'd stalked him to pitch him my screenplay."

Jason's hands around mine are the only thing grounding me as I speak. I don't tell him everything: how distinguished Rhett looked in his suit and blue tie, tugging on his lapels. How I secretly craved his attention. The sound of my high heels clicking across the marble tile floors as we left the party.

"He said he wanted to go somewhere more private where we could 'talk.' I should have seen the red lights on the dashboard. I guess I just wanted it so badly—the opportunity, the dream. Even when it became obvious we weren't talking about screenplays, I told myself it would be worth it for the foot in the door." I pause, remembering the slippery bedspread, the musty hotel room smell. "Afterward, he looked at my screenplay for, like, eight seconds, and then told me it wasn't good enough. *I* wasn't good enough. Neither one of us was 'special.'"

I risk a look at him, damp curls ringing a soft expression. His voice is tender. "My dad always said there's no such thing as 'special.'"

"Do you believe that?" I ask him.

"Don't you?"

I bite my lip to keep the tears at bay. "I really don't."

"That's a shame."

For a moment, only the ocean speaks.

I continue. "After I found out I was pregnant, I went to one of his premieres to tell him. He had this whole entourage. We made eye contact across the room, but…I couldn't do it. I chickened out, left, went back to Florida. Had the baby. Never came back. Until now."

"Oh, Emmy—"

"So—" I cut him off with a fake smile because the last thing I want right now is Jason Connor's pity. "Maybe you weren't there for the birth, but at least your baby knows who his daddy is. Besides, birth isn't something you necessarily want to watch. There's a lot of yelling and…bodily fluids."

His face lights up in a meme. "Are you kidding? Bodily fluids are my favorite!"

I giggle, relieved that the tension is broken. Since we're being all honest, I should tell him about the scene in the book so I won't have to worry about it anymore. Maybe it won't be so bad. Maybe he'll forgive me, seeing how pathetic I am right now.

"Jason, there's something I need to tell you. About the book. There's a scene—"

He stops me with a hand up. "No spoilers! I told you I was going to read it."

"It's kind of personal."

He rolls his eyes. "If there's a dirty sex scene in there, Emmy, don't worry about it. We're both adults."

"It's not— Well, there is a sex scene…it's tasteful! But that's not what I'm talking about. There's another scene…"

"Okay. I'm listening." Jason waits with an expectant, innocent smile. I imagine that smile melting away, all the playfulness draining out of his eyes when he discovers I exploited his real life and pain for my fake story. I can't do it to him. I just can't. Besides, what the hell am I doing worrying about a stupid scene in a book when I have the man of my dreams, Jason Connor, dripping wet right in front of me and talking about dirty sex?

My favorite dessert is éclairs, and when I order one at the French bakery, there's this thing that happens between the time I place my order and the moment the velvety chocolate and rich cream hit my taste buds. An unbearable wanting springs up inside me, like a vitamin deficiency that will kill me if I don't have it. Looking at Jason Connor's wet shirt clinging to his chest, the shadows exaggerating his perfect, square jaw and that mouth I've already tasted, I'm getting that same physiological reaction. I'm starving for Jason Connor. I want him. Right now. Nothing else matters.

"Emmy?" His voice cracks on my name.

That sound fuels my desire even more, and I close the space between us in the hot water. "There's a scene," I lie, "where Nora tells Gage all the reasons she fell in love with him."

"Oh really?" Jason says. "Miles must have cut that from the movie."

With a finger, I trace a little square of collarbone visible above the neck of his wet T-shirt. "Reason number one is this spot right here." I lean in and kiss it.

His expression shifts electromagnet fast to something darker and hungrier. "Then let me give you better access."

In one movement, he yanks his shirt off. I continue tracing the little piece of his collarbone with kisses, my lips playing across his hot skin. When I look up, he's watching me with eyes as indigo dark as the Pacific.

"What's the second reason?" he asks, voice husky.

I offer my worries and fears like sacrifices to the surging moan of the sea. I trail my fingers up his neck to his ear, where the tips of his curls cling to damp skin. "Reason number two is this spot right here." I suck a droplet of water off the lobe, my hands moving down to his chest, all muscle and sinew under my touch.

"And reason number three..." I bring my open mouth to his as he grips my upper arms and we inhale each other's quickening breath. "Is right here." The kiss is deep and uninhibited. Delicious. I lose myself in it, tasting him, relishing the way he tastes me. Before I realize what's happening, he grabs the fabric at my waist and pulls my hoodie and shirt over my head, balling them up and tossing them aside. When they strike Possessed Baby, she falls to the patio floor with a sickening sound we both ignore. Then he lifts me up like I don't weigh anything and sets my hips on the edge of the hot tub.

"Permission to redo my submission for the hugging contest?" The crack in his voice is still there, but this time there's a dangerous edge to it.

Half-naked and shivering on the edge of the hot tub, I grant it.

All at once, his arms are around me, my body igniting at the feel of so much of his bare skin against mine. He presses closer, forcing my thighs farther apart, and all my major muscles go weak. One of his hands tangles gently in my hair while the other wraps across my entire back, pressing me into him so hard I gasp. His chin scratches my cheek; his breath warms my ear.

"Don't you ever say you aren't special, Emmy Ellison," he whispers. "You *are* special. You're special to me."

I shiver from the weight of his words more than the chill of the air.

"Are you cold?" He propels himself out of the water and returns with a huge, soft towel. He wraps the towel around both of us, making a cocoon. Inside this safe, warm place, he holds me against him and kisses me slowly, deliberately, like I'm a thing to be cherished. His hands leave hot trails across my back. I kiss him harder, and he hikes me up off my feet. My legs cinch around his waist as our teeth bang together in ever more desperate kisses.

"Tell me you're mine, Jason Connor," I rasp.

"I'm yours." He says it without hesitation, pushing open the French doors and carrying me into the warmth of the house, to the bedroom, *his* bedroom, with the rumpled white duvet and the view of the Pacific. When we reach the foot of the bed, he trips, and I cry out as my back hits the mattress and the satisfying weight of his body pins me down.

I smile as I tease a dripping curl away from his perfect forehead. "Say it again, Jason Connor," I whisper, drinking in every line, every curve, every movement. Beneath the gravity of his body, every part of me is spooling up. "Make me believe it."

His face changes. It's all at once tragic and beautiful and certain and uncertain. He traces my lips with his thumb and kisses my mouth so very gently.

"I'm yours, Emmy Ellison," he whispers. "I promise. I'm all yours."

Chapter 26

How many Baby Yodas had to die to make this drink?

Jason

THE FIRST THING I see when I roll over is the tangle of brown hair on my pillow and the bare, suntanned shoulder peeking out from under the covers. I brace myself for the usual feeling of dread I get after a hookup, but instead I feel this thing I believe is called...happiness. Instead of wanting to get away as fast as I can, I want to scoot closer and fit her muscular curves against me. Do a repeat of last night. Maybe add a scene or two.

Mattie's chirps drift in from the hall, and I know I need to get up. Before I do, I lean over and study Emmy's sleeping face. It's half-buried in hair, her fists tucked under her chin. I can't see the tiny mole on her eyelid. I can barely see her face at all. Only the line of her jaw leading to her sensual, slightly open mouth.

Looking at that mouth brings back more memories from the night before. Again I feel zero regrets. Maybe there's something different about what Emmy and I have. Had. Might have. Might have had? Grammar was never my strong suit. I was more of a PE kind of kid.

Speaking of wrecking the English language, I said a lot of things last night that probably made it blush. I've always been a talker during sex, mostly in my younger years when I fell in love as often and as easily as the surfers outside my bedroom window tumble into a wave. Last night was the first time in a long time that I've done that.

She started it. She asked me to say *I'm yours*, and I did. Several times. Then I told her I wanted her. That I'd wanted her from the very start. I told her all the things I wanted to do to her right before I did them. I asked what she wanted, and I told her I'd do it, say it, manifest it. Whatever she wanted, I would make it happen. She could drag me to the bottom of the sea, and I would let her. I'd hold my breath forever. I feel like I'm still holding it.

It's not a bad feeling, being underwater. Maybe if I don't breathe out, I can hold on to this feeling forever. She picked me over all the others and said all those nice things about me. I don't know why that makes me feel so invincible. I have a lot of fans. Tons of people tell me I'm great. It's just that I don't believe any of them.

Somehow, I believe her.

Mattie's noises get louder, and carefully, I roll off the far side of the bed. I dig some pajama pants out of a drawer and throw a T-shirt onto the bed for Emmy. I don't know if she'll use it, but it would be a treat to see her in it. I leave the door open as I slip out.

I get Mattie set up with cartoons in front of the TV and head to the kitchen. The blender makes enough noise pumping out two green smoothies that she finally emerges from the bedroom. I smile seeing those muscular legs under the hem of my Jackson Hole shirt. She's got her phone and charger in hand.

"Good morning." I meet her sleepy steps halfway with a glass of vitamin-rich protein-kefir-kale deliciousness in each hand. But instead of taking one, she puts her arms around me and melts into my bare chest. I can't hug her back because my hands are full, so I kiss the top of her head instead.

"My phone is dead," she murmurs into my chest. Her breath makes a hot spot on my breastbone.

"I'll call the police and report the murder. In the meantime, there's a plug at the breakfast nook." I press a glass of green liquid into her hand.

She scrutinizes it. "How many Baby Yodas had to die to make this drink?"

I muster Sean's conservatively offended face. "People pay eight dollars a glass for this at the Acai Palace. And his name is Grogu."

"Oh, I'm aware." She takes a sip and turns her back to me, leaning forward on the counter to plug in her phone. The hem of my shirt lifts up as she does, revealing the bottoms of her boy shorts and giving me a cheap thrill. Once the device powers up, she holds up her green smoothie and snaps a selfie.

I wrap my arms around her from behind and smile over her shoulder. "Why don't you get one of us both?"

Our faces look relaxed and happy on the screen as she snaps the picture. Suddenly, I remember she's leaving tonight on the red-eye. I won't see her again until the promo tour in December.

"Will you send that to me? I'm going to want something to remind me of you when you're gone."

The ends of her mouth turn down at the corners, and she makes three taps on her phone. "Done."

Behind me on the counter, my phone dings. The sound is almost as wistful as the look in her eyes. If Mattie wasn't here, I'd take her back to bed right now. I'd spend every moment we have left looking at her, touching her, losing myself in her. I'd beg her to drown me again. The way she's looking at me, I can tell she wants the same thing. Instead, I turn to the coffee maker.

"So, what's on the agenda for today?" I ask.

"Let's check your popularity." She pulls a rubber band off her wrist with her teeth and twists her long hair into a ponytail. Then she hops onto the counter. With nothing on but my T-shirt and underwear, it's über-erotic. Tethered to the wall by the charger, she dangles her legs and taps around on her phone. A snorty little pseudo-laugh escapes her.

"What?"

"They love you again, Jason Connor."

"That quickly?"

"See for yourself." She turns her phone toward me.

I bring the coffees over. Sweet and plant-milky for her. Black for me. Her eyes are extra golden in the shifty morning light. Sliding a hand around her waist, I let it fall on her bare thigh and peer at the phone screen.

> @thefunnyJason, you are still adorbs. C'mere and I'll work with you on your yoga skillz.

I chuckle. "Tempting, but no."

Emmy reads the next one out loud. "*Hey @thefunnyJason, sing a song for us!*"

"Don't mind if I do." I launch into "Every Little Thing She Does Is Magic" by the Police.

She interrupts my long note with a kiss. Her kisses are never light, never playful. When they show up, you know you're about to have a bag thrown over your head and get shoved into a car. With Mattie here, though, I can't afford to get kidnapped, so I pat her leg and pull back.

Her expression is teasing and apologetic. "I'm a sucker for Sting."

"Aren't we all? Dude is sexy!" I move to the sink and rinse out the blender. Emmy pulls her legs up and sits cross-legged on the counter. I make myself look away.

"It's our last day," she says quietly. "I have a couple more ideas for videos we can shoot, but the ones I uploaded are doing really well and several more are queued up to go, so I'd say mission accomplished."

I shake my head, amazed. "From what land forthwith came thee?"

She hops off the counter. "I don't speak German."

Then her arms are around my neck, and her mouth is on mine, relentless. When I taste her coffee-laced tongue, I give up altogether. Go ahead. Take me to the second location. I'll have the waterboarding and the Stockholm syndrome, please. Anything to keep feeling this way.

"Daddy?"

We peel apart at Mattie's voice. He's standing only a few feet from us in Spider-Man pajamas with a book in his hands. It's Emmy's book, looking crumpled and misused. He holds it out to me. I take a deep breath and try to settle everything down.

"Thank you, buddy. Where'd you find that?" I smooth the cover and then glance at Emmy with a teasing grin. "Should I read a random scene out loud?"

"No!" Her eyes widen. "I mean, I thought you didn't like spoilers."

The fact that she's so vehement about it makes me want to do it more. With a grin, I start flipping pages.

"Stop, Jason, no!" She reaches for the book, trying to swipe it out of my hand.

"What's wrong? I just filmed the whole dang movie. It's not like I don't know what happens."

"I don't like hearing my stuff read out loud."

I've got a good eight inches on her, so when I start riffling through pages over my head, she can't reach it even as she jumps. I choose a random page and read the words out loud.

"Come here, Mattie." She lifts him onto her shoulders. "Get the book! Get the book from Daddy!"

It's an effective strategy because the kid is a velociraptor. Two ferocious little hands yank at my hair and scratch at my face as he lunges for the book. I can't have my face getting all marked up, so I relinquish it. Emmy sets Mattie down and, giggling, he hands her the book. She turns and launches it Frisbee-style into the dining room. She's wagering on my laziness. It's a good bet. I'm not going after it.

"You still need to autograph that for me, you know."

Once it's clear she's won, she's back on her phone. My own phone dings again, and I grab it. Mattie whines at me to pick him up, and I do it absently.

"Crap," I say, reading the notification.

"What?"

"I totally forgot. Sean is hosting this gala tonight, part of the children's hospital initiative. The whole *Lost Star* cast is going. They're gonna auction off props from previous seasons. It's a big deal. You want to go?"

"Yes, I want to go!"

Of course she does. This is Emmy we're talking about.

Honestly, I'd rather just have another evening at home with her and Mattie. Watch her read books to him. Swim in the pool. Walk on the beach. Do more silly videos that somehow don't feel like marketing and instead feel like two people getting to know each other. Have more amazing sex.

But this is work, and it's for a really good cause. "It's going to suck," I warn. "There'll be an open bar. Celebrities everywhere looking all…celebrity-ish."

"Sounds great!"

"It's on this scandalously huge yacht."

She bounces on the tips of her toes. "I already said yes!"

I smile. "Fine. We'll go. It's seven to nine, so there'll still be plenty of time to get you to the airport."

"I need to call Val." She whirls back to her phone.

"'Nana," Mattie says in my arms.

"You want a banana?"

"'Nana." He nods.

I grab one off the counter and put it to my ear. "Hello, Banana? Mattie wants to eat you. You okay with that?"

My boy giggles and snatches it from my hand. I give him a noisy smooch on the cheek. Margarita is scheduled to pick him up at five o'clock today, and at that thought, the coffee goes acidic in my stomach. I suddenly seem to recall having mentioned the gala to her a month or so ago and her perhaps having added it to her calendar, although we haven't spoken about it since. Is Margarita planning on being there? If she's seen the videos I've been making with Emmy, the answer will be a definitive yes.

Oh well. At least I got to be happy for a minute.

Chapter 27

I might turn into an actual lovesick washcloth.

Emmy

WE WALK TO the end of the dock at Marina del Rey, and all I can think is *wow*.

Jason said the fundraiser was happening on a yacht, but the words *scandalously huge* don't do it justice. It's like calling Robin Williams "that kinda funny guy" or Oprah Winfrey "that talk show host from the '80s." When we step aboard, I look up, and, seriously, I can't see any sky.

Jason's eyebrows go up. "What do you think?"

"I thought it'd be bigger."

He laughs as we make our way to the gangplank, but it's Val who's the real hero here. I finally understand what he means by "butter." I'm in a slinky, low-cut, yellow Carolina Herrera dress kind of like Kate Hudson's in *How to Lose a Guy in 10 Days*, but knee-length and with a built-in bra. He straightened my hair, which now reaches halfway down my back. He also added a couple of really thin braids in there, hippie-style, which, believe it or not, pair really well with Jason's fitted navy suit.

The boat has many, many decks, all brilliantly white. As we make our way around, I note the most important areas are the bow for when you want to be "outside," the bar (actually there are two of them, a big one on the main deck and a smaller piano bar belowdecks), and the "disco" with a full DJ and video game floor so you can do a VR version of *Just Dance* or something like it.

Sean spots us and gathers us into a group hug. He's wearing a ridiculous rainbow-colored crocheted sweater and yellow pseudo-sunglasses. I can already smell the whiskey on his breath. "Snack, if this party gets boring, I may ask you to take your shirt off."

Jason doesn't miss a beat. "Of course."

I could get used to this so easily! "Don't worry, Sean," I say. "This party is *not* getting boring. Not if we can help it."

He looks at me with desperate joy and leans forward open-mouthed like he's about to plant a huge, sloppy kiss on me. I scream/laugh and dodge out of the way. The kiss winds up landing wet and scratchy on my cheek.

"It doesn't mean anything!" Sean cries as Jason tugs me out of his reach.

"Get your own."

We run into Ramirez, who's talking to a very rich-looking lady holding a papillon. I reach out to pet it, and it growls at me.

"Bellatrix is not very friendly," she apologizes as I retract my fingers.

We greet Amanda, Andrew and Renee, Kayla, and some

of the crew. Jason hands me a tumbler of something orange. "Mimosas on the lido deck." The glass is thick and expensive.

"Can we look at the things they're auctioning?" I ask.

"But of course, madam." He holds out his elbow all Hugh Jackman–like, and I take it.

As we climb the stairs to the next deck, the engines rumble in my teeth as the yacht prepares to leave dock. Up here, the tables and turquoise lounge cushions are covered with carefully laid-out items from the show, and people with an obvious overabundance of cash peruse them. There isn't even the tiniest indication in their eyes that I don't belong.

"This is the laser gun Sean used for the first three seasons." Jason hands me a gray blaster.

I heft it. "It's so light."

"That was the problem. You could tell there was no weight to it, and Sean had to constantly compensate to make it look like it wasn't a toy. Plus, it would always fly out of his hand. We named it after Thor's hammer—Mjolnir."

I set it back into its place. "Is that the original Orbit?" I snatch up the blue furry puppet. "Oh my gosh, it is! This is the one Ruby smuggled onto the ship in season two—the one that used mind control to make people take care of it before it got crossed with Mittens in a transporter accident."

"The one that tried to kill everybody in their sleep—yes, that's him. Although I never understood how crossing a hostile alien with a cat made it *less* nasty." Jason slips the thing over his hand and changes his voice as he works the mouth. "Take me home, Emmy. Feed me. Love me."

"Sorry, Old Orbit." I shake my head. "My best friend hates puppets. Besides, New Orbit is better."

"Yeah. He's quite popular." Jason gently replaces the puppet onto its spot. "If you put him in a celebrity crush poll, he'd probably win."

We move on, and though we're careful to keep everything looking professional, when Jason's fingers brush the bare skin of my back, it sets off a chain reaction, and all I want to do is drag him into some closet full of smelly ropes and join the "mile-out-to-sea" club. At the very least, I wish I could press myself to him right now and kiss him. After the night we shared, it doesn't seem fair that I can't. It makes me feel kind of cheap, to be honest. What's so wrong with us being together? I know the network wants him on his best behavior, but what we had wasn't some tacky hookup. It was special. And beautiful. At least, for me it was.

Jason continues pointing out all the auctioned items and how they were used in the show. Zipping my feelings up, I write my bid down for a leather jacket he wore for two seasons before they changed his uniform. It's a first for me—writing four figures down on an auction sheet. Heck, I'm a *New York Times* bestselling author, firmly hanging on to the number two slot! Why not? One day, those royalties will come rolling in. In the meantime, there are always credit cards.

Speaking of my spot on the list, the smoothie selfie I took this morning has been burning a hole in my gallery. It's the opportunity I've been waiting for: my hair is sex-tousled, and Jason is shirtless in the background. Of course, there's no proof our disheveled looks are related to nighttime escapades, and I've blurred the background with a vignette so you can't even tell where we are. My hope is there's enough innuendo in it to make Jill happy and boost the book, but not enough to hurt Jason's image.

I haven't shared it yet, and every time I think about it, I get a sick, sinking feeling in my stomach. I don't know why. Nobody ever got canceled over a smoothie—that I know of.

I dart a glance at Jason, all dapper and smiley, chatting with a middle-aged couple about a futuristic-looking plastic box with clear tubes sticking out of it that I only sort of recognize. In midsentence, Jason catches my eye and winks, sending flutters from my stomach all the way to the tips of my fingers and toes. Last night was even better than my fantasies. The things he said. The things he did. His rock-hard body mine to explore and discover. How slowly, delicately, he brought me teetering to the brink until I couldn't stand it anymore. Then, together, we plunged.

Jason ends his conversation and grabs my hand for a quick, secret squeeze as we move farther down the line of items. If this keeps up, I might turn into an actual lovesick washcloth.

He waggles a penlike prop between his fingers. "This is the injector I supposedly used to stay alive before they discovered the cure for my mysterious space illness in season three."

"Mm-hmm." I try not to look too distracted. Right next to the smoothie-after photo in my gallery is the other selfie we took in the kitchen with his arms around me. That one would make Jill happy, too, but I don't want to share it with anyone else. That one's mine. It's the one I'll take to bed with me at night as I weep into my pillow because, oh yes, that's coming. I may be soaring on cloud nine right now, but that just means one thing: there's nowhere to go from here but down.

But I don't want to think about that right now.

I sneak a hand under his suit jacket and run it over his back and around his waist. A gentle hand removes it with a playful-yet-warning eyebrow raise. It's not a rejection, but it feels like one.

"Not here," Jason whispers.

I force my frown into a weak smile. I shouldn't feel hurt—he did warn me. But I do anyway.

The line of items up for auction comes to its end, and that's when I see *her*. Exquisite in white with a silver shawl, her hair pulled away from her perfect face, her lips as red as the imaginary shirt I'm wearing, Margarita is here.

I turn to warn Jason, but a second later, she's next to us, like a phantom.

"Hello, Emmy. I missed you at the house." When I don't answer, she clarifies. "I was there to pick up Mattie."

She knew I was at the house? Of course she did. Margarita would have recognized that the videos were done on Jason's patio. "Oh, ummm, I've been...out...with my stylist..."

"Mattie had a bit of a stuffy nose last night," Jason interrupts. "You might want to keep an eye on it."

The way her eyes move from me to him is smooth and void of emotion. Her face looks puffier than I remember but still gorgeous. Again, I can't tell what she's thinking. If this were a video game, I'd have to level up at least six times before I could fight Margarita.

"Relax, Jason. I was simply hoping Emmy would autograph this for me." She holds up a copy of *#CelebrityCrush* and a pen. "I thoroughly enjoyed it."

"Oh, thank you." I take the book and the pen from her. Her eyes tell me nothing, but her barely there smile feels like a threat. Surely she knows about Jason's fight and the arrest. She would recognize the scene! I open the book to the inside cover, trying not to fumble, and click the back of the pen. *To Margarita*, I write. *Thank you for bringing Nora to life.* I sign my name with too many humps on the *m*'s and hand the book and pen back to her, almost dropping them.

"It's very well done." Margarita catches both deftly, totally in control of her hands and everything else. "Have you read it yet, Jason?"

And there it is. She's about to out me.

I gulp down the rest of my mimosa. "Oh, look at that. My glass is empty, and I'm so thirsty! I'll be right back."

I duck out and swoop down a level to the main bar, my heart racing. If Margarita intends to complete my downfall, she's going to want me there to witness it. I'll just avoid her the rest of the party. I fly out tonight. My bags are in Jason's car. I can tell him the truth later over the phone. Or...never.

Or maybe she'll just tell him anyway, whether I'm there or not. Maybe she's doing it right now!

Of course she's doing it right now. She doesn't need me there. She's got the proof in her hands—I just autographed it.

My reckoning has come.

We're chugging our way up the channel out to sea, the sky dulling from perfection blue to something edgier and secretive. "Another one of these." I slide my glass across the varnished surface toward the bartender. I tap my nails until he serves me an overfilled replacement, which I slurp down to a reasonable level with a self-conscious look around.

I recognize some more familiar faces from Sean's party, but mostly it's just rich people who've paid huge sums of money to hang out with their favorite celebs. Amanda is caught up in a conversation with a tall, lanky man who can't seem to stop talking. Ramirez has been cornered by yet another Golden Girl. Poor Kayla stands in the middle of a group of well-groomed young men looking like a deer surrounded by hungry wolves. Andrew, cool as a cucumber, entertains two couples with practiced poise while keeping one hand on the small of Renee's back. A few days ago I would have been fangirling hard right now, but now I see the cast for what they are—regular people who just happen to have a job that makes people love them—Jason's friends, maybe mine, too, if I can carve out a place here. Jason will surely hate me, but the rest of them may never know why.

I reach into the tiny Michael Kors purse Val picked up for me and dig out my phone. I snap a few pics of the crowd on the boat and post them to my Stories. *Here I am at a swanky fundraiser with the Lost Star gang. It's so fancy. It's so fun.* That's the image I project to the world. I use all the right hashtags. I tag all the right accounts.

But Jill will tell me it's not enough, and I know she's right.

Side by side in my camera gallery, the pictures of Jason and me from this morning glow brightly in the dim evening light. I tap them and swipe through them for a better look. The story everyone wants to hear is written in our easy smiles, mussed hair, and the subtle yet unmistakable intimacy of the moment. These are the photos that will complete my fake Cinderella story. They are the ones that will go viral and launch me to the moon, because the real happily ever after is off the table now. It was never on the table in the first place.

My thumbs tremble over the screen. What am I waiting for, anyway? Nobody's going to hand success to me. Rhett didn't, and Jason won't, either. It's up to me to get my name on everyone's lips so I can sell the next book, the next screenplay, and the next, and the next. Hollywood's on the ground with my knee at its throat. I did that. All that's left is to sink the dagger.

Why am I hesitating? Why won't I just do it?

Elbows on the bar, I log in to my scheduler and draft a quick post with the first smoothie-after photo. A wave of nausea passes over me, like I've just been dosed with radiation. It's the way I felt when Rhett told me I didn't have any talent. And again when I read those comments on Jason's profile calling me *low-hanging fruit*. Just minutes ago, his tiny rejection and Margarita's thin smile brought on the same feeling. They're stars, after all, and I'm the expendable, forgettable redshirt. I always will be as long as I'm unwilling to do what I have to.

Take off and nuke the site from orbit. It's the only way to be sure.

I stare at my screen. Then, with a few swipes, the posts are launched across the digital universe. All at once. On all platforms.

The phone makes a solid *thunk* on the bar as I let it fall from my hands. It's not like Jason and I had a future together anyway. And if we never had a future together, then what am I really sacrificing? The picture isn't that bad anyway. It shouldn't get him into too much trouble.

At least I hope not.

I take three slow, deep breaths and a big gulp of my drink. Whatever. It's done, and I'm on the brink of all my dreams coming true. I feel like a Cylon, waking up with a blinking detonator in my hand. Except the Cylons didn't know they were traitors. I chose it.

Just then, Jason barrels down the stairs. "Come on, let's go get some air. There's something I want to talk to you about."

Chapter 28

I've got Matt Damon on speed dial.

Emmy

THE YACHT IS anchored just off the coast and rocks gently on the waves. We grab a couple 100 percent recycled-plastic bottles of water and head out to the bow to catch the tail end of a California sunset. I brace myself for Jason to confront me about the scene in the book. I don't know what I'm going to say. I have no excuse, no explanation worth giving. But he doesn't launch the attack right away. Instead, he leans on the rail, gazing out at the explosion of oranges and pinks and reds sinking into the sea.

"You have these, too, don't you? West coast of Florida, right?" he asks.

I disguise my deep, heart rate–lowering breath to look like

I'm enjoying the salt air. "I live near the water, so I get to see sunsets like this almost every day. I love them."

"Social media marketing pays well, I guess."

My first instinct is to agree, but I'm already weighed down with dishonesty. I don't want to tell him any more lies. "The rent for my trailer hookup is only eight fifty a month." My gaze drags from the horizon to the angles of his almost-too-handsome-for-this-world face surveying the water.

"You gonna stay there now that you're a big shot author?"

I smile, partly with relief that he wasn't shocked by my lowbrow lifestyle and partly because the wind off the water ruffles his curls in a way that makes me want to run my fingers through them. I don't know where he's going with this, but in my experience, adding humor never hurts. "I've got a call in to NASA. We're gonna outfit the trailer for Mars and launch it on the back of an Atlas rocket. I've got Matt Damon on speed dial, so I'm feeling pretty confident."

He chuckles, watching as the last sliver of sun is swallowed by the relentless ocean. The sky turns the color of avocado toast and magic. What's happening here? Did Margarita tell him about the scene, and instead of being angry, he's just disappointed? Or is he testing me? Giving me a chance to fess up? Did she say anything at all?

I take a deep breath. "What did you and Margarita talk about a minute ago?"

He turns to me. "We didn't. This pair of physicists waylaid us to explain wave-particle duality. It was interesting, but I think a piece of my brain shriveled up."

I feel a pang of inappropriate but totally justified jealousy. I've always wanted to have quantum physics explained to me by a physicist. "I'm sorry I missed that."

If he's telling the truth, that means Margarita didn't throw me under the bus. Or, at least, she didn't get a chance to. Crap, I shouldn't have posted that photo! I need to tell him about it. I need to tell him everything.

"Do you ever think of moving somewhere other than Mars? Like LA?" he asks.

My confession evaporates on my tongue. "Wh-what?"

"You could finish what you started."

I don't know if he's talking about us or my Hollywood dreams or both. Regardless, I'm knocked completely off base. I have a life back in Florida. A daughter. A home. Yes, it's been my dream to move back out here, but I never got past the dreaming part. A physical move would be a big step, for a lot of reasons, one that wouldn't be easy to undo. And if Jason is suggesting I come out here for him, what is he really suggesting? I can't touch him in public because us being together is bad for his image. If I lived here, would that change? Or would it always be hot and cold, yes and no, like his relationship with Margarita? I have to consider what's best for Peyton and me.

And, apparently, he still doesn't know I screwed him over. *Twice.*

Jason waits for me to say something, but I can't tear my gaze from the blurring horizon to give him something, *anything.* The pulsing music stops. Sean is on the mic again, introducing Miles to talk about the charity.

Jason stabs his thumb in Sean's direction and gives me an out. "I'm probably gonna have to take my shirt off any minute now."

I open my mouth to protest, but I'm interrupted by yelling.

"Oh my goodness! Oh my goodness!"

It's Jason Ramirez's lady friend with the papillon. Except she doesn't have the dog in her arms anymore. She's leaning over the edge, looking down. There's a small, tan blur in the dark water.

"She just jumped out of my arms! Oh, Bellatrix!"

Jason and I exchange a look. "I'll go get the captain," he says, taking off.

"Just keep an eye on her," I tell the woman. "Don't let her out of your sight."

"She loves to swim! It's not a pool, Belly!"

It's about twenty feet down to the water from where we're standing. A small crowd is gathering at the railing. One of the onlookers is a greasy-haired kid wearing a blue-and-white-striped crew shirt.

"Hey," I call to him. "You have to rescue that dog!"

His face registers boredom and a desire to be anywhere else but at work. "The employee handbook says we only have to go in for people."

"So you're just going to leave it out there to die?"

At my words, the woman's face whitens, and she wails. "Bellatrix! Oh, my Bellatrix!"

I catch her shoulders. "He's not going to do that." I aim my next words at the kid. "He's *not going to do that*, right?"

He shrugs. "I'm not jumping in."

I look around. There's no sign of Jason. Miles has been replaced at the mic by Jason Ramirez, also giving a speech. The sound system is fantastic. Even out here on deck, I can hear him telling my joke about the two guys in the bar on the top floor of a skyscraper.

I kick off my shoes and throw my leg over the railing.

"What are you doing?" The deckhand cries in a high-pitched voice.

"I'm saving the damn dog. What do you think?"

"Don't do that, ma'am!" He lurches toward me. "Please don't do that!"

Jason appears just as I'm leaning out over the waves. "Make sure that guy puts the ladder down at the back," I tell him.

His eyes go wide, but I don't wait. I jump.

It's a long way down, and when I hit the water, it makes the Waldorf Astoria pool feel like a bathtub. I gasp as I surface. Luckily, Bellatrix is only a few feet away from me.

"Emmy!" Jason shouts down.

I give him a thumbs-up and then turn back to the dog, my teeth chattering. "Don't bite me!" I mutter. But if Bellatrix saw me as a threat before, I'm her best friend right now. She dog-paddles toward me and lets me tuck her against my shoulder as I swim us toward the stern of the boat.

It's kind of nice to be in the ocean, even if it is cold. The yacht is all lit up and beautiful. The sky is a cobalt backdrop. I can still hear the speakers as I kick my way aft through the dark water. Jason Ramirez has given up the mic. Now Margarita is up, which is strange because she's not even a member of the *Lost Star* cast.

"Good evening, everybody. First of all, I also want to thank all of you for your support today. I know I haven't been around to many of these events lately. I've been busy filming *Hashtag Celebrity Crush*. If you haven't heard of it yet, I have the book right here. It's a fun read, and the movie is going to be even better."

I ignore the subtle dig at my writing skills and imagine her holding up the book I autographed for everyone to see. That's nice of her—promoting my book. But why would Margarita do something nice for me? It doesn't make any sense.

And then I have a terrible thought. What if she's planning to read out of the book? What if she reads the bar scene out loud right now?

"The author of the book is here, Emmy Ellison. Where is she? She should come up. Emmy, where are you?"

I swim faster, but it's not easy to do a breaststroke one-armed with a dog in tow, and the boat is over a hundred feet long. I scan the deck for Jason to no avail.

"What? She's not here?" Margarita's laugh echoes over the microphone, and if I didn't know better, the sound would make me smile. "Well, never mind. I'm pretty sure she'll turn up. She can't go too far. It's a boat, right?"

I turn onto my back and kick furiously, reaching behind me in a half backstroke. I have to get back on board. I have to stop her before she reads that scene in front of Jason and everyone else. The stern is still twenty feet of dark water away.

"Anyway, the real reason I'm up here is to share something with you. Many of you are my friends, and I wanted to take this opportunity to announce that...I'm pregnant."

I miss my stroke and gag on a mouthful of salt water. *What did she just say?*

"Six months along. Thank you! Thank you! Jason, come up here. You should be up here, too."

Why is she calling Jason up there? This can't be right! I tread water, desperately scanning the deck for him. Finally, I spot him. His back is turned to me, still as a statue. I shout his name, but he doesn't turn around. Instead, like an automaton, he heads toward the stage, disappearing from view.

Heart pounding, I paddle the rest of the way to my destination, where the deckhand is leaning over the ladder, waving me in like a frantic swim team mom. Beside him, the dog's owner thanks me profusely and fans herself with one hand.

"You're crazy, lady," the kid says, stepping aside as I climb back on board. Bellatrix's owner folds her into a towel, and as soon as I've released her, the dog proceeds to growl and show me her teeth.

"Really, Bellatrix?" I snap.

Out of the water now, I'm freezing, and Margarita's announcement has turned my insides to ice as well. Someone hands me a towel, and I wrap it around myself and run barefoot up the sharp metal steps to the main deck. At the top of the steps, I halt, dripping. Jason is on the dance floor with Margarita, receiving congratulatory handshakes. His eyes are blank behind the occasional flat smile.

How can this be happening? I home in on Margarita's figure. Her stomach in the white dress *is* slightly rounded, but only in the way of someone who forgot her Spanx. It's still small for six months along. Maybe she's not pregnant at all. Or maybe she is, but it's not his. He said he hadn't been with her for months.

This is ludicrous. I can't just stand here. I need to say something. I start in their direction.

"Oh no you don't, Ariel."

The arm around my shoulders is strong, the voice melodious and self-assured and unmistakable. Sean O'Sullivan steers me not so gently around a corner and down the stairs to the piano bar, where a handful of introverts sip drinks on stools.

"Out!" Sean shouts. "Everybody out!"

I fall into a booth while he dismisses the bartender with a handful of bills and gets to work behind the shiny mahogany counter.

"She's lying." Without asking what it is, I accept the large, strong-smelling drink he serves me. "She's jealous of us. There's no way."

Even as I say the words, I know I'm protesting too much. Jason never told me the last time he was with Margarita. Under my bare feet, the engines rumble to life as the boat prepares to head back to the marina.

"I wouldn't put it past her." Sean slides into the booth across from me. He's ditched the yellow glasses, and his eyes are two emerald shards. "But you and I have something else to discuss: the photos you posted."

"What?" I bury my face in a corner of my towel. Margarita just announced that she's pregnant with Jason's baby, and Sean is worried about my stupid smoothie picture?

Sean's icy tone says he isn't kidding. "Did you or did you not post photos of you and Jason at his house this weekend?"

"We posted a bunch of photos," I say miserably. "Videos, too."

He rolls his eyes. "*Provocative* photos, Emmy."

I scoff. "There was one that was *suggestive* maybe, but not provocative." I rack my brain for something that will prove Margarita is or isn't pregnant with Jason's baby. "Oh my God, that face she made at the filming when I suggested the buffet! Was that morning sickness?"

"Emmy! Focus!" Sean's palm smacks the table, and his face is as serious as a Reaver attack.

I scowl. "What's your damage?"

"My damage? *This* is my damage!" He unpockets his phone and swipes around with his ring finger, the oddest way I've ever seen anyone swipe. He shoves the phone in my face.

Oh no, oh no, oh no.

I grab it from him. It's the TMZ website, and these are *not* photos of my green smoothie with Jason in the background. These are photos of Jason and me on his patio last night. Multiple photos. In the hot tub and out of it. Both of us with our shirts off, our mouths pressed hungrily together.

A firing squad of expletives explodes from my mouth.

He snatches his phone back. "Are you trying to tell me you didn't share these?" Sean's voice is pissed now. Truly furious.

"It wasn't me!" My voice catches in my throat.

"Who did then?"

"I don't know! Nobody else was there. Maybe it was paparazzi."

"Paparazzi don't come to your house. By law."

I can't formulate a coherent explanation. My hands fly up in the air, not knowing what to do. Sean seizes them and lowers them to the table, and that's when I notice how badly they're shaking.

"Emmy, you need to understand something." His green eyes blaze. "Jason is going to lose his job over this. So if you know anything about these pictures, you need to tell me. Now."

"I don't know! I don't know! I promise!" Heat spreads through my body. Oh God, I'm going to spontaneously combust! I've read about that—people who just burst into flames. I yank my hands away so I don't take Sean O'Sullivan with me. I'd never be forgiven for that.

"Stay here." He holds a finger up and then disappears.

How are those photos even possible? I pull in deep breaths, forcing myself to think logically. We were on the patio. Anyone could have been outside with us, on the beach. But Jason has a pool cage and a lot of landscaping around his property, so we would have been hidden. The photos are close up and weirdly angled. It's hard to tell from what direction they were taken. Could it have been a drone?

I sip the awful beverage Sean brought me. It tastes like a Long Island iced tea laced with strychnine. I push it aside. Someone took those photos. Who? And how?

I left my purse up on deck when I jumped in the water. Sliding out of the booth, I slip out of the bar and head for the stairs. I need my phone. And I need to talk to Jason.

"You're not going anywhere." Sean catches me before I get any farther. He shoves my shoes and purse into my hands.

"I need to find Jason."

"Listen, Emmy, this is for your own good. A lot of people on this boat love Jason and hate you right now."

"Does he really think I did this? How could I? I'm in those pictures, too!"

Sean's face is stone. "Oh, I don't know. A strategically placed phone with a video app? Fifty bucks and an accomplice? Shouldn't be too hard for a social media expert to figure out."

My voice is small. "But I didn't."

"Here." He replaces the wet towel over my shoulders with Jason's old Hadron jacket. "You won this in the auction. You can make the donation through the website."

I thread my arms through the sleeves. It still smells like him: citrus and musk. It might be all I have left. Sean steers me back to the bar and pushes the drink at me again, but I don't want it. I should go back out there, face the hate, find Jason, and defend myself. I didn't do anything wrong! I don't deserve this!

No, that's a lie.

This is what I was planning to do to him all along. Use him. Exploit him. Climb him like a ladder, complete with foot in face, all the way to the top. Of course he believes I posted those terrible photos. It's only a few steps up from what I actually did. I'm no different than any of the talking heads and internet trolls and know-nothing gossip column junkies that are always trying to make him into something he's not. Except what I did was worse because I was supposed to be on his side. I was supposed to care about him.

I drop my head onto the table. I never meant to hurt Jason, but I had to fight for my dream. Nobody was going to hand it to me. Not Rhett. Not Hollywood. Not Jason Connor. And why am I trying so hard to hold on to Jason anyway? We were never going to be a real, normal, happy couple. Relationships don't work when both people are too busy thinking about themselves.

Nose pressed to the tabletop, I roll my gaze toward Sean until the smooth lacquer cools my cheek. "What now?"

His reply is gentler than I expect, his hand on my head kinder than I deserve. "I'm taking you to the airport, Emmy. You're going home."

Chapter 29

Well, hooray for evolution!

BETTER READS PODCAST, AUGUST 11

BETH: Good afternoon and welcome to *Better Reads*, your favorite source for everything bookish. I'm Beth Yang, and I'm here today with Emmy Ellison, who, unless you've been living under a rock or holed up banging out that latest manuscript, you know as the author of the *New York Times* bestselling novel *Hashtag Celebrity Crush*. Welcome, Emmy!

EMMY: Thanks for having me, Beth.

BETH: So, Emmy, you recently hit number one on the *New York Times* list. Congratulations! That's quite an accomplishment!

EMMY: Thank you.

BETH: It's pretty much the holy grail for authors. Of course, you had help from your own promotional efforts as well as publicity surrounding your real-life celebrity crush, the superhot, all-you-can-eat special, Jason Connor. You know we were all rooting for you, right?

EMMY: Thanks. Reaching number one is… great.

BETH: I'm not talking about *that*. I'm talking about you scoring a touchdown and an extra point with Jason.

EMMY: [*coughs*] What happened between Jason and me wasn't planned, Beth. And I have no idea what you mean by "extra point." We were just doing some social media marketing together, and things… evolved.

BETH: Well, hooray for evolution! Care to share any details for us, Emmy? Any between-the-sheets stories? Does he like it when—

EMMY: No details, Beth.

BETH: Okay, okay, I understand! Those pictures were something else, Emmy. You still claim it wasn't you who leaked them, am I correct?

EMMY: It wasn't me. I would never have done that to him.

BETH: Oh yes, he ended up getting fired from *Lost Star* over those pictures. A shame. I loved him in that show. I heard they offered the role to Zachary Tay, and he's accepted.

EMMY: Do you have another question for me?

BETH: You seem upset, Emmy. Did you really care about Jason? Because in all the interviews I've seen with him lately, he says you used him specifically to build buzz for your book and the movie.

EMMY: It wasn't like—

BETH: That was brilliant! I bet he never saw it coming. Give me a high five! Here's your heroine, ladies. Emmy Ellison. Turned the tables and seduced Jason Connor instead of the other way around.

EMMY: Can we not use the word "seduced"?

BETH: Of course! How about landed that fish. Captured that flag. Buttered that biscuit.

EMMY: Beth, please stop.

BETH: You're truly an inspiration, Emmy. I know I speak for a lot of people when I say thank you! Thank you for showing us what can be accomplished when you truly set your mind to something.

EMMY: I'm sorry, are we talking about the book now?

BETH: No! We're talking about Jason Connor. Oh, give me another high five! I just can't get enough of them. We're all dying to see what kind of trouble you get into on the promo tour in December. Don't disappoint us! All righty, that wraps up today's podcast. Join us tomorrow for a brief chat with Stephen King's best friend. So proud of you, Emmy.

Chapter 30

Mom, do you want me to tell them anything else?

VLOG, *RANDOM YOGA POSES*, SEPTEMBER 25

PEYTON: Hi, everybody. This is *Random Yoga Poses*. My
name is Peyton Ellison. That's my mom Emmy on the
floor there. She's not feeling very motivated today, so I'll
be doing the vlog. I guess we'll go ahead with Child's
Pose today. That's the pose my mom is in at the moment;
she's been doing it for about an hour now. You just
basically kneel down and let your face fall to the floor,
and then you just lay there. You can put your arms out in
front if you want for a stretch. Or, like my mom, you can
let them lay alongside you like dead tree branches. You
can turn your head to the side or prop your forehead on

your hands. Or, again, as my mom is demonstrating, you can just have your face right on the floor. Just... you know... staring right into the carpet with your dead tree branch arms lying next to you. Rrrrright. Okaaaay. Mom, do you want me to tell them anything else? Mom?

Chapter 31

The pit of hell has excellent lighting.

Emmy

JOSIE BARGES INTO my room. "Emmy, this has gone on long enough! You've been living in this room for three months. Get out of bed!"

I roll over onto my laptop, which has become my perpetual and only bedmate because, hey, a girl's still gotta work, and dig myself deeper into my nest of misery. "Leave me alone," I moan. "I'm meditating."

Josie huffs. "This is unacceptable. Peyton, bring a candle!"

I yank the covers off my head and squint. "Did I forget to pay the electric bill? Did a hurricane hit? Is it my birthday?"

"Relax. I'm just going to freshen up this room. It smells like dirty laundry and depression. Alexa! Stop playing Death Cab for Cutie."

I sit up. "Is that tea in your hand?"

"It is." She hands it to me. The cup is warm. It's one of the mugs Peyton made me with *Best Mom Ever* written on it in her thumbprints.

"I love you." My face crumples. "I love you both so much."

"No!" Josie shouts at me with the intensity of an early *Battlestar Galactica* episode. "No more crying! No more wallowing! You have to pull yourself together. We're leaving for the premiere in a few weeks." Josie pushes my knees aside and makes room for herself on the bed.

Peyton appears in the doorway with a candle in her hands. "It's your favorite scent, Mom."

"The Pandora ride at Animal Kingdom?"

She nods. "Frozen Lake."

"Gracias, niña." Josie pushes her out the door. "Let me talk to your mom for a minute."

I blink in the early afternoon light shining through the tiny window in my tiny bedroom. Through the smeary glass, I can see a little bit of the Gulf of Mexico. The never-ending song of seagulls filters in through the cracks, and I discover a crumb of joy while sniffing the candle and taking a sip of my tea. At least the world hasn't totally come apart. It's not *Infinity War*.

"He still won't answer my texts," I say. "He still thinks I leaked those photos."

"I'll kill him with my bare hands," Josie growls.

"He just went right back with her. Immediately. He didn't even miss a beat."

"And after I kill him, I'm going to push him down the stairs."

"Did he feel anything for me? I don't think he felt anything for me!"

"And then I'll drag his body into that big fire ant mound in the parking lot."

We've had this same conversation at least ten times, but it never helps. I press my cheek against the warm cup in my hands. "Josie, stop with the support, please. It's not helping. I think I need you to give me some real advice."

Josie puts on her bad-news face, which kind of looks like she has a live hamster in her mouth. "You're not gonna like it."

"Just shut up and tell me."

"Okay then." She takes a deep breath. "Emmy, you always believed that Jason was a good guy even when the media said otherwise. Now that he's trying to do right by his family, you're going to fault him for that?"

She's right. I hate this. "I don't fault him for anything. I just want him to know I didn't mean to hurt him."

Josie's eyebrows go up. "You didn't? Because I thought that was the original plan: use him for fame and fortune."

"I never meant for him to lose his job. I just wanted to catch up with my dreams. You know."

"I know." She picks up the face down framed picture that I secretly peek at when I want to torture myself—our morning-after photo. The one I didn't share on social media. The one I kept just for us.

"That's a lie from the pit of hell," I grumble.

She shrugs. "The pit of hell has excellent lighting."

I fall back on the pillows with a groan.

"Emmy, try to look on the bright side. You're a hugely successful author with a movie deal! You should be enjoying this.

So things didn't work out with Jason Connor. So what? He was always just the gravy. You got the meatloaf."

"I like gravy. I want gravy."

"I always worried about this with you, you know."

I frown. "What do you mean?"

"I don't think I can say it. You're gonna be mad."

I smack her with my pillow. "Say it."

"No." She drops the framed photo on the bed, snatches the pillow out of my hands, and throws it on the floor. "It's not supportive."

I smack her with my other pillow. "Say it!" She grabs at that one, too, but this time I manage to keep it out of her reach. "Say it, Josie! I need to know."

"Fine, I'll say it!" She blows out a sigh. "With you, nothing's ever enough."

I halt with the pillow brandished in midair. "That's hurtful."

"I know. But it's true." She pins me with her warm brown eyes. "Five years ago, I met a girl who wanted to publish a book. She published a book. Then she wanted a movie deal. She got a movie deal. Then she wanted to meet her favorite actor. She met him. Then she wanted him to fall for her. He fell for her, and don't say he didn't"—she shakes the framed picture at me—"because you don't get a photo like this any other way."

I scoff.

"Don't scoff yet! I'm not finished. *Then* she wanted to be number one on the bestseller list. She did it. And now that she's achieved all that, how does she spend her free time? Moping around pining for the one thing she can't have. And I bet you, even if she got that, even if she patched up things with Jason Connor and woke up in that fluffy, white-sheet den of pleasure every morning, it still wouldn't be enough. She still wouldn't be happy. Because you, Emmy Ellison, have a problem that not even the love of a superhot movie star can fix."

A rumbling happens in my chest, like an alien creature awakening. I want to argue with her, but I'm also dying to know what my problem is. "Go on."

"You have to decide, when is it going to be enough? Because at some point, enough has to be enough to make you happy."

I open my mouth to protest, but no words form, because I realize that she's probably right. Maybe I'm climbing a never-ending ladder. Or worse yet, maybe I'm climbing a ladder with nothing at the top.

I drop the pillow to my lap. "I'll think about it. But in the meantime, what do I do about Jason?"

She studies the photo some more and shrugs. "Do whatever you want to do. You want to kill Jason? Kill him. You want to jump his bones? Jump his bones. You want to apologize and then kill him and jump his bones, do it. Whatever you want to do, I support you."

"No!" I shout, using her own weapon against her. "Josie, no. For real. Not *what do I want to do?* What's the *right* thing to do?"

Her face softens, and she brushes the hair off my sweaty, greasy forehead. "The right thing to do is to tell Jason how you feel...and then try to be okay with whatever happens next."

Chapter 32

Cue the orchestra. Roll the credits.

Jason

MY RED NIKES pad across the gold and maroon hotel carpet. I've walked this path many times, for many promo tours. Only the overly polite assistants change.

"Jason Connor? This way. You'll be here. Can I get you some water, sir? Ice?"

"I'm good, thanks."

Breathing in the fusty smell of conference room air-conditioning, I settle into the chair with my name on it. When no one is looking, I wiggle the flask out of my back jeans pocket and take a swig of whiskey. It goes down hard and hot. I take another. If anyone sees, they don't let on.

Ten feet to my right, Margarita sits with hands clasped on

the table. The baby is big now, and Margarita's dress celebrates every curve. The last ultrasound said everything was good. I pasted on a smile as we watched the black-and-white smudges moving around on the screen. It's a girl this time. I know I should be happy, although "happy" is a bit ambitious for me lately. It would be nice to feel anything, honestly.

Emmy walks in wearing skinny jeans and a macramé vest, and my numb brain summons an emotion: anger. A staff member leads her to a chair ten feet away on the other side of me. Our eyes meet, and I look away.

There's another emotion—hurt. Forget I said anything about wanting to feel. Feelings suck.

The flask is calling to me. *Drink me. I'm here for you, bud. You and me. I'll get you through it.* I take another swallow and grimace as a tall, grinning suit makes his way over to the chair across from me.

"Storm Morowitz." He holds out his hand. "Celebrity Roundup."

"Nice to meet you." I tuck the flask back in my pocket. "Shoot."

He launches into the usual round of questions about the movie. Margarita and Emmy are also both being interviewed by people I vaguely recognize. I could probably recall their names and publications if I tried hard enough. If I cared hard enough.

"What kinds of fans do you see the film appealing to?" Storm asks.

"Oh, you know." I rub my temples. "Unhappy, middle-aged women and hormonal teenage girls. The usual."

He emits a stuttering laugh. "What was your favorite part of the filming?"

"When we could finally turn off the Duran Duran music."

"Did you do your own stunts?"

"You mean the thrilling action scene where I ate sushi with wasabi? Yes."

Time's up, and Storm Whatever His Name Was thanks me and takes his voice recorder away with him. I use the short break to steal another glance at Emmy. She looks as miserable as I feel, although maybe it's just her guilt showing.

She's texted me at least twenty times between the fundraiser and now, telling me she wasn't the one who posted those photos, but I don't know who else it could've been. How convenient that the photos were anonymous, and then the very next week, her book hit number one on the bestseller list.

Maybe I could've been convinced to give her the benefit of the doubt, except in all my downtime after getting fired and finding out I'm having another kid I can disappoint, I finished reading her book. That was a real punch in the nards.

Amanda warned me about Emmy, but I didn't believe her. Miles tried to, too. I was supposed to be her celebrity crush! She was supposed to actually like me, at least a little bit.

I lengthen my legs under the table and stretch way back in my chair so there's no chance of looking her way. Why does everything hurt? When I lift my head again, Harper Rose is there. I'm actually relieved, and that's the second time today my brain has surprised the hell out of me.

"Hello, Harper," I say semi-cheerfully.

"Hello, Jason." Her smile is even bigger and faker than usual under her coiffed blond updo. "Excited to be a new dad soon?"

Big eyes and lots of teeth are how I choose to answer that.

"Any luck finding a gig as good as *Lost Star*?"

She would go there. Harper Rose has a heart the size of a garbanzo bean inside a body of indeterminate age—she's either a vampire or she's hired the best plastic surgeon in California.

There's no point sugarcoating things, so I tell her the truth. "Not yet." I don't mention Cameron dumped me, too, so I'm not only out of a job but also out of an agent.

"I'm sure it'll happen." She says it in the same way grocery store baggers say, *Have a nice day.* "Are you and Emmy on speaking terms yet?"

No need to lie about that, either. "Nope."

"And Margarita? She's gotten quite serious with one of her producers, at least that's what I've heard."

I trail my finger down the faux wood grain on the table. "That's what I heard, too." This is supposed to be a premiere interview. We're supposed to be talking about the movie, but leave it to Harper to pour salt in my wounds instead.

"What about you? Anyone giving you comfort and solace lately?" The slow, sleepy way she asks the question makes me look up. She's got that smile on, the one that tells me yup, that's exactly what she meant.

"No comfort, Harper," I admit. "No solace."

"That's too bad." She reaches across the table and puts her hand on mine. I catch a glimpse of Emmy out of the corner of my eye. She's watching us.

I know it's a sucky thing to do, but vengeance is a dish best served with a side of suck. I flip my hand over so Harper's fingers can find my open palm. Then I switch on the smolder to level two of ten. Barely there, but *there*. Subtle but powerful. Harper's smile widens.

"Did you have another question?" I purr.

"What are you doing tonight?"

"Tower Bar," I say.

"Maybe I'll see you there."

I give her the finger gun. It wasn't much of an interview, and

I won't be seeing her at the Tower Bar. As she walks away, hips swinging in her pink suit skirt, I steal another glance at Emmy. She's staring straight ahead at the empty chair, pretending she didn't see any of that, but I know she did. I get more feelings, kind of tangled-up ones. Satisfaction mixed with guilt. Vindication wrapped around despair. Desire all tied up with...

I pull out the flask again and check my phone. How many more hours of this?

There's a notification for a missed call from a *Lost Star* network flunky harassing me about a promo I'm still contracted to do for a show they fired me from. I made the mistake of answering their initial calls a month ago, thinking maybe it was good news. Nope, just a waste of everybody's time. I delete the voicemail without listening to it.

Screw them. I'm not Hadron anymore. Zachary Tay is. Write the promo shit into *his* contract.

When the interviews are done, I hurry out before Emmy can catch me. Turns out I didn't need to. When I glance back, she's not chasing me. She's talking to a purple-haired, artsy-looking woman in a beret—must be her friend Josie—and Peyton. I should go and meet them, especially Peyton. It's the right thing to do, but Jason Connor isn't a guy who does the right thing, is he?

Instead, I duck my head and continue the long, fast walk to my car. When I press the ignition button on the Alfa, Duran Duran blares on the stereo. I quickly switch it to Smash Mouth. My eye jumps to the photo I stuffed face down into a crack in the dash. I tug it free and flip it over. It's the pic Emmy mailed to me of us in the kitchen. God, who is that guy and why is he such a sucker?

Did she plan to use me all along? If so, she should be acting, not writing. Maybe it was too good an opportunity to pass up, a moment of weakness at my expense. With my history, I'm probably not even allowed to be mad about that.

I open the glove box, toss the photo in, and slam it shut. Then I take a deep breath and hold on to the steering wheel. Only two more days of interviews and then a game show with Emmy, hosted by Terica. The premiere is next week. Then it'll all be over. The baby will come, then Christmas. I'll start auditioning for work in the New Year. Emmy Ellison and all my memories of her can fade out. Cue the orchestra. Roll the credits.

Yup, that's what I want. That's what I need. That's what I deserve.

I shift into first and head for the liquor store.

Chapter 33

Parents, send your kids out of the room.

CELEBRITY STRAIGHT TALK, DECEMBER 3

AMIL: Have you seen the interviews from the promo tour for *Hashtag Celebrity Crush*? Talk about painful.

ISLA: Seriously, it's like they want us to hate them. Do they want us to hate them? Are they Gordon Ramsay?

AMIL: Hidey ho! This is Amil Nair, host of *Celebrity Straight Talk*. And this is my cohost, Isla Wallace.

ISLA: Hi-la, it's Isla!

AMIL: So, let's talk some more about how cringey it was to watch Jason Connor and Emmy Ellison talk about this movie. Yikes!

ISLA: Mmm, so true, Amil. Looking at Jason Connor, you'd think it was a zombie flick, not a rom-com. He looks half-dead!

AMIL: Well, in his defense, dealing with a pregnant Margarita Ayala would suck the life out of any man. She's not always such a sweetheart.

ISLA: Mee-*yow*!

AMIL: I'm just sayin'. It might not even be his baby.

ISLA: Poor Jason. Someone should take him home.

AMIL: Nurse him.

ISLA: And feed him.

AMIL: He doesn't need anyone to feed him, Isla. He's starting to pork out.

ISLA: Probably eating carbs.

AMIL: He needs someone to make him some kale chips.

ISLA: I make a mean kale chip.

AMIL: I'm sure your kale chips are the meanest, Isla.

ISLA: [*laughs*]

AMIL: [*laughs*]

ISLA: No, seriously, Amil. You know who'd probably like to do that is Emmy Ellison.

AMIL: Oh, pancakes! Are we talking about her now? Parents, send your kids out of the room. They shouldn't have to hear this.

ISLA: Her interviews could be summed up in one word: pitiful.

AMIL: Actually, I'd go with "sappy."

ISLA: Did she even speak words or did she open her mouth and just exude pure wretchedness?

AMIL: I used to like her, Isla.

ISLA: Me too.

AMIL: Now she's pathetic.

ISLA: Amil, I heard that, with the way these two are torpedoing their personal lives, several premiere events around the country have been canceled already. They may even scrap the red carpet here in LA and throw the film out to the public on December fifteenth.

AMIL: How horrible, Isla! A Jason Connor and Margarita Ayala film treated like some B movie.

ISLA: I bet that wasn't part of Miss Emmy Ellison's plan when she went all sexy librarian on Jason.

AMIL: But, Isla, she still denies having anything to do with the photos.

ISLA: Nobody believes her, Amil.

AMIL: Why not?

ISLA: Do you believe her?

AMIL: No.

ISLA: Me neither. It was a genius move for book sales.

AMIL: Yeah, but when it comes to Jason, she shot herself in the footnote.

ISLA: Hashtag ouch!

AMIL: Hashtag medic!

ISLA: Hashtag too bad, Emmy.

AMIL: At least you got your fifteen minutes of fame.

ISLA: And we just gave you, like, three more.

AMIL: Hashtag you're welcome! [*laughs*]

ISLA: [*laughs*]

Chapter 34

We'll give you that one out of sheer pity.

Emmy

VAL WIGGLES A mascara wand in front of my face. "You need to do better, Katniss Everdeen. Look up."

I look up.

He lengthens my lashes and then grabs the eyeliner. "This is your time and you're squandering it. Look down."

I look down.

He thickens the line at the edge of my lids. I hear a lipstick tube open. "You are not gonna let that boy ruin this for you. Relax your face."

I relax my face.

He paints my lips. "You're gonna go out there, and you're gonna kill it." He hands me a tissue. "Blot."

I blot.

Val leans back and admires his work. Across the hotel room, Josie is doing Peyton's makeup, both of them perched on plush burgundy chairs in front of a filmy white curtain ten stories up in our hotel room.

"I'm done," Val concludes. "Now all that's left to fix is your attitude."

I move to look at myself in the hotel's full-length mirror. For the game show, Val has me in couture ripped jeans and a silky black Kate Spade blouse with cat eyes and silver eye shadow. I check my smartwatch. We leave in fifteen minutes, and I'm nervous.

No, that's a lie. I'm terrified.

The live *Celebrity Showdown* episode will feature Terica as a guest host and is supposed to be a fun follow-up from our initial meeting on her talk show, but since Jason won't speak to me, I'm not sure how that's going to go.

"Eyes on the prize," Val continues. I watch him packing up his makeup kit behind me in the mirror's reflection. "Movie tickets sold means books sold. You sell that movie, girl. You were made for this."

In the monthslong vacuum of news about Jason and me since our so-called affair, book sales have fallen along with the temperatures. I dropped off the bestseller list in October.

"I'm not sure it'll be enough," I confess, plopping onto one of the queen beds. "People have lost their enthusiasm for *Hashtag Celebrity Crush.*"

"Well, no wonder! Y'all are depressing," Val says. "You need to bring up the energy, Emmy. This is not about what's really going on. This is about what you want people to *think* is going on."

"What do I want them to think?"

"That you're having fun! That being famous is great! That it's Disneyland on steroids with lots of glitter and champagne and a bunch of rich white people laughing."

"You can do hard things." Josie stops applying Peyton's lipstick to wave imaginary pom-poms.

"I can do hard things," I repeat.

"Like first-degree murder," Josie adds, still waving pom-poms.

The game show studio has no greenroom, so the staff seats us in the studio audience. That means Jason's here somewhere, too, if he bothered showing up. As we get settled in the orange chairs in the front row, at least half the audience recognizes me and either waves or grins at me. Peyton is smiling ear to ear. Josie looks uncharacteristically nervous, while Val has the cagey look of a bodyguard in drag. Everything is over-the-top decorated for Christmas, including the stage, the curtains, and even the staff.

"Mom, look," Peyton whispers, pursing her lips. Since I taught her it's rude to point, she does this thing where she points with her mouth. I follow the trajectory of her lips to find Jason walking across the front of the stage, led by one of the crew. He's wearing a red sweater that's way too preppy for my taste and dark pants. The sweater is too tight. He's really put on weight. She brings him to the chair next to mine, and he falls into it.

"Hi," he says.

"Hi." At least we're on speaking terms.

"Jason Connor!" Peyton's face is all eye shadow and braces. She's on her knees on the chair, which I'd normally correct her for but don't bother doing today because, frankly, there's too much going on for parenting. I introduce Jason to Peyton and then to Josie. To his credit, he resurrects the charm for them. I'm grateful for that.

Once the audience is seated, Terica kicks off the show. The crowd goes wild as we head to the stage. Terica greets us with a look that says, *I know what's going on, but you better not eff this up.* I catch Jason's eye. He nods his agreement. Good. We're doing this.

"Okay!" Terica turns to the audience. "You're in for a treat today! If you remember earlier this year, superhunk Jason Connor and author Emmy Ellison met on *The Terica Show* about her book *Hashtag Celebrity Crush*. Now that book is a major motion picture premiering this Friday, December ninth! See, kids, dreams do come true!"

The audience cheers. I give an exaggerated wave, exerting as much energy as I can muster. It's my dream she's talking about, after all.

"So, Jason and Emmy are going to play a few games with us, and don't forget, this is live streamed, so text your friends and family and tell them to tune in right now. We're going to start with Wrong Word." She turns to us. "So, who wants to give the clue and who wants to get spattered?"

Jason and I just look at each other.

"Come on, no need to be polite," Terica teases. "How about this? Who *deserves* to get spattered?"

Jason says dryly, "I'll do it."

"Great! Chivalry's not dead. Here are your glasses, Jason. Go on up and sit on the stool."

I bounce on my toes and smile at Peyton, who is antsy as a kitten in her seat in the front row. As Jason gets into position, Terica explains the rules. "Emmy is going to get a card with two words on it. One is the right word, and one is the wrong word. She's got to use one-word clues to get Jason to say the correct word. If he says the wrong word, something's going to happen that he's not going to like. Are we ready?"

"Ready!" I blurt.

Jason gives a reluctant thumbs-up.

Terica presses a blue card into my hand with the correct word, *famous*, and the wrong word, *celebrity*. Tricky.

"You!" I say.

Jason slumps on the stool, hands clasped in front of him. "Unemployed?"

The audience laughs. I don't. Terica widens her eyes at me but doesn't say anything.

"Let's try again." I grin at the audience. I go for the movie title: *"Almost..."*

"Done?"

The audience mutters. His attitude is a total buzzkill.

"Sean!" I try again.

"Celebrity."

"Oh no! That's the wrong word!" Terica cries. "Get ready, Jason. Here it comes!" She presses a button, and purple goo squirts from a pipe and splatters him. It's surprisingly violent and copious. He startles in his seat, meme face automatically coming into play. It's hilarious. I can't stop myself from laughing.

"That was awesome." Jason's tone is laced with venom. "Thanks, Emmy."

"The word was *famous*. You're the one who got it wrong." I can't help but think this is righteous retribution. Yes, I used Jason for a leg up in Hollywood, but he used me, too, and then dumped me like a hot potato. And he's been a jerk ever since I got back.

Terica jumps in. "Okay, Emmy, another."

This time the right word is *romance*, and the wrong word is *love*.

"Heart," I say.

"Love."

The audience, who can see the words on a screen, goes wild.

"Oh no, Jason, you said the wrong word again!" Without fanfare, Terica splatters him a second time. "The right word was *romance*."

"You did that on purpose." Jason glares at me, and even though I can't say 100 percent that I didn't do it on purpose, I'm laughing too hard to protest.

I fake a cheerleader voice. "We can do this, Jason! I know we can. Next card, Terica." I grab it out of her hand. The right word is *chocolate*, and the wrong word is *dessert*.

"Candy," I say confidently.

Jason is doing his fierce face, except it's less theatrical because he really is pissed. "Rubber," he guesses through gritted teeth.

I try again. "Cake."

"Mushroom." Is he throwing the game on purpose?

Terica's lips purse. "I don't know if you guys are playing this right."

"Dark," I say, switching gears.

"Vader."

"Oh no, Jason, that's three strikes." Terica shakes her head. "You didn't say the wrong word, but you didn't get the right word, either, so you get splatted anyway." She pushes the button, and now Jason is covered in purple goo from head to toe. I bend over, holding my stomach, the tension in my muscles evaporating with my laughter. It would be more fun if Jason wasn't being such a sore loser, but there's nothing I can do about that.

Terica turns to me. "Well, Emmy, I think you have

something to add to your Venn diagram, because you didn't do too well at that."

I shrug mock apologetically.

"No problem, because you're going to get another chance. Jason, come on over. It's your turn to give the clues. Emmy, have a seat."

Oh to the crap, I hadn't thought about the tables being turned. Jason nods at me with a Dexter face as we pass each other on the very messy stage. He hands me the sticky, goo-covered glasses.

"Get ready," he says.

I take a deep breath and wiggle onto the stool, slipping the glasses over my eyes. The stage and the audience are purple and smeary through the plastic lenses, but I can still make out Peyton bouncing in the front row, Josie grinning like an alligator, and Val sitting cross-legged and judgmental. I'm sure he's not pleased that his hard work is about to turn into that ectoplasm scene from the original *Poltergeist*.

"Okay, Jason," Terica says. "You've got your words. Go ahead and give Emmy a clue."

He shifts his shoulders, and a slow, confident smile spreads across his face. "Cat."

I take a guess. "Pet."

"Oh no!" Terica frowns. "That was the wrong word! The right word was *dog*!"

I close my mouth a fraction of a second before purple goo the consistency of half-solidified Jell-O assaults me. It's cold and shocking and everywhere. I hold out my spattered arms and shoot Jason a death glare. "Since when is 'cat' a clue for 'dog'?" Grape-flavored spittle flies from my lips.

"Next one!" an apathetic Terica crows.

Jason checks his card. "Cruel."

I scrunch up my face, trying to work out the psychology. If he wants me to say the wrong word, it's probably *evil*, which means I won't guess that. What's something kind of like *cruel*, but not? Maybe the opposite? I feel like I'm in the poisoned wine scene from *The Princess Bride*.

"Friendly!"

I wince, but it's not the wrong word.

"Unforgivable." Jason gives the second clue.

What is he getting at? I could just guess crazy stuff from out in left field, but I'll still get splattered if I do. "Villain?"

That's wrong, too.

"Liar."

Now all I can think of are movie villains. "Thanos?" He wasn't a liar, though, just misguided.

Terica doesn't bother saying anything before pushing the button and soaking me again. "The right word was *dolphin*, and the wrong word was *shark*. I don't know what that was all about, but we're moving on to the next game."

"You cheated!" I accuse Jason, wiping purple goop off my face and arms as Terica buys us time to clean up with her banter. "What does *cruel* have to do with *dolphin*?"

"I guess it's just the word association I had going on in my head."

A burly guy with a Santa hat ushers us back into the lights and commotion, but not before I catch Jason taking a swig from the flask he's been carrying around all week. A couple of girls in *Celebrity Showdown* T-shirts and elf shoe coverings strap us into jump seats on circular platforms. Terica is grinning at us, and Peyton is cheering and flailing so violently in her chair that it might require an exorcism. Meanwhile a sinking feeling overwhelms me. I know this game.

"Lucky, lucky Jason and Emmy. You get to play Spinning Hits! That's where I give you a word, and you have to come up with a song that has that word in it. Emmy, we all know what a great singer you profess to be, so this should be fun."

Beside me, Jason sniggers. It comes across pretty funny, seeing as he's strapped into a seat, too. But despite my anger, I really want to talk to him. I need to tell him how I feel, like Josie suggested, and this is probably my only opportunity since he can't get away.

"If you can't name a song, or you get it wrong, you get spun really fast for five seconds," Terica says. "And I promise it'll be the longest five seconds of your life. Okay, let's start. The word is 'didn't.' Emmy, ladies first."

My cheeks fill with air as I scavenge my brain while also stressing about my nonexistent singing skills. Luckily, while my voice is terrible, my memory is a steel trap. I struggle through the first line of "This Night" by Billy Joel.

Terica holds up her cue card. "Well done, Emmy! And only a little off-key. Only a little." She scrunches her nose at me, and I aim a grateful grin her way. "Jason, you're up with 'didn't.'"

He doesn't hesitate, singing the song title. "'I Didn't Mean to Turn You On.' Robert Palmer!"

"That's legit," Terica says.

"And apropos," he adds.

I frown and whisper out of the side of my mouth. "Was that really necessary?" Suddenly, he's grinning and bopping like he's having the time of his life. The audience loves it.

"Emmy," Terica says, "another with 'didn't.'"

I can't think of one, so I make up lyrics to the tune of Ariel's song from *The Little Mermaid*. "I didn't send. Those pictures in. It had to be someone else. Someone in the bushes…Oh no, don't!"

My song is cut off as my seat launches into a spin. Everything blurs, and Terica is right—it's the longest five seconds of my life. When the spinning finally stops, my head is swirling, and the grape taste in my mouth is no longer even remotely pleasant. Even though I'm drenched in purple, my face must be green because the audience laughs uproariously, and Jason is cackling without the slightest shame or apology.

"Next one! Jason, you're up. The word is 'love.'"

Again, he's lightning fast with "Love on the Rocks" by Neil Diamond, promising to pour me a drink and tell me some lies in an enviable tenor.

"Done and *done*," I hiss.

He smiles sweetly, and that makes me even madder. How did I ever think there was anything between us?

"Emmy, your turn—"

But I've already started. "*L* is for the way you used to look at me. *O* is for the only person you want to listen to being yourself. *V* is very, very selfish and unfair."

"Okey dokey, I think we know what you were going for, so we'll give you that one out of sheer pity." Terica blows out a loud breath.

Jason launches into Def Leppard's "Love Bites" before he's even invited to. The audience takes over for him, and he turns to me and sings, more softly, "Love exploits you. Love pretends to care about you..."

"Jason, I think we've found your game!" Terica says. "Emmy, you got another?"

I don't. I'm not having fun anymore. My heart is pounding, and I can't think straight. I squeeze my eyes shut as off I go again, launched into a grape-smelling tornado of hell. Jason is laughing too hard for it to be a real laugh.

"Well how about that? Jason didn't get spun once," Terica says matter-of-factly.

"Well, he *is* the performer." I swallow hard as my chair slows and shudders into position. "He'll do anything, sing anything, say anything. All the world's a stage, right, Jason?"

"Guess what?" Terica blurts. "It's time for Falling for Trivia!"

"Get me out of this thing," I mutter to the crew as they free us.

Jason is still dancing and humming "Love Bites" as he lifts up his arms to get unstrapped. I stagger when my feet hit the stage, and I have to think about the smell of brownies to stop the queasiness. Then up the rattly metal stairs we go into the rafters to the top of the Falling for Trivia platform. We'll have to answer a bunch of questions until we get enough wrong and the trapdoors open under us. Then we'll plummet thirty feet into God-knows-what at 9.8 meters per second squared. I learned the exact speed of a falling object while helping Peyton study for her science test last week.

I glance over at Jason, who's standing only a few feet away from me on another trapdoor. He pulls out his flask again and takes a quick swig while everyone is focused on Terica. I put a hand over my mic and make my voice extra condescending. "You know, it's really sad seeing you like this."

He doesn't even bother covering his mic. "There are three hundred and fifty-nine other degrees. Why don't you look at one of them?"

"You know, you were supposed to meet me at the back of the yacht," I hiss. "What if that deckhand hadn't put the ladder down for me? I could have been left behind, floating in the Pacific."

He shoots me a look that appears genuinely hurt. "Give me a little credit, Emmy."

So he did make sure I was safe. Well, at least that's something. He takes another swig, right there in front of everyone.

"I never meant to hurt you, Jason. Truly."

His Adam's apple bobs as he swallows. "When, Emmy? When did you never mean to hurt me? Was it when you posted those photos?"

I roll my eyes. "*A*, I told you that wasn't me, and *B*, do you really think I would share photos of myself like that when I have a twelve-year-old daughter—"

He cuts me off. "*Or* did you never mean to hurt me when you put my personal life in your book?"

My mouth claps shut. He finished it. After everything that happened, I didn't expect him to actually finish reading it. I try to say something, but nothing comes out.

He looks away. "Yeah, that's what I thought."

I'm still scrambling for a reply when the lights go up and the cameras are on us.

"All righty! Jason and Emmy are in position and ready to play Falling for Trivia. Since it's just the two of them, this is how we're going to do it. I'm going to ask a question, but if you get it wrong, you only fall if the other person gets theirs right. Got it?"

I give a weak thumbs-up, but inside I'm reeling. "I really wanted to tell you about that scene," I whisper to Jason, who's glaring straight ahead at the far wall of the studio. "It was a mistake. I shouldn't have done it. I'm really, really sorry."

"Okay, kids! Jason, you get to go first this time. You guys both love movies, so we'll start with some movie questions. In the film *Monty Python and the Holy Grail*, what type of bird was discussed regarding its ability to carry coconuts?"

"A swallow, Terica," he says.

"A swallow is correct!"

I try again, covering my mic and whispering, "It was selfish of me. I wasn't thinking."

He replies through gritted teeth, "I told you that story over the phone. What orbital mechanics were going on in your head that you didn't say anything right then?"

"Okay, Emmy, your turn! How many movies were made of the *Hunger Games* series?"

"Four!" I shout with confidence before turning my attention back to Jason. "I didn't know what to do. I tried to tell you and just couldn't."

"Jason! What famous actress played the lead role in the 1998 film *Sliding Doors*?"

He sighs. "Gwyneth Paltrow. Emmy, forget it. It's not like we had a future anyway. Next time, do me a favor—pick someone else for your celebrity crush. Pick Sean. Pick Ramirez. Pick Zachary Tay. Anyone but me. Because I don't want the job."

I don't know if there's anything he could have said to make me feel worse. My knees go weak. Everything feels like it's swirling downward, into a drain of regret.

"Emmy, yoo-hoo!" Terica calls. "Look over here!" I drag my gaze toward her. "Finish the name of this Mike Myers movie: *So I Married…*"

"*An Axe Murderer.*" I drop my voice again for Jason, and it comes out small, defeated. "I said I was sorry. Are you really not going to forgive me?"

He doesn't hesitate. "Nope."

"You guys are too good at this. I think it's time to change topics. Let's do science."

My heart is pounding. My smartwatch, the one he bought me, flashes along with all the lights on my dashboard. I tear it off my wrist.

"Jason, which is the larger category for scientific classification? Phylum, family, or class?"

I fling the watch, and it bounces off his chest. With impressive reflexes, he catches it and stuffs it in his pocket. "Phylum."

"Correct!"

"Fine!" I blink back tears. "Let's get through this and the premiere, and then we never have to see each other again."

Jason's perfect jaw moves in a way I've never seen it move before, like he's grinding metal with his teeth. "I lost the best job I ever had over you, Emmy, and I don't care anymore what happens with the movie. I hope the press is so bad that they cancel the LA premiere, because I don't want to do any more of these events. In fact, I'm going to do my best to make sure that happens."

Terica's voice is a little desperate and a lot annoyed. "Guys, let's not talk shop in the middle of Falling for Trivia, 'kay? Emmy? Your answer, please?"

My eyes tear up. Jason's going to tank the premiere on purpose, destroying everything I've worked so hard for. This is just another rodeo for him. But for me...this is my golden ticket! If this movie fails, I may never get to work in Hollywood again.

"Emmy?" Terica warns.

I snuffle and squeeze my eyes shut, fighting back tears. "Can you repeat the question, Terica?"

"Sure. No problem. We're not on a schedule or anything. How fast does an object fall?"

Oh, thank God and Tom Hanks, there's some mercy in the universe after all. "Nine point eight meters per second squared." I turn to Jason, my voice begging. "You wouldn't do that. I know you wouldn't do that."

"Watch me." He raises his voice. "Terica, I have a Falling for Trivia question for Emmy."

Oh to the craaaaap! I shake my head at Terica, desperately mouthing "no" at her.

"Well, that's highly irregular and probably a really bad idea…"

Jason cuts her off. "Emmy, when you came to LA, were you thinking *A*, I'm going to break into Hollywood with a crappy romance novel and a gimmick, or *B*, I actually have the talent to make it in this business?"

Red hotness rises up my neck into my cheeks.

"Oh no," Terica says.

I turn to him. "I've got a question for you, too, Jason. When you drink out of that fancy flask of yours, do you think you look like *A*, Benedict Cumberbatch, or *B*, Fat Thor?"

His glare is icy. "Fat Thor was still hot!"

"Can we cut to commercial?" Terica makes hand signals to the crew. "Guys, you need to cut it out up there." She waves and raises her voice. "Guys?"

"Emmy." Jason's face is turning as red as mine. "What is the thing you suck at most? *A*, singing; *B*, baking things in round pans; or *C*, thinking about someone other than yourself?"

"Jason!" I counter at the top of my lungs. "Why are you really all alone? *A*, because your playlist sucks; *B*, because green smoothies are not breakfast; or *C*, because you're a hypocrite?"

Terica stacks her cards. "That's it. Drop 'em."

The trapdoors open under us, and we plummet.

Chapter 35

My trainer says no more bread.

Jason

I ALWAYS HATED this sweater anyway. In fact, it doesn't matter if the goo comes out or not because, when I get home, I'm gonna burn it. Burn it down! Burn it all down!

God, I drank too much.

Emmy. Emmy. Emmy. She called me Fat Thor. Where's the exit? I've never been to this studio before. Have I been down this hallway already? Where is the goddamn exit?

I turn a corner and catch Emmy eyeing me as she dries her hair with a towel. I whirl in the opposite direction, but when there's no exit door there, either, I'm forced to head back her way. I trudge down another hallway and get even more lost. I'm banging my forehead against the wall when she appears at my side.

"You're not driving home, are you?" Her hair is wet and stringy and still beautiful. I know she's mad at me, but her hazel eyes are soft. I'm not used to seeing her in black. She's more of a color person. "I'll call you an Uber."

"I don't want to leave the Alfa here," I say to the wall.

"Then I'll drive you home."

I don't want that. I don't want her anywhere near me. It's too hard. It's too confusing. I just want to be home and be alone and not think. "No. I'll just wait until I sober up." The keys are in my hand, jangly and hard.

"Let me drive you, Jason. I want you to be safe. For Mattie."

It's hard to argue with her beautiful face, even though I'm angry. But she's right. It'll be a long time before I'm fit to drive. "Okay. But you were mean."

Her hand touches mine, but just to take the keys. "Stay here."

I lean against the wall and wait. She's probably telling her daughter and her friend that she's driving me home. She's probably being all responsible. I feel irresponsible. I feel like a loser. I can't even get myself home. And Mattie's with me. Margarita has let me have him more often since the pregnancy, and he's at home with the babysitter. Ugh, this purple stuff has a smell to it, like fifty-year-old Kool-Aid.

Emmy comes back and takes my elbow. "Okay, Jason, we can go."

I love hearing my name in her voice, even though I know this whole situation is *no bueno*. She asks me where the car is, and I know the answer to that question. See, I'm not totally irresponsible.

"Why'd you park so far away?" she asks.

"Margarita always says that." I know she'll hate that answer. Good. I'm so mad at her. She used me. She got me fired from the best job I ever had. Why'd she do that? I thought she liked me.

It's a long walk, and she wraps her arms around herself in the cool night air. She's always cold anytime it drops below seventy degrees. There's the Alfa on the curb, right where I left it. Everything is dark and wet. It must've rained. The streetlamps reflect off puddles in the street, and that makes me sad. Then it makes me queasy. Suddenly, everything in my digestive tract ignores the one-way signs, and I reach for the passenger door handle, lean over, and puke.

"Okay." She lays a hand on my back. "It's okay."

She helps me inside and straps the seat belt across my chest. When she taps HOME on the GPS, I know I'm going to be okay. Bon Jovi roars over the speakers.

"Did you mean it?" I turn down the volume. "Does my playlist really suck?"

She smiles, and it's beautiful and naughty. I forgot how beautiful and naughty it was. "No, I just said that."

"Why?"

"Because I'm mean." She switches the music to Duran Duran anyway.

We splash through a puddle as she pulls out. Everything smells like wet asphalt and minerals. I let my head fall back against the cold headrest and loll with the motion of the car. It feels good letting someone else drive. No, *good* isn't the word. It feels like *relief.*

I close my eyes. Then I just say it. "I don't know if it's my baby."

She turns the volume down until the *do-do-do-do*s are a barely audible buzz and the water under the tires is louder. "Did you do the math?"

"It's possible, but...she's been seeing someone else for a while now."

Her face twitches like she wants to say something, but she's being careful. I wish we didn't have to be careful. I wish we could say everything.

"It doesn't matter." I spare her the trouble of figuring out what to say. "Even if the baby isn't mine, she'll still be Mattie's little sister."

"It's a girl?" Her smile is weak, but there.

"Yeah." I smile back. "It's a girl."

I wake up to her tugging on my arm, telling me to get out of the car. My head is swimmy as I cross the foyer and collapse onto the couch in the den. I smile and say hi to Leah on the way as Emmy mumbles something to her. I already paid Leah before I left, so there's really nothing to mumble about. Something hard pokes at the soft flesh under my right thigh. It's Possessed Baby. I toss her across the room, where she lands in the corner, mouth open, silently cursing me and all my progeny for eons to come. I close my eyes.

"Don't go to sleep!" Emmy's voice jolts me.

She presses something into my hands. It's a sandwich.

"My trainer says no more bread," I whimper.

"We're way past that."

I take a bite, tasting lunch meat and avocado and lots of mustard. She remembered I like mustard. I close my eyes and chew.

"I'm going to put Mattie to bed," she says.

Mattie's still up? I start to rise, but her hand is on my shoulder.

"Just eat," she says. "I got this."

I feel ashamed and small and like Fat Thor, but I eat the sandwich. I need to do better. Right now, though, I'll just eat and try not to fall asleep before swallowing each bite.

The clock reads midnight when I wake up.

The TV is on. Emmy's sitting on the floor on Mattie's bean bag chair watching the ending of *Rogue One*, the part where the blast that kills them is coming and you know everyone is about to die. Jyn Erso and Cassian are gripped in each other's embrace. It's a moment you can't look away from.

"I love this scene," I say.

She turns to me, a tear in her eye. "I do, too."

Four months have passed since our night together in this house, and I feel the weight of that. The weight of everything. I lick my parched lips.

"I brought you water." She points to the side table.

I take a sip and then gulp the whole thing down. When I finish, she's got more tears in her eyes. Something's wrong. Something more than the stuff that I already know is wrong. "What happened?"

She holds up her phone. "They canceled the LA premiere. The red carpet. All of it."

I can't look at her as I set down my glass. My chest seizes up, and I don't know why. It's what I wanted, isn't it? To not have to be at events with both Margarita and Emmy. To hurt Emmy the way she hurt me. Except now I just feel like an atomic dick. After all the terrible things I said and did, she took care of me tonight. Me and Mattie both. Someone has to really care about you to do that.

Maybe I was wrong about her. Maybe she didn't take the pictures. And I can tell she's truly sorry about that scene in the book. She apologized for it... I just haven't accepted it.

"I guess I'll go now." She gets to her feet.

Reaching out, I catch her wrist. "Emmy, wait. I'm sorry." I wish I had more than just words to offer. "I was an asshole today. No matter what, you didn't deserve that."

Two tears race like falling stars down her cheeks. She swipes them away. "I did deserve it, Jason. I exploited you in my book. I didn't know you back then. I was just being selfish—you were right about that—but that's no excuse...and then I did it again."

I give a tight-lipped nod as understanding dawns. "So you did leak those photos?"

"No." She shakes her head. "I told you that wasn't me. I'm talking about the smoothie-after photo."

"The smoothie-after photo?"

"You didn't see it?"

I shake my head. She sniffs and swipes around on her phone. Then she turns the screen to me. I squint at it, bracing myself for the worst. All I see is Emmy with messy hair and a glass in her hand. "You're on the wrong photo."

She glances at the screen. "No, I'm not."

I look again. "Are you talking about this one? Where you're drinking a green smoothie and I'm a big blur in the background?"

She tsks. "My hair is sex-tousled. And you're shirtless."

"It looks like a Jamba ad. You can't even tell it's me."

"Don't you see? I posted it so people would pick up the innuendo."

"It looks like you posted it so people would pick up a healthy breakfast."

She smirks. "Smoothies aren't breakfast, or don't you remember?"

Her joke takes twenty pounds off my shoulders. It isn't lost on me that she was worried about posting this silly picture, worried it might hurt me. Someone who cringes at a photo like this would never have shared those other shots with TMZ.

Shit. I've been unfair. Colossally unfair. I start to say so, but she beats me to talking.

"Jason, about what I wrote...I really am sorry." Unshed tears magnify her amber irises. "I wish I could take it back."

That awful scene in the book. When I read it, it was like a machete ripping through me. But I should forgive her for that. It happened a long time ago, and I need to get over it. I meet her worried gaze with my nonchalant face. "It's okay. I was going through a bad time. That's not really who I am."

Her eyebrows go up. "Wow, did Jason Connor just admit he's not a total jerk-in-the-box?"

"More like jerk-in-the-box adjacent."

"No." She shifts and looks me straight in the eye—no coyness, no teasing, nothing at all to get in the way. "Who you really are is a guy dedicated to his little boy. A guy who, when he does a charity event, gives it his all. A guy who is always the first to say yes to his friends and fans, no matter what. A guy who buys a smartwatch for a girl he hardly knows because he remembered she ruined hers..."

"Emmy..." I interrupt her, embarrassed.

"I'm not finished." She sniffles and sits up straighter. "A guy who stands by a woman he doesn't love, who's pregnant with a baby that might not be his, just so she doesn't have to do it alone."

I don't even know what to say to that.

Two tears slip down her cheeks, and each one is a knife in my chest. Her next words start out on a hiccup. "You're a good person, Jason. You've always been a good person. I'm the real jerk-in-the-box. I can't believe I was so determined to reach some vague idea of success that I was willing to hurt you to get there." Her face crumples. "I'm sorry."

Whoa, whoa, whoa. I can't let her do this—take all the blame.

"Hold up a second." I sit up and take her hands in mine.

They're warm and small, and I want to hold them forever. "I love how you see me, Emmy, I do. It's one of the many things I love about you. But when you met me, I was already neck-deep in quicksand. I did that all by myself."

One side of her mouth quirks. "Yeah, well, I wish I'd been the girl to pull you out rather than shove you the rest of the way under."

My chest tightens. I squeeze her hands and gaze straight into the golden-hazel depths of her eyes. "You *were* that girl. You *did* pull me out. You were the only one who could've."

I want to kiss her, but my mouth is this unsavory place where salami and whiskey and puke breath are still trying to keep the party going. So instead, I bring her head to my chest and plant a smooch in her sticky waves. She feels warm and perfect in my arms. For a long moment, I just hold her, and she holds me, and we don't say anything. I know it won't make all our problems disappear, but right now, it's everything I need and want and choose. To be with someone who makes me feel like five million bucks. Someone who sees things in me I don't see in myself. Someone who could, maybe, with time, make me see them, too.

She likes long hugs. Even the sheepherders in Nepal know that by now, but eventually, I feel the gentle movement as she pulls away, and I know it's the end of our moment.

"Jason!" She jerks away from me, her eyes glued on something across the room. It's Possessed Baby, lying on the floor where I threw her earlier.

"Did she move?" I ask. "Please tell me you didn't see her move."

"No, but...her mouth."

"Is there a big black centipede crawling out of it? Because she and I had a heated discussion about that."

"Jason, no..." Emmy pushes off the couch, retrieves the doll, and begins to undress her.

"I don't think she'll like that very much," I say nervously.

Emmy's face goes dark, and her lips press together in a line. "I think I figured out where those photos came from." She shows me the cracks in Possessed Baby's skin where the batteries go, the little slot for the SD card, and the shiny lens deep inside her dreadful, gaping mouth.

Oh shit. "Mattie's doll is a nanny cam?"

She nods.

"The doll Margarita got our son is a nanny cam? And she didn't tell me?" I know it's wrong to disparage a pregnant woman, but I aim a barrage of curses at Margarita anyway.

Emmy puts a hand on my chest. "Easy, big guy. Sun's going down..."

"She leaked those pictures! She had no right!"

"She had no right, but it's done."

"We have to tell everyone... the media."

Emmy shakes her head. "First rule of marketing—don't resurrect bad press. Let it die, Jason."

"But..."

"Trust me. It won't change anything."

I think about how angry I've been with Emmy for something she didn't even do. How I threw a tantrum on the show today and got the premiere canceled. This was Emmy's dream, and I stole it from her. Although maybe it's not too late to make it right.

"Well then, Emmy Ellison, social media influencer extraordinaire..." I tuck a sticky lock of her hair behind one beautiful ear. "If we're not going to clear your name, what insane stunt are we going to pull to get your premiere back on?"

She lays Possessed Baby face down on the couch. "I think

I'll just take Peyton on a studio tour and go home." Her smile is weak. "Let's face it. I don't really fit in around here anyway."

I blink at her in disbelief. "Are you kidding? I don't think I've ever heard a more ridiculous statement, except that there's such a thing as too many *Jurassic Park* movies. You were made for showbiz. You fit in here better than I do."

Her mouth twists to the side. "I had my fifteen minutes of fame, but now it's over."

"No way!" I shake my head. "I don't believe that. The world wants more Emmy Ellison, I'm sure of it. More dolphins telling their fortune..." She smiles. "More flames and skulls..." A half-hearted chuckle. "More awesome books and more sexy pool parties. I know I want more of all of those things, especially that last one."

She hugs herself. She's squeezing so hard that her shoulders tremble. "I think I'm done."

"What about us?"

Her sad, little laugh is something I've seen actors struggle to imitate. Turns out pretending your heart isn't broken is a really special skill set. "I want to be with you, Jason, I do. But the truth is... I don't think it would work out no matter how hard we tried. Our worlds don't intersect. You've got a baby on the way with Margarita—"

"I don't even know if it's mine."

"Is that going to change whether or not you take care of her?"

I don't say anything.

"I didn't think so. And I wouldn't expect anything different. Your dedication to Mattie is part of what made me fall in love with you, and I know it'll be the same with Margarita and this baby. There's no room for me here, Jason. Or Peyton. Because I have a child to think about, too." She pauses. "Let's face it. Your celebrity dance card is already full."

My precarious world starts to fall to cinders around me. I don't want to lose her. I know that now, but I don't know if I can give her what she wants, what she deserves. The desperation must be written all over my face because Emmy touches my hand.

"It's okay." Her desert eyes flash like liquid fire in the den's yellow light. "We always knew this story wasn't going to have a happy ending."

She stands up, and I roll to my feet and stand with her, face-to-face. The way she clutches the strap of her purse, the way her shoulders roll inward, I don't dare touch her. I only have my words.

"Please don't leave," is all I can manage.

She touches my face. "You're not my boyfriend, Jason. You're just my celebrity crush."

Then she turns her back on me and heads for the door.

Chapter 36

I was wishing I'd been anesthetized.

CELEBRITY STRAIGHT TALK, DECEMBER 8

AMIL: Happy holidays, everyone! I'm Amil Nair with *Celebrity Straight Talk*, and this is my cohost, Isla Wallace. Love the reindeer antlers, Isla.

ISLA: Thank you, Amil. I brought a pair for you, too.

AMIL: Oh, aren't you on the nice list! So, last night we all got to experience the colonoscopy-level discomfort of Jason and Emmy on *Celebrity Showdown*, and I'm not talking about Emmy's singing voice.

ISLA: Yes, I was wishing I'd been anesthetized, Amil.

AMIL: It was their last chance to resuscitate a dying promo tour.

ISLA: And now that promo tour is officially dead.

AMIL: There'll be no premieres, no red carpets.

ISLA: No nuthin'.

AMIL: I kind of wish they hadn't canceled it, though, Isla, because there's something so captivating about those two.

ISLA: Never a dull moment, that's for sure.

AMIL: I heard something on the street. Maybe you heard it, too, Isla?

ISLA: That Jason might be trying to win her back?

AMIL: Yes! But what about Margarita?

ISLA: She's about to have her tethers loosened so she can float away! [*laughs*]

AMIL: [*laughs*] What?

ISLA: Just kidding. She looks radiant.

AMIL: Maybe they're going to share him.

ISLA: A friendly little love triangle?

AMIL: More of a love trapezoid. Rumor has it Margarita's dipping her pita chip in a different flavor of hummus.

ISLA: Amil, I don't know how you do that when the hummus you have right in front of you is so gosh darn delicious.

AMIL: That hummus *is* delicious, but it's also a fool. Jason needs to stay away from Emmy. Focus on his family. Focus on damage control for his career.

ISLA: Agreed, Amil. Except Jason's been posting on social media that he's going to be out at the Pershing Square ice skating rink tomorrow night with, get this... *a big surprise for Emmy.*

AMIL: What could it be?

ISLA: I have no idea, and he's not letting on.

AMIL: Do you think she'll show up?

ISLA: I don't know. He did hijack *Celebrity Showdown* and get the premiere canceled.

AMIL: That was pretty awful.

ISLA: But she's no angel, either.

AMIL: If these two are really ready to forgive and forget in front of the whole world, this is going to be epic.

ISLA: Maybe he'll give her a huge present.

AMIL: Oooh! Like a ring! Or a Tesla.

ISLA: Maybe it's a trick. Maybe he'll throw hot chocolate all over her.

AMIL: Yes! And then they can beat each other to death with giant candy canes.

ISLA: Here's a thought: maybe they'll act like normal people and just go ice skating.

AMIL: [*laughs*]

ISLA: [*laughs*]

AMIL: Honestly, I would wait an hour to see any of those things.

ISLA: Me, too.

AMIL: Save me a spot, Isla?

ISLA: Always, Amil.

AMIL: Happy holidays, everyone!

Chapter 37

There's no other plausible explanation for
that amount of screaming.

Emmy

"YOU. ARE. GOING."

"I'm not going, Josie."

"Did you read those texts? Because if you had read those texts—"

"I read them."

"He's practically begging you to come to Pershing Square."

"Well, technically he *is* begging me."

"Hence, why I repeat. You. Are. Going."

A knock sounds at the hotel room door. It's not polite or reserved or in any way normal. It's the knock you use to warn people there's a Terminator in the building. I whirl on Josie. "You called Val?"

Peyton, the little traitor, opens the door. Val, dressed all in white, is like a great gust of winter air swooping into the room, laden with shopping bags.

"I'm sorry they wasted your time." I plop down on the bed. "I'm not going."

The room erupts with protests.

"Listen!" I bark, lasering my gaze on each of them in turn. "I appreciate all of you, but you've got to stop. Jason and I didn't work out. If we drag this out, it's just going to be one disappointment after another, and I can't take any more."

I bite my lip so the tears don't come. Walking away from him was the hardest thing I've ever done. I don't even know how I had the guts to do it. I wanted so badly to just climb into his arms, curl up, and let him hold me forever. But I don't fit into his complicated Hollywood life, and Peyton and I deserve better. If there's one thing I've learned from this, it's that I'm not bulletproof, and honestly, I don't want to be in a relationship where I have to be.

No one challenges me for about ten seconds. Then a high-pitched little girl voice starts to read from a phone she's not supposed to know the password to. *"Emmy, I know things didn't end well the other night. It doesn't have to be this way. Let me prove how I feel about you. Come to Pershing Square tomorrow night at eight."*

"You little sneak!" I reach across the bed to snatch my phone from her. Peyton squeals and tosses it to Josie, who continues reading.

"I haven't heard from you. But I'm doing this. I need you to be there. Please, Emmy. Tell me you'll come."

"Stop it!" I lunge for Josie, but by the time I grab her hand, the phone is already flying over my head to Val. He squints at the screen.

"Besides, your loyal stylist has the perfect outfit for the occasion, and it would be a travesty not to wear it."

I give up and drop my hands to my sides with a huff. Val glances up from where he was pretending to read.

"You guys should be supporting me, you know," I grumble.

"Oh wait, I remember how to do this!" Josie clears her throat and puts on a bored voice. "Emmy, we support you. The man of your dreams discovered the error of his ways and apologized to you. He wants you to meet him in a Cali winter wonderland and profess his love for you in front of millions of people. You'll regret it forever if you don't at least go hear what he has to say. But you know what? Let's just stay in the hotel room and binge Netflix instead."

Val tosses the phone back to me. "I miss the Emmy Ellison who was bent on total world domination."

I thumb the screen absently. "Total world domination is a big responsibility."

"That's why every villain needs a sidekick." Val's eyes flash. "And that boy wants to be yours."

I glare back at him. Maybe I should go and see what Jason has planned. Josie's right—if I don't go, I'll always wonder. It might be good publicity for the movie, too. At this point, with today's premiere canceled, we need all we can get.

"What do you say, Mom?" Peyton's big eyes are imploring. "We haven't been to Pershing Square yet."

I take a long, deep breath, then roll my eyes in my best Tony Stark impression. "Fine."

"Woo-hoo!" she cheers, bouncing on the bed. "And shawarma after!"

⭐

An hour later, all four of us are in an Uber. I'm rocking my "butter" brand, the winter edition: wool camel-colored pants, fitted white angora Fendi sweater, black fleece-lined leather jacket, and shiny ankle-high red leather boots with garish Christmas tube socks all the way up to my knees. My lipstick is a red I didn't even know existed. My eyelashes go on forever. My hair is in one long Elsa braid, throwing itself over my shoulder with sparkly, hair-sprayed abandon.

Val turns around from the passenger seat for the gazillionth time. "Don't you dare let the back of your head touch that seat."

I lean forward obediently. Val's work is a level of perfection you don't mess with.

The crowd is insane. As we pour out of the car, I'm swamped by fans asking for autographs. There must be five hundred people here. The air smells of desert night and lattes. The networks are here—camerapeople checking their equipment, announcers tapping their earpieces. Social media influencers cackle and pose into their phones. I catch a glimpse of Harper Rose and those two mynah birds, Amil and Isla. I don't know what Jason is planning, but whatever it is, everyone is here to see it.

At exactly eight o'clock, a crew pushes the crowd back from a makeshift stage I didn't notice was there until now. I think I spot Sean tugging a long, green-and-white-striped stocking cap down on his head, trying to look inconspicuous. And what the...? Is that Amanda leaning on the rink railing? I move in for a closer look as the DJ cuts off the holiday music, a final note bouncing across the night.

Then the *Lost Star* theme song swells over the speakers, and from the crowd, the whole team emerges onstage. All of them are wearing some kind of holiday getup. Jason Connor's in a Santa hat with Yoda ears. Kayla wears a long, girlie nightgown with a Cindy-Lou Who hairdo. Andrew, with Orbit in his arms, sports snowflake leg warmers over his jeans. Amanda is wearing a Mrs. Claus apron, Jason "Mount" Ramirez's ugly sweater has every winter holiday represented, and Sean's stocking cap is jauntily placed.

Once they're in position, the music changes, and, flash mob–style, they launch into the big dance number from the season finale of *Lost Star Dance Troupe Saves the Universe*, season 4. It only aired a few weeks ago, so everybody recognizes it. My mouth drops open as the gang executes their moves to the pulsing music. It's been months since they last danced this number, so it's a miracle they even remember it. The best part, though, is that none of them are 100 percent in character. They're laughing and carrying on and having a great time. At one point, Kayla gets turned around and panics. Ever the pro, Ramirez swoops in like Captain America, lifts her up, and deposits her in the right place with a spin in between. It's supercute, especially with her Cindy-Lou Who outfit and the fact that Ramirez is four times her size.

Jason Connor, in a leather jacket and that Yoda hat, is obviously loving this. Snagging a giddy teenager by the hand, he hauls her under the ropes and throws her back and forth a few times before giving her a gentle push back into the audience. Her friends freak out, and I laugh, imagining how she'll still tell this story when she's fortysomething and married with teens of her own. At the same time, my heart aches as I watch him. This is the real Jason, the amazing guy I've fallen in love with. I'm going to miss him so much.

For the record, Fat Thor *is* still hot.

Sean swoops his arms upward, telling the crowd, *More! More! More!* They respond in a staggering wave of noise. Even the skaters on the rink have congregated to this side of the ice to see what's up. I don't think I've ever seen Harper Rose look less bitchy.

The *Lost Star* song ends on a surging note, and everyone but Jason exits the stage, either ducking under the ropes or, in Sean's case, leaping over them like a stocking-capped parkourist.

Jason grabs a cordless mic from a guy in a headset.

"That was just to get your attention. Thanks, team! You were great! Weren't they great?" The audience howls in reply. I join in, my hands forming a megaphone. Jason's gaze finds me in the crowd, and he can't contain his million-dollar smile. "Thank you, everyone, for coming out! I appreciate each and every one of you, but there's one person in particular who I'm especially glad is here because this would've been a colossal fail without her."

Josie jostles my shoulder. Hundreds of heads turn and bob, trying to get a look at me.

"Nine months ago, I met Emmy Ellison on *The Terica Show*, and the truth is I fell for her that very day. Now, you guys know her as the author of *Hashtag Celebrity Crush*, but I know her as so much more than that. She's beautiful. She's funny. She's talented. And she's five foot three inches of pure, hundred-proof fearlessness! She jumped into the Pacific Ocean to save a dog. I bet you didn't know that. Who does that?"

He's still breathing hard from dancing, and his eyes shine beneath the fuzzy trim of his Yoda-eared Santa hat. I don't know if all the tingles in my body are from the chilly air or the fact that he's telling all of LA how great he thinks I am. My mouth smiles against its will.

"And she doesn't care what anybody thinks—not you, Harper. Not you guys, either, Amil and Isla. She's the smartest, funniest, coolest person I've ever met, and I can be myself with her. She actually helps me be better than that. I know we've had our problems, but don't believe everything you read on the internet. Emmy, will you come on up here? They can't see you out in the crowd."

Someone—I'm pretty sure it's Josie—shoves me from behind. The crowd parts as I totter on wooden legs to the barrier and duck under it. Taking my place beside Jason, I survey the dizzying number of people who are here cheering me on, and who are also, at the moment, probably expecting me to say something. I lean sideways into the microphone. "I'm five foot five, actually."

The audience rumbles with laughter, and Jason surprises me with a quick kiss on the cheek. God, he's gorgeous close up. Why does that always shock me? I should be used to it by now. His arm around my shoulders is strong and warm.

"If you haven't met her yet, this is Emmy Ellison," Jason says into the mic. "She's a *New York Times* bestselling author, and the movie based on her book is coming out on December fifteenth. That's only a few days away! You're not gonna want to miss it, and the book is even better than the movie. I wanted to introduce you all to her because she's *my* celebrity crush. Every time I see her, I get all sweaty and swoony. I know it's hopeless because she's way out of my league. In fact, she's already told me to get lost, but I couldn't stop thinking about her. Maybe I should ask her to dance. What do you think? Who knows? Maybe she'll say yes."

He's been peeking at me throughout his entire outrageous speech, but now he full-on turns to me as the crowd roars their encouragement. "Emmy, will you do the *Hashtag Celebrity Crush* dance with me?"

I sputter out a cough. It's been months since we did that dance for Operation Keanu Reeves. I don't even know if I remember the moves. But colored holiday lights dance over my head. The collective murmurs of hundreds of people are in my ears. Jason's blue eyes are imploring me with his curls poking out from under that ridiculous hat. Everyone is waiting for me. Everyone is rooting for me. Heck, I'm even rooting for myself.

I grin. "Sure, why not?"

He does the overly excited face, first to me and then the audience. "She said yes!"

He relinquishes the mic, and his hand closes over mine, warm and familiar. I plant my feet as the noise level drops to whispers. We share a smile just as Duran Duran's "Rio" takes over the night.

Then we dance.

I don't know if any of these people saw our video of this dance or not. It's possible they recognize it from the movie trailer, or maybe they're just feeling the magic of Christmas in Cali under the stars. Either way, to say that the crowd is freaking out would be an insult to them. They are losing their ever-loving minds, and it's glorious.

As for me, I'm already lost. Everything is muscle memory at this point, and I get to be Nora/Margarita/Emmy, spinning and swaying and moving and surrendering. *Hands up! Push, push. The wave! The wave! Then it's the whole thing again, but faster.* During the parts where I'm in Jason's arms, I'm Baby in *Dirty Dancing*. Other times, I'm Alex in *Flashdance*. I'm not that great. I know I'm not. Jason's ten times better than me, but I can't stop smiling, and the overwhelming energy surging through this place fills in all my gaps.

Jason called me his celebrity crush! Jason organized this crazy flash mob for me. Jason is looking at me in a way that only ever used to happen in my dreams. I don't know what's going to happen next, but one thing's for sure...I'll never forget this.

The song starts to fade, but something else is coming up at the same time—a salsa. Jason yanks me into his arms, our feet automatically switching to the one-two-three-skip beat. I remember to keep my elbows out and tap my toe in just the right place. Jason turns me, throws me, moves me this way and that, but the thing he taught me about the salsa is that as long as you keep up with the footwork, it all looks good.

If the crowd was wild before, they are a mob now. I swear, if I didn't know any better, I'd think alien ships had come down and started sucking people up into them—there's no other plausible explanation for that amount of screaming.

Our gazes lock, our feet doing all the work, upper bodies hardly moving. I can barely hear the music for all the cheering. The lights swirl like tiny nebulae in the sky above as Jason tips me into the final dip. Then the song is done.

But, apparently, we're not.

The next song kicks in. It's the Renegade TikTok dance. Jason gives me a nod, and on the starting beat, we hit the *whoa, clap, scoop, wave.*

"Come on, TikTok fans!" he shouts. "If you know it, join in!"

As the ocean of people roars their approval, Jason's helpers haul away the ropes and now the stage and dance floor are open. With a *wooooooo!* Peyton appears beside us, renegading it up like the adorable little maniac she is. Jason taps her on the shoulder, and the two of them double-time it, mirror image–style. My face hurts from smiling as I watch them.

The DJ plays a bunch of other popular TikTok clips in a row. I catch Sean slow dancing with Josie to some other song nobody else can hear. I think I even spot Terica in the crowd. When our show is done, the DJ cycles back to regular programming so everyone can free dance to holiday music.

I whirl, looking for Jason, but Sean kidnaps me in an embrace first, swaying me to "Last Christmas."

"You did good, Florida." His eyebrows are up, mouth serious. "I gotta admit, I almost gave up on you there for a minute."

"Thank you," I say, because I didn't get a chance to before. "For everything."

He shrugs it off. "That's just what you do. The Sean O'Sullivans look out for the Jason Connors. But I don't have to worry about Snack anymore. He's got you."

I love this side of Sean, the warm, gooey middle inside the insanely confident candy coating. I give him a sly grin. "You were actually the best hugger."

His whole body reacts like volts of electricity have been channeled through it. "I knew it! I knew it!" Then he relaxes and gives me a wink.

"I don't know what's going to happen with Jason and me," I say.

His response is quick and wise and unapologetic. "You'll figure it out. Ope! I think someone wants to cut in."

Sean whirls me in a circle twice, fast, and then releases me into Jason's arms as the opening bells of "Do They Know It's Christmas?" ring through the square. Together we rock side to side, Jason's arms cinched around me, my cheek against his chest. I can feel his heart pounding, or maybe it's mine. It reminds me of the hug I asked for months ago, but this time it's more.

He opens a gap between us so he can pin me with those Gulf of Mexico eyes. "How'd I do? Do you think it'll make up for the premiere?"

"This…" I look around at all the happy commotion. "Is even better than a boring old premiere."

His expression softens. "And us?"

I take a deep breath, tearing my attention away from the flashy Hollywood splendor back to reality. Because despite all of Jason's efforts, our situation hasn't changed. I reach up and trace one sideburn down his perfect cheek and square jawline all the way to his superhero chin. "Listen, Jason, I love what you did for me tonight, but—"

He cuts me off. "I pick *you*, Emmy. I don't care what anyone has to say about it. I'll find another job. I can still be there for Margarita and the baby. But there will always be room on my dance card for you. You and Peyton both. I'll love her, too. I promise."

I don't say anything. According to Josie, I'm supposed to be content with what I have. To decide what's enough. But Jason Connor just offered me the whole universe. What am I supposed to say to that?

My internal organs launch another Klingon fire drill, and it's all forehead prosthetics and anarchy in there. But my heart is drumming out a steady beat, and I'm counting on it to keep those losers in check. I open my mouth to respond, but something catches the corner of my eye. It's Margarita and her new boyfriend, or date, or whoever he is. Except I recognize him. Oh, God and Tom Hanks, I recognize him! How could I not?

Chapter 38

That's a Josie-level-terrible suggestion!

Emmy

RHETT CASTLE DOESN'T look that much different, just older and more distinguished. His hair is way too black, meaning he dyes it, but it falls in the same thick, tousled way I recognize from brushing Peyton's hair almost every morning for the past twelve years.

Jason's arms tighten around me even as the shock plays across his face. Apparently, he didn't know Margarita was dating Rhett, either.

A noise escapes me that's something between a choke and a whimper.

"Emmy, it's okay." He rubs my arms. "Take a breath. Come on. Do it with me."

I try to breathe with him. My whole body feels like it's shaking, but on the inside.

"You're okay. Say it."

"I'm not okay," I gasp. "I'm going to spontaneously combust!"

"You're not going to spontaneously combust. I promise. You're okay. Say it."

"I'm okay."

It sort of works. I don't burst into flames, and I muster the courage to peek around his shoulder. Margarite and Rhett are still there, mingling. Only ten feet away, Peyton is holding Mattie's hands, dancing with his little feet on hers.

"I can't do this right now. He's the father of my child. And she's here! And neither of them knows it!"

"Maybe we should go say hello."

I pull back from him with a horrified noise. "That's the worst suggestion ever! That's a Josie-level-terrible suggestion!"

"You think you're going to avoid him forever?"

"Yes!" I swivel my head, desperately searching for an exit through the throng.

"Emmy, this crowd is here for you. You've earned this! Don't let a guy you haven't thought about for over a decade ruin it."

It's not true that I haven't thought about Rhett. Every time I looked at my daughter and saw a little girl without a dad to love her, I thought about him. Every time I ended a relationship because I didn't trust the guy to do right by my daughter, I thought about him.

My voice is small. "What if I tell him and he doesn't want anything to do with her? What if he doesn't believe me? What if he disappoints her? Hurts her?"

"You don't have to tell him anything right now. All I'm suggesting is that we go say hello."

"Hello, Emmy. Hello, Jason."

I jump. In typical Margarita fashion, she appears at our side, soundlessly, like a pregnant wraith heavy with an enormous wraith baby. I don't want to, but now I'm forced to face her enigmatic smile and *him.*

"Hello, Margarita," I say. "You look beautiful. How are you feeling?" Dang it! Even after she posts half-naked pictures of me all over the internet, I'm still starstruck by this woman.

She doesn't answer. Instead, she turns to the man beside her. "This is Rhett Castle. Rhett, you know Jason, and this is Emmy."

Rhett's smile is one I can't read. "Ah, the infamous Emmy Ellison! We've actually met. Congratulations, by the way. You've come a long way."

I try to say *Thank you*, but it won't come out. The words that want to come instead are, *You have a daughter, Rhett. She's ours, and she's here, just over there, and I know she would love to meet you and know you and have some kind of relationship with you. So what's your opinion on that?*

"She's earned it." Jason takes my hand and gives it a squeeze.

Margarita's smile is slightly less enigmatic and more uncomfortable. Rhett has obviously been following me on the news, but I'm not sure he's told Margarita about us. Does he know I have a daughter? Does he suspect she's his? I don't think so. If he did, his face wouldn't be so smug.

"You must be very happy," Rhett says to me. "I heard Miles made some magic out of that gummy little romance novel you wrote."

I'm just getting some strength back in my legs when the words sink in. Oh, hell to the no! He did not just call my book "gummy." What does that even mean?

"I'm glad we're getting a chance to chat," he continues. "Last time I saw you, I don't know how many years ago, you were this overzealous college girl trying so hard. It was adorable."

His words, the set of his jaw, the way he tugs on his lapels—all of it drags me back through the years to that day. Suddenly, I'm that overzealous college girl all over again, feeling small and used.

He goes on. "Somehow in the last decade, you figured out some great formula. Write a book—it doesn't have to be great, just write it. Build some crazy hashtag campaign around it. Then hook yourself a handsome movie star to help you promote it. I don't know how you did it, Emmy, but congratulations, girl! You managed to elbow your way into Hollywood despite everything. I never would've expected it."

Rhett's smile is bland. He can't even emotionally invest in attacking me. I swallow hard. There's a break in the crowd to the left. I could make a beeline for it. Forget Jason's offer. Forget Hollywood. Forget telling Rhett about Peyton, and Peyton about Rhett.

Except something odd is happening. I have no desire to run, not even a little bit, because the voice I'm hearing—Rhett's voice—is all too familiar. It's been echoing in my head for thirteen years, and frankly, I'm sick of it.

Jason said I belong here, and the people who came out tonight to see us confirmed it. Josie said my problem is that nothing is ever enough. Now I know why. I've been dosing myself with Rhett Castle's poison every day since I met him, and apparently doing a way better job of it than he ever could. I let this man's opinion of me define me for thirteen years. And that's extra sad because he's not even a major player in my story. He's a redshirt. And I let him steal the show.

Not anymore.

A chuckle escapes me as I lift my chin. "Thank you, Rhett, for reminding me how naive I was back then, and also for accusing me of cheating my way into Hollywood with a mediocre book and a great marketing campaign. Regardless, I'm enjoying being a bestselling author with a movie deal and a huge career ahead of me. *Hashtag Celebrity Crush* has been a dream come true, and it's also given me a chance to meet some amazing and talented people. Yes, there's been some drama"—my eyes flick to Margarita— "but I never meant to hurt anyone. So, if I did, I hope they'll forgive me."

For a second, Margarita's mouth forms something that's not a smile of forgiveness but also not a withering frown. I'll take it as a victory. But that was the easy part.

I glance over to where Peyton is dancing with Mattie and Josie. Beautiful in her lanky tweenness, she's a magical creature you want to protect from all the ugly things of the world. An elf. A sprite. A skittish, ephemeral thing. It's all I can do not to cry as I say the next words because she's not bulletproof, either, and she shouldn't have to be.

"It was actually *thirteen* years ago, Rhett, to be exact, when we met at that party. The reason I know this is because that night changed my life in a big way. I didn't have the guts to tell you when I should have, but I'm telling you now."

I point semi-discreetly in Peyton's direction. I expect Rhett will get my meaning since they look so much alike. Jason nods once at me in encouragement. Meanwhile, Rhett's smug countenance dissolves into an expression I don't think he can control, all his load-bearing walls falling, one by one.

I suck in a breath. "Her name is Peyton. She's twelve years old. She's an amazing kid who is good at everything she does, whether it takes her one try or a hundred thousand tries to get there. She's sweet and caring and funny, and she's the best person I've ever met. And oh crap, she's coming over here."

Peyton has noticed all our eyes on her and, of course, the fact that the beautiful and talented Margarita Ayala is part of the group. I pull her into a hug as she approaches, and Mattie wraps himself around Margarita's leg.

"I love all your movies," Peyton says to Margarita, eyes and braces shining. "I've always wanted to meet you."

Margarita smiles and thanks her. Then Peyton looks at Rhett.

My heart jumps. Here goes nothing. "Peyton, honey, this is Rhett Castle, big-shot Hollywood director...or producer now, I should say. He..." *Oh God, how am I going to do this?* "He wants to talk to you about movies," I finish.

"Hi," Peyton says shyly.

My breath is trapped in my lungs, throbbing and burning. I'm terrified Rhett is going to choke. Or say something stupid. Or react badly. He was an ass thirteen years ago, and from what I've seen today, I doubt he's changed. But if he hurts my daughter right now, I swear to God and Tom Hanks, I'll pull a Jason Connor and punch him in the face.

Rhett lifts his arms halfway, tentative. "Peyton, wow." It's the softest I've ever heard him speak. "It's so nice to meet you."

"It's nice to meet you, too," my polite daughter replies.

"So...uh...what's your favorite movie?"

Fear and threats of violence give way to relief as I listen to Peyton rehash the plots of the *Descendants* movies for Rhett. When he catches my eye, I give him the tiniest head shake *no*.

I'll tell her the truth, eventually. I will. But not right now. First, Rhett has to earn it.

Beside me, Margarita winces and leans forward, letting out

a slow breath as Mattie clings to her pant leg. It doesn't take me long to recognize what's going on.

"You're in labor."

"For the past two hours." Her expression is, dare I say, conspiratorial?

"I'll bet you're ready for this. Come here, Mattie." I whisk him up on my hip. "You're like ten days overdue, aren't you?"

She gives me a dark look. "I'm due the fourteenth. But, yes, I'm ready. Do you not see the size of me?"

My brow furrows. "I was sure Jason told me you were due December first."

"No." Her beautiful dark eyes confess the rest of what she's unwilling to admit as she breathes through the pain. The math problem works itself out in my head.

"It's not Jason's." I say it matter-of-factly, my insides untangling as the words come out. "But you let him think it was."

Margarita's beautiful face twitches with annoyance, as if there's nothing more reprehensible than being forced to explain herself to me. "Jason's a great dad," she huffs. "I wanted to believe it was his, that it was meant to be... a second chance for us. Sometimes we lie to ourselves...until we can't anymore." She straightens up and blows out a long breath as the contraction tapers off. "I didn't want to have to do this alone. It was so hard with Mattie, and my family was not supportive the first time. I dreaded having to go through all of that again. I..." She pauses, as if realizing she's telling me too much. "After my announcement on the boat, I didn't expect Rhett to stick around, but he did." She looks away, her voice going wistful as she whispers, almost to herself, "He stuck around."

I follow her gaze to Rhett, who, hands in pockets, is rocking on his heels and nodding in response to Peyton's animated chatter.

From zero to two daughters in one day. Wow. I almost feel sorry for the guy.

I almost feel brave, too. Brave enough to confront Margarita, and not just because she's got an obvious handicap and couldn't possibly beat me in a footrace. I lean in, looking around to make sure no one else hears us, not even Jason. "Why did you leak those photos from the nanny cam? You hurt Jason more than you hurt me, you know."

"What are you talking about? That was you."

"It wasn't me! Why doesn't anyone believe me?"

Even with a seven-to-ten-pound brand-new person slowly making its way out of her, Margarita's face is a serene mountain pool with one tiny ripple on it. "We have a lot of history, Jason and I, but I would never do something so awful to him. Yes, I was angry with you, with both of you. I read your book, and I was convinced you were using him. On the one hand, I wanted him to get hurt. It felt like poetic justice. But on the other, he's the only person who's been there for me these past three years, even if it was...dysfunctional." Her gaze shifts from me to Mattie, who is painting his face with the end of my braid. I expect her to snatch her precious son out of my boyfriend-stealing arms, but instead, her expression softens. "Maybe Jason is right. Maybe we both deserve to finally be happy." She leans forward again, lips pursed in a long intake of breath.

At the mention of his name, Jason clues in and heads our way. "Oh my God! Is it time? Is this happening? I'll go get the car."

"No." Margarita holds out a hand in the universal sign for *just give me a minute, I'm finishing up a contraction.* When it's done, she straightens. "Can you and Emmy keep Mattie while I'm in the hospital?"

Jason cocks his head. "Aren't I going with you?"

"No." Her eyes lock on his, and if I didn't know better, I'd have said they were apologetic. Then she smiles at me, and it's the first real smile she's ever given me. Even after everything, it makes me feel all warm inside, like I'm part of a secret club with only a handful of members who probably hate me.

"Wh-what's happening?" Jason is flashing meme faces at warp speed.

"Come on, Jason." I hook his elbow in mine. "Let's get Peyton and give Margarita a minute alone with Rhett."

Chapter 39

Even better than *Firefly*.

Emmy

WE LEAVE THE kids with Josie and help Margarita into the car when Rhett pulls up. As she takes her purse from me, I'm surprised at the rush of compassion I feel for her. How must it have felt being pregnant with Mattie, knowing it was never going to work out between her and Jason? What's it like raising a child with a man you don't love, who doesn't love you, either, and you both know it? I guess sacrificing for your kids is always hard, no matter how famous you are.

"Do you think Rhett suspected it was his?" I ask Jason as they speed off.

He wraps his arms around me under the oversize Christmas balls and shiny icicle decorations. The smell of his leather jacket and the way he rocks me gently from side to side give me a sleepy, safe feeling.

"I don't know," he replies, "but is it wrong if I still want to kill Margarita over that nanny cam?"

"It wasn't her." I nuzzle into his chest. "We had a talk about it, and I believe her. But if you want, we can still push them both down a hill and keep the baby for ourselves."

He lifts my chin and kisses me gently on the lips. "Nah, we don't need their old baby. If you want a baby, I'll give you a baby."

There are a lot of ways I could respond to that super-loaded statement, but gazing into his eyes, I ask, "Are you sorry that Margarita's baby isn't yours? Were you getting your hopes up?"

He tilts his head, and a red Christmas light blinks on and off, throwing his perfect face into shadow one second and illuminating it the next. "No, I'm not sorry. Honestly, I'm relieved not to have that job anymore. I'm glad she has someone. Maybe he'll do better by her than I did. Because there's somebody else I want to do better by. You."

My organs settle into their jump seats. The dashboard is quiet. Everything is perfect, so perfect, except... "We fly home tomorrow."

He shrugs. "You don't have to. You could stay."

He's right. Peyton just met her dad. Margarita is having her baby. School break is right around the corner. There are so many reasons to just...not leave. See how this plays out.

When I don't say anything right away, Jason goes on. "Or I could come with you." His face lights up, excited. "We could drive your trailer cross-country! I don't have a job right now. We could travel with Mattie and Peyton. Have an adventure!"

Great. Now he's added a crazy road trip to my decision tree.

"What do you say, Emmy?" His eyes are shining. "Let's move

you out here to California! You see how good we are together, not just us, but our kids, too. Let's take all our broken pieces and make something beautiful."

I blink under the colored lights. The picture of the one-way trip he's painting forms in my brain. A life with the four of us seems perfect, but moving here would also mean dealing with Margarita, and maybe letting Peyton see Rhett, too. As scary as that feels, it's also exhilarating, in a real-life, non-Hollywood way.

I think about how Jason promised to love us, not just me but Peyton, too. For the first time, something like that feels possible.

Jason cradles me in his arms, waiting for my answer. He's holding the wormhole open for me; he'll hold it open as long as he can, but just like in season three, episode nine of *Lost Star* and every single other sci-fi show involving wormholes, it's up to me to take the plunge.

I tilt my head up to him. "We'll have to stop and see the Grand Canyon."

His fingers smooth the hair out of my face, his touch deliciously tender, his smile even more so. "My family in Ohio, too."

"The biggest tumbleweed in Texas."

"A nude RV park."

"Eww, not with the kids!"

"Oh yeah, I forgot they were coming."

I giggle, but I can't let this conversation end on a joke, because there are serious matters at hand. "It'll be complicated."

He turns off all the faces. "I'm not afraid of complicated."

"Won't this be bad for your career? Hollywood's hashtag bad boy in a relationship with the greedy author who played him for book sales?"

He looks pensive. "My ex-agent says there are plenty of porn producers who would be happy to have me."

I grimace. "Jason, *no.*"

He squeezes me. "In all seriousness, though, I don't care about any of that. I want to be with you." His voice cracks, and his gaze is filled with the same tragic certainty of our night together.

I hold my breath. I'm pretty sure I know what he's going to say next because, well, I happen to be an expert in Jason Connor expressions.

"Hashtag I love you, Emmy Ellison."

My heart swells with something I don't entirely recognize. Maybe it's the feeling of finally reaching the top of the mountain. Of my cup runneth-ing over. Of having everything I ever yearned for with no empty spaces. Nothing left to want. The feeling of being, for once, satisfied, even without a red carpet.

"Hashtag I love you, too, Jason Connor." I push up on the tips of my candy apple–red boots and ambush his open mouth with a kiss so deep and long that my insides go liquid. He pulls me against him like he'll never let me go. It's perfection. Even better than *Firefly*.

Suddenly, a blinding whiteness assails us. We break apart as a car pulls up to the curb—a luxury SUV with a vanity plate that reads PRINZR33SE.

"You've got to be kidding me," Jason mutters, folding in on himself. "Is he here to take you, too?"

Zach Tay steps out of the car in a tux and the shiniest shoes I've ever seen. "Jay-*son!*" He presses his key fob, and the lock beeps. Then he pumps Jason's hand energetically and nods to me. "I know I'm late, but Margarita invited me."

"She went into labor," I tell him. "She's gone to the hospital."

"I really came to see you anyway." Zach's gaze settles on Jason, and he shifts uncomfortably on his feet. "The Hadron thing isn't really working out for me. You know?"

Jason shakes his head. "I'm sorry, what?"

"It's not my speed. I've been trying to reinvent myself, you know? Go more serious. Less…music-y, if you know what I mean?" Jason looks like he's catching flies in his mouth. "I really don't."

"Anyway, the part's yours, man, if you still want it. The network's willing to have you back. They've been trying to get a hold of you. You gotta answer your phone from time to time, sport." He claps a speechless Jason on the shoulder and winks at me. "You *are* taking it, right? Because I already picked up another gig—this Rocky Mountain true-crime series with a paranormal twist. It's"—he makes a sword-slicing motion through the air—"*edgy!*"

I elbow Jason.

"Yeah! Of course!" he chokes out.

"Great. Next season tapes in the New Year. Tell Margarita congratulations for me." They shake hands again, and then Zachary Tay pumps mine so hard I'm afraid I might get tennis elbow. "You two let me know if you ever need anything. You need anything—I'm there. You got that?"

He gives us double finger guns.

"Thanks!" I double finger gun him back.

As Zach zooms away, I grab the front of Jason's jacket and shake him. "You got your job back! And Zachary Tay is such a nice guy!"

Jason wraps an arm around me, still looking shell-shocked as we trudge back to the skating rink. "Yeah, Zachary Tay's not so bad, is he?"

"Maybe I should have gone with him," I muse.

"Ouch, Emmy."

"You know I don't mean that."

"I wouldn't blame you, honestly."

"Oh, shut up."

Chapter 40

Mom, be quiet.

EMMY ELLISON'S PERSONAL VLOG, DECEMBER 30

EMMY: Hey, everyone, this is Emmy Ellison with Jason Connor coming to you, as promised, with a photo slideshow from our road trip from Florida to California!

JASON: Howdy.

EMMY: If you look at the background, you can see we're in Joshua Tree National Park. Almost home! Let's take a look at the trip from two weeks ago up until today. Jason, would you start the slideshow? Okay, here we are pulling out of my old park and waving goodbye to my parents and my best friend. Notice the license tag on the trailer?

JASON: It says FERRARI. With a 3 instead of an *E*.

EMMY: A little homage to Terica since she promised Jason a Ferrari for winning my poll. We're gonna tag her on that one.

JASON: Here we are watching Florida State play UF at the FSU football stadium.

EMMY: Jason ate, like, six hot dogs that night.

JASON: I skipped the buns, so it only counts as three.

EMMY: Here we are at the Georgia Aquarium in Atlanta. And here are the kids eating s'mores at the campground in Daniel Boone National Forest.

JASON: As you can see, my son's creepy doll made the trip with us.

EMMY: Jason! Her eyes are glowing in that photo. Do you think her eyes are glowing?

JASON: Don't look or you'll get a phone call right before you're murdered.

EMMY: We stayed a few days with Jason's family near Cincinnati. There's your mom. Look at her smiling at you!

JASON: There's my brother Keith and his wife and all their kids.

EMMY: Mattie had a really good time. Look at his face.

JASON: Mattie also got his hair cut by one of his cousins. That's why he's got a buzz cut in the rest of the pictures.

EMMY: Peyton feels terrible about that.

JASON: Well, it's not Peyton's fault. You can't put a twelve-year-old in charge of eight little kids. It was *Lord of the Flies* up in there.

EMMY: Here we are at another campground in Missouri, where we sang karaoke with this lovely couple named Earl and Shasta. They thought Jason was Luke Bryan. That was hilarious!

JASON: I didn't correct them.

EMMY: Oh, here's the Grand Canyon! And here's Jason pretending to chuck Possessed Baby into the Grand Canyon and Mattie crying about it.

JASON: Stellar parenting moment. Ah, there's the one of Emmy and Peyton looking beautiful as they dare each other to touch a cactus. And a few frame-by-frames of that whole installment.

EMMY: And here we are arriving at Joshua Tree National Park. Wait, Jason, what are you doing?

JASON: I'm giving Peyton the phone so she can take a video for us.

EMMY: Why is Peyton taking a video for us? Peyton, why are you taking a video for us?

PEYTON: Mom, relax.

EMMY: Jason, are you injured? Why are you on the ground?

PEYTON: Mom, be quiet.

JASON: Emmy Ellison, in front of our children and the world and a bunch of really weird trees featured in a 1990s U2 album...

EMMY: Oh my God!

JASON: Will you marry me?

EMMY: Jason Connor just asked me to marry him! Oh. My. God.

PEYTON: Answer him, Mom!

EMMY: Yes! Of course! Yes, I'll marry you!

PEYTON: Mom, don't knock him over. Let him put the ring on you.

EMMY: Wow, look at it! It's like an ice cube on a keychain.

JASON: Show it to the camera, Emmy. Peyton, hon, zoom in, will you?

PEYTON: Zooming!

JASON: Is it okay? Do you like it?

EMMY: I love it. And I love you.

JASON: I love you, too. Peyton, you can zoom out again.

PEYTON: Oops! Sorry! Zooming out!

EMMY: I can't believe Jason Connor asked me to marry him!

JASON: Hashtag believe it.

EMMY: Hashtag we're getting married!

JASON: Hashtag we are.

Chapter 41

I don't know who she is, but I hate her already.

CELEBRITY STRAIGHT TALK, JUNE 15

AMIL: Look lively, folks! We've got some wedding photos for you today!

ISLA: Yay! I love wedding photos! Even if I'm viciously jealous!

AMIL: This is Amil Nair coming at you with *Celebrity Straight Talk*, and beside me, lovely as ever, is my cohost, Isla Wallace.

ISLA: Hi-la!

AMIL: Well, surprise, surprise, it was all "Hashtag I do" during a beach wedding for Jason Connor and Emmy Ellison! The ceremony was held behind their Santa Monica home with a small reception on the Spanish colonial revival patio. Look at those photos! I gotta tell you, Isla, I had my doubts about those two, but they sure look happy.

ISLA: That's it then. Jason Connor is officially off the market. And I'm officially on antidepressants.

AMIL: I've been crying into my pillow at night, too, Isla.

ISLA: [*wails*]

AMIL: [*wails*] Okay, that's enough. Here are some photos of the reception. There's Rhett and Margarita with their baby, Eva. She's about six months old now. Pretty little thing.

ISLA: That's Emmy's daughter Peyton with Jason's son Mattie.

AMIL: And who is that woman with the purple hair hugging Sean O'Sullivan?

ISLA: That's Emmy's maid of honor. She seems to be

enjoying herself from what I can tell from the back of her head.

AMIL: Can you blame her? There she is again, hugging Jason Ramirez. And again! Andrew Valentine.

ISLA: I don't know who she is, but I hate her already.

AMIL: Me too! [*laughs*]

ISLA: [*laughs*]

AMIL: Speaking of photos, did you see they finally discovered who leaked those R-rated pics of Jason and Emmy back in December?

ISLA: Yes, I did. The babysitter! Who would have thunk it?

AMIL: I always say, you've got to look really closely at what kind of car your babysitter drives to see if they're getting some extra funds on the side.

ISLA: What kind of car does she drive?

AMIL: I don't know. Anyway, Emmy's got something else to celebrate as well. She's got a new book coming out. Some crazy science fiction novel that's, like, a thousand pages long. When that thing prints, you'll be able to prop the garage door open with it. Congratulations, Emmy!

ISLA: And Jason's enjoying being back on the *Lost Star* team. It's hard to believe that Zachary Tay isn't as perfect as we all thought.

AMIL: Yes, apparently the director described his dancing as "Austin Powers standing in a fire ant hill.

ISLA: So, what's left for these two, Amil? Seems like all their dreams have come true.

AMIL: I think they still need an air fryer. It was on their registry, and no one bought it.

ISLA: What? I'll get them the air fryer.

AMIL: Let's both get them the air fryer and the recipe book that goes with it.

ISLA: Deal! So, who are we going to swoon over now?

AMIL: How about Sean O'Sullivan?

ISLA: Ooooh, Sean O'Sullivan. Good idea. He's got a great mouth.

AMIL: He does have a great mouth, doesn't he?

ISLA: Kind of loose and pouty.

AMIL: Irreverent, too.

ISLA: Just the way I like it.

AMIL: [*laughs*]

ISLA: [*laughs*]

Acknowledgments

Woo-hoo! *Celebrity Crush* is finally a book! First of all, thank you to my wonderful agent Cathie Hedrick-Armstrong and equally wonderful editor Alex Logan for taking a chance on me and also for thinking this book was funny even though neither of them got any of the sci-fi jokes. Thank you to my husband, Mark, who was the original author of several of those jokes; to my mom, Lucia, for being my biggest fan; and to my dad, Jim, the inspiration for my very first "book"—"Mr. Paul's Parrot." Thanks also go to my brother Jimmy, who made me consider writing a book in the first place; my mother-in-law, Donna, for her constant support; and my sister-in-law Cristy for being my official event planner. Also my four wonderful daughters: Megan, who introduced me as an "author" well before I'd earned it; Kira, who designed the cover for my very first manuscript (it was a YA sci-fi novel and, at age eleven, she drew a mean postapocalyptic dolphin); Ocean, at least one of whose quirky little blurts made it into this book; and Shea, for her fierce and furious loyalty over every rejection—every writer needs someone like that. I can't forget my son-in-law, Taylor, and my three grandsons, Ashur, Ezra, and Malachi, as well as my extended family. And, of course, my BFF, Minna, who cheered me along and also provided much of the inspiration for Josie.

Nobody ever gets to this point without having a mountain of other writers lifting them up. For me, this includes my dear Sprinters: Emily Colin, Lisa Amowitz, Rachael Peery, Angela Sierra, John Klekamp, and Sarah Anderson (a special thank-you to Lisa for her cover design help and Angela for being my sensitivity reader). Also huge thanks to the Write Squad: Kelly Ohlert, Shannon Balloon, Joel Brigham, Kyra Whitton, Audrey Burges, Kelly Kates, and Laurel Hostetter. Joel gets an extra special thank-you for his editing suggestion for the hook and for pitching this manuscript for me. I wouldn't be here without him. Thank you to Elsie Howe and Linda Bernfeld for giving me a place to run away to where I could focus on writing. Thanks to Heather Montgomery, Keiti Pierce, and Ann McIntosh for Monday night sprints at Barnes and Noble. I also want to acknowledge the very first person in the writing world to ever give me a professional critique, who pointed out all my rookie moves so gently and masterfully that I felt empowered and excited and fueled for the rest of this crazy journey, and that is the amazing Lorin Oberweger. Thank you also to Michelle Hazen for her expert editing advice, Debbie Ellis and Warren Rourke for their early support, and Fred, Sarah, and the rest of the gang at Ready Chapter One for sharpening my skills. And then there are my wonderful beta readers: Jessica Cleveland, Becki Lee, Rachel Murphy, Bekah Kline, Meri Munn, Jennifer Dickinson, Dustin and Emily Angell, Damara Hutchins, Megan Polak, Michel Daw, and Jody Perry Clair. If you had any part in this journey and don't see your name here, know that it wasn't intentional. I appreciate and love you.

To the fantastic folks at the Purcell Agency, including Tina Purcell (who also beta read for me) and Bonnie Swanson, who reps my sci-fi with so much enthusiasm, thank you. I also want to thank the entire team at Hachette Forever. I didn't get to meet every one of you, but I appreciate all the professionalism and care that went into your contributions: Leah Hultenschmidt, Estelle Hallick, Alli Rosenthal, Carolina Martin, Caroline Green, Grace Fischetti; Daniela Medina and cover artist, Cannaday Chapman; Anjuli Johnson, Eric Arroyo, and Marie Mundaca for production; Sara Schaller and the manufacturing team; the sales reps, Mary Urban, and the digital sales team; Ghenet Harvey and the audiobook team; and Francesca Begos and the subrights team. To the booksellers, librarians, Bookstagrammers, Book-Tokers, book bloggers, reviewers, journalists, book clubs, festival and event organizers, and podcasters, thank you for all you do!

Lastly, I have to thank the inspiration for this book. *Celebrity Crush* is, at its heart, a love letter to the entertainment industry. I wrote it while bingeing the Marvel movies during COVID quarantine, and being able to lose myself in epic superhero stories with all the feels made a really scary time less scary. I know I'm not alone in feeling this way—good storytelling matters! On a more personal note, as a debut writer, I was still figuring out my process when I wrote this, and I discovered that, once in a while, if I wasn't quite sure how to write a scene, I could just imagine how one of my celebrity crushes would play it, and suddenly... problem solved. So I guess I have that to thank them for, too. ;)

About the Author

Christy Swift writes smexy rom-coms and is a sci-fi fangirl who loves it all, from *Star Trek* to *Firefly* to the MCU. She daylights as an award-winning freelance writer, editor, and social media content provider with a focus on medical writing and conservation. Christy has lived in many places, including Spain, Mexico, Canada, and all over Florida. In her free time, you can find her on or near the ocean, in front of the TV, or playing the nerdiest board game you've ever heard of with her husband, kids, and friends. To learn more, visit ChristySwift.com.